THE MERMAID MURDERS

Special Agent Jason West is seconded from the FBI Art Crime Team to temporarily partner with disgraced, legendary "manhunter" Sam Kennedy when it appears Kennedy's most famous case, the capture and conviction of a serial killer known as the Huntsman, may actually have been a disastrous failure.

The Huntsman is still out there…and the killing has begun again.

The
MERMAID
MURDERS

JOSH LANYON

JUST JOSHIN'
PUBLISHING INC.

THE MERMAID MURDERS (Art of Murder Book I)

March 2016

ISBN:978-1-937909-83-3
ISBN-10: 1937909832

Published in the United States of America

JustJoshin Publishing, Inc.
3053 Rancho Vista Blvd.
Suite 116
Palmdale, CA 93551
www.joshlanyon.com

This is a work of fiction. Any resemblance to persons living or dead is entirely coincidental.

TABLE OF CONTENTS

To Jenna Bennett

CHAPTER ONE

*F*rom out their grottos at evenings beam,
the mermaids swim with locks agleam.

— Walter de la Mare, "Mermaid"

Summer heat shimmered off the blacktop.

In that shivery, humid light, the big, blond man casually leaning against the silver government-issue sedan—and checking his watch—looked a little like a mirage. No such luck. Senior Special Agent Sam Kennedy was not a trick of the light.

Kennedy looked up, spotted Jason, and grimaced. Maybe it was supposed to be a smile. Probably not, given Kennedy's reputation.

"Special Agent West," Kennedy said. His voice was deep, and he spoke with a suggestion of a drawl. "I thought maybe you stopped off to see if you could solve the Gardner Museum heist on your way over here."

Funny guy, Kennedy. Special Agent in Charge Carl Manning had already warned Jason that Kennedy was not thrilled to be partnered again, let alone partnered with an agent seconded from the Art Crime Team. That's what happened when you screwed up your last high-profile investigation to such an extent the governor of Wisconsin denounced you on the nightly news. An agent with less seniority would have been "on the beach" for the foreseeable future, but Kennedy was a legend in the Bureau. One of the great "manhunters." His career would survive, but he was under a cloud, no question. His kind of success earned enemies—and not just from the usual suspects. A successful career wasn't just about closing cases—and Kennedy didn't strike Jason as the tactful type.

"Nice to meet you too," Jason said, reaching the car. Kennedy did not offer his hand, so Jason shoved his own in his pocket. "Just to be clear, I'm supposed to be on vacation. In fact, I busted my ass to get here. I was in Boston about to catch a flight home to L.A."

"Duly noted." Kennedy turned away, going around to the driver's side of the gleaming sedan. "You can throw your bag in the trunk." He reached in and popped the trunk hood.

Jason opened the trunk and slung his brown leather carryall next to Kennedy's black Tumi. That was some serious luggage. The luggage of someone who lived out of his suitcase. Primetime TV notwithstanding, it was rare for agents in the Behavioral Analysis Units to leave Quantico and travel around the country, but Kennedy was the exception that proved the rule.

"We need to hit the road. That girl's been missing over eight hours already." Kennedy threw that comment over his shoulder, before sliding in behind the wheel.

Jason started to answer but restrained himself. SAC Manning had clued him in to a few facts about his new—temporary—partner. And, ostensibly, this urgency to get to the crime scene out in rural Kingsfield was all part of what made Kennedy so good at his job—not to mention the reason they were meeting in a diner parking lot instead of the division office at One Center Plaza.

He slammed shut the trunk, walked around to the passenger side, and climbed in. The car was still cool with air-conditioning, so Kennedy hadn't been waiting long.

Kennedy turned the key in the ignition. More cold air blasted out along with news radio. "So you know the area? Your family used to have a vacation home in Kingsfield?"

"That's right."

"How nice." Kennedy's tone was more like *Why am I not surprised?* He wore too much aftershave. The fragrance as aggressive as everything else about him. Top note sandalwood, bottom note obnoxious.

"I guess so."

Kennedy threw him a sardonic look as they exited the parking lot. Or at least the twist of his mouth was sardonic. The dark Oakleys he wore concealed his eyes. He looked to be in his mid-forties. Not handsome, but he had the kind of face you didn't forget easily. Although Jason was going to try his best the minute this case was over.

Jason said, "Clarify something for me. The Kingsfield Police Chief asked specifically for you because he thinks he might have a copycat killer on his hands?"

"It's too soon to say, but yeah. That's the concern, of course. No girl is going to go missing in Worcester County ever again that people aren't going to fear it's some kind of copycat crime." Kennedy began to bring Jason up to date on the case.

It was a swift and concise summation, but then the facts were few. Rebecca Madigan, the teenage daughter of wealthy local residents, had disappeared Friday night while hosting a party for friends. Rebecca's parents were out of town. The housekeeper had reported the girl missing. A search had been organized, but so far there was no sign of Rebecca.

"There could be a lot of reasons a teenage girl disappears," Jason pointed out.

"Yep. But like I said, the folks of Worcester County have long memories."

Yes. With good cause. Jason stared out the window at the slide-show of skyscrapers and historic buildings. Parks, playgrounds…ponds. *The dazzle of bright sunlight on green water. The echo of a young girl's laughter…* He removed his sunglasses, passed a hand across his eyes, and replaced the shades.

Worcester was an old city with a modern attitude. It was only about twenty-four miles from Kingsfield, not much more than a forty-five-minute drive, but it could have been a different planet.

He said, "I remember the original case. You were behind the capture and conviction of Martin Pink."

"I played a role." Kennedy was displaying unexpected—and undue—modesty. There was no question the Kingsfield Killings had stopped thanks to Kennedy's efforts, which was no doubt why the police chief had been so quick to call him in this time. It was a little surprising the Bureau hadn't waited to see how things developed in the Madigan case, but maybe this was as much about putting Kennedy on ice as finding a missing girl. That was certainly the way it had sounded to Jason when SAC Manning had asked him to cancel his vacation.

"What kind of a party was it?" Jason asked.

"What do you mean?"

"It's June. Was it a graduation party? Birthday party? Sweet sixteen? Secret baby shower?"

Kennedy's laugh was without humor. "It was the kind of party you throw when your parents are out of town for the weekend."

"Was everybody invited, or was it private?"

"We don't have the details yet. You know everything I know."

Yeah, probably not. Kennedy was old school, one of these lone-wolf types who no doubt preferred to "play his own hand" or whatever bullshit macho phrase his generation used to excuse not being a team player. It made for good TV, but in real-life law enforcement, not being a team player was how people got hurt.

Sometimes you got hurt even when everyone on the team had their eye on the ball. Jason's shoulder twinged, and he rubbed it absently.

There was a large heart-shaped sign by the side of the road on the outskirts of town. The sign read: IN OUR HEARTS FOREVER Honey Corrigan.

The sign had not been there the last time Jason had driven this road. It was probably familiar to Kennedy. He must have passed it a hundred times that long ago summer.

Neither of them spoke, and a couple of minutes later they were out of the dense green woodland and into the shady streets of the picturesque and rustic village of Kingsfield. It was classic New England. Pretty and quaint. White clapboard houses surrounded by wide lawns or gardens of old roses, renovated nineteenth century commercial buildings of red and yellow brick, war memorials—that would be the Revolutionary War— white churches with tall steeples, all artfully positioned around the large and lush village green. Nothing like California, that was for sure. But then that had been the point of spending summers here.

It was a quiet little place, but even so it seemed deserted for a Saturday afternoon.

"Just like you remember?" Kennedy's voice jarred Jason out of his thoughts.

"Doesn't seem to have changed much."

And that was the truth. It was almost eerie how untouched by time the village seemed. Talk about back to the future. They passed Beaky's Tavern. Bow windows and a hanging, hand-painted sign featuring a bewigged gentleman with a hooked nose like a hood ornament.

"When was the last time you visited?"

"Years." His parents had sold their vacation home right after Honey had disappeared, and Jason had not been back since. He was not going to share that information with Kennedy—even if Kennedy had been listening.

Which he wasn't. His attention was on the information his GPS provided in crisp, mechanical tones. His large hands moved with easy assurance on the steering wheel, his gaze raked the pretty little shops and cafes.

The police station was located in the center of the village, housed in the former Town Hall building. It was a two-story structure of faded brick, complete with a clock tower. Gray columns supported the front portico. The arched windows had a nice view of the Quaboag River, a blue shadow in the distance.

They parked in the rear beneath a row of maple trees, green leaves so shiny they appeared to be sweating in the heat.

"I'd expect to see a lot more cars here," Jason said, studying the nearly empty lot.

"Everybody is out searching," Kennedy replied.

His tone was neutral, but yes. Of course. Of *course* the entire town—or at least every able-bodied and available resident—would be out combing the extensive surrounding wilderness areas for the missing girl. This child was one of their own. The fact that hadn't immediately occurred to Jason simply underlined how long it had been since he'd worked a violent crime.

Or at least since he'd worked a crime where there was an expectation of violence. People were always unpredictable. Especially when they felt cornered.

He walked beside Kennedy around the building, feet pounding the pavement in dusty rhythm. The air was hot and humid, scented of warm stone and daylilies. Kennedy didn't say a word from the parking lot to the front portico. It would have been helpful to have some kind of briefing on what they were walking into, but Kennedy was not a chatty guy.

They pushed through the old wood-frame glass doors, passed a long row of bulletin boards papered mostly with flyers and notices for community events, though there were a couple of wanted posters too. A matronly-looking officer was busy answering the phones. She barely glanced at their IDs, indicating with a nod that they should proceed down the dark-paneled hallway and then calmly answering the caller on the other end of the line.

They located the incident room on the main floor. Folding chairs had been set up in neat rows to face the cluster of photographs of a very pretty girl—white, mid-teens, blue eyes, and blonde hair—plastering the front wall. The room was abandoned but for one lone uniformed officer who was erasing something on the large, portable dry-erase whiteboard. Jason's heart sank as he recognized Boyd Boxner.

Hell. Of all the gin joints—or police stations—in all the world...

It had been a long time, but Boxner hadn't changed all that much. Square shoulders, square jaw, square head. Well, maybe his head wasn't square, but his towheaded crew cut gave that impression.

"Kennedy, FBI." Kennedy offered his ID again. "This is Special Agent West."

"We've been expecting you," Boxner said. He glanced at Jason without recognition—nothing like a badge and shades for camouflage— and that was fine with Jason. "Chief Gervase is directing the hunt for Rebecca. He asked me to escort you to the search site."

"Let's get moving," Kennedy said.

Jason threw him a quick, startled look.

"Or," Jason said, "maybe we should set up base here and start reading through the witness statements. There are going to be a lot of eyewitness accounts to sort through, and it's possible there's some overlooked indicator as to why she might walk away voluntarily. Though I'd also like to swing by the girl's house. Take another look around."

A crime scene was a unique and fragile thing. You really only got one chance at it because with each subsequent visit by law enforcement, the scene—and your perception of it—changed, altered.

Kennedy looked as though he'd forgotten Jason was present. He'd removed his sunglasses. His eyes were blue. Arctic blue. A hard and unforgiving color. He turned back to Boxner. "We'll liaise with Chief Gervase."

Clear enough. Kennedy was the senior on this investigation. This was not Jason's field of expertise. By the same token, he wasn't only there to fill a second suit. He wasn't trying to challenge Kennedy's authority, but Kennedy was assuming the local police had already done the groundwork investigation. Jason didn't like to assume anything.

He also didn't like getting smacked down in public.

He said, matching Kennedy's blank face and tone, "Why? Are they short of volunteers? Isn't the point of our being here to look at the case from an objective and impartial viewpoint?"

Kennedy stared at him for a long, silent moment. It was not a friendly look. Nor the look of someone considering another viewpoint.

"You want me to leave you two to work it out?" Boxner was examining Jason more closely now.

"If you don't mind, I'd like to have a word with my colleague," Kennedy said with ominous calm.

"Right. I'll bring the car around." Boxner was clearly in no doubt as to who would win this round. The old floorboards squeaked as he departed with the air of someone tiptoeing away from a bomb site.

Kennedy didn't say a word until Boxner had vanished down the hall. He turned to Jason.

"Okay, pretty boy. Let's get something straight." His tone was cold and clipped. "We both know your role here is to run interference between me and everybody else. All you need to do is stay out of my way and smooth the feathers when needed. And in return you'll be the guy who gets to pose in front of the cameras with Chief Gervase. Fair enough?"

"The hell," Jason said. "I've been asked to try and make sure you don't step in it again, sure, but I'm not here to hold your cape, Batman. I'm your partner on this case whether either of us likes it or not. And, for the record, I *don't* like it—any more than you do."

"Then make it easy on both of us," Kennedy said. "You stay out of my murder investigation, and I'll let you know if I hear about any paintings getting stolen."

He didn't wait for Jason's answer. He turned and followed Boxner down the hallway.

CHAPTER TWO

"I thought they discontinued that model," the officer behind the reception desk remarked as Jason followed Kennedy out of the incident room. Her name badge read A. Courtney.

Kennedy, several strides ahead, was already disappearing through the glass doors. He had kept his voice down, but it was a carrying kind of voice. Or maybe Officer A. Courtney had ears like a bat.

Jason said, "The engine still runs. But we'll never find replacement parts for that carburetor."

She gave a snort of amusement, though all traces of humor disappeared as the phone rang and she reached to answer it.

"No. No news," she was saying as Jason followed Kennedy outside.

Jason would not have been entirely surprised to find Kennedy had left him at the station house—but no. The black and white idled in front of the portico, spilling exhaust into the sultry summer air.

Jason climbed into the backseat behind the cage partition—which was probably exactly where Kennedy believed he belonged. The too-warm interior smelled of drunks and dogs. Or possibly drunken dogs.

Anyway, he and Kennedy needed to work together long enough to bring this kid safely home, and then he'd never have to deal with Kennedy again. He wasn't sure who he was more irritated with: Kennedy, SAC Manning for talking Jason into this, or himself for agreeing to join an investigation where he was not going to be able to add a whole hell of a lot of value. The "pretty boy" comment had stung more than he wanted to admit.

Boxner hung up his radio and put the vehicle in motion. "Rebecca's a wild girl, but she wouldn't take off in the middle of her own party. She was only wearing her bathing suit, for one thing. Her car is sitting in the garage. The housekeeper says none of her clothes are missing. Her purse is still at the house. Her cell phone was left on a table on the deck."

Kennedy grunted, which could have meant *yes, no,* or *don't talk when I'm trying to think.*

Jason asked, "How wild is wild?"

Boxner shrugged. Once again his dark eyes studied Jason in the rearview mirror as though trying to place him. Unlike in Boxner's case, those sixteen intervening years had made a big difference to Jason. He'd filled out, lost the braces, and cut his formerly shoulder-length dark hair. Nobody who'd known him then would have expected to find him working for the FBI. Including Jason.

"Nothing that required jail time."

The Madigans were a wealthy local family, so what did that really mean? Did it matter? In most cases the character of the victim determined the initial focus and direction of investigation. If the Madigan girl was the randomly chosen prey of a psychopath, which is what Kennedy and everyone else around here suspected, then character was irrelevant. Victimology was immaterial. Rebecca was just a pawn in a gruesome game of chess.

"Are the Madigans longtime residents?" Jason didn't recognize the name.

"They moved here from New York about four years ago. Mr. Madigan is a big deal in commercial real estate."

So Rebecca had moved to Kingsfield right around the time she started high school. New social dynamics. New friends. New enemies. "How did Rebecca fit in?"

"She fit in okay."

"Is she an only child?"

"No. There's a younger brother. He's away at summer camp. They both fit in okay. *Her* problem is too much money."

"That's not such a bad problem to have."

"No. It sure as shit isn't," Boxner said with feeling.

* * * * *

Crime scenes were always chaotic, but the volunteers behind the New Dominion housing development had accidentally stirred up a wasps' nest, which added to the furor. A dust storm of stinging insects was moving across the ragged field like a small and irate tornado, and the searchers had temporarily retreated to cars and the porches of neighboring houses.

Kennedy observed the situation with his usual deadpan expression and went to seek out the police chief. Judging by the variety of uniforms, it looked like law enforcement personnel from at least two other townships as well the State Police had shown up to aid in the search.

Seeing the number of people gathered—so many tense and tired faces—reminded Jason of the search for Honey sixteen years earlier. He'd done his best to forget, but it was all coming back now. Of course he and Kennedy needed to be here. They needed to understand the scope of what they were dealing with. And if they could see and get a feel for all the players, it gave them an added advantage. He probably should have kept his mouth shut back at the station. If he was going to lock horns with Kennedy, it needed to be over something that really mattered.

He scanned the row of expensive new homes that hadn't existed sixteen years ago. They were all of the McMansion school of architecture. Oversized and bastardized Colonials or Casa del *Huhs*.

Between each house stretched a discreet square of landscaping, wide enough to foster the illusion of privacy without eating up too much acreage. Behind the row of houses to the east was a large empty meadow and then the woods. Kingsfield was surrounded by both state parks and wilderness areas, and despite the uptown airs of New Dominion, this was rural Massachusetts with ten percent of the population living below the poverty line. Some people in these remote areas went entire weeks without seeing another human. The deep woods provided home to deer, bobcats, otters, raccoons, and occasionally larger critters like bear and moose. Jason even remembered stories of a local hunter bagging a Russian boar one autumn.

The real predator haunting these woodlands had not been four-footed.

"Chief Gervase," Kennedy called.

A man in uniform—medium height, trim and fit as a career soldier—turned from the insignia-decorated circle of men he was speaking to. Just for an instant his weary, strained expression relaxed into surprised relief. "Special Agent Kennedy. You came."

Until that moment, the only face Jason had recognized had been Boxner's, but he remembered Police Chief Gervase.

Back then he had been Officer Gervase, not Chief. The then-Chief of Kingsfield, Rudy Kowalski, had been a bluff and beefy man, well-suited to appeasing the town fathers and keeping rowdy teenagers in line. He had been completely out of his depth when the slaughter began. But that had come later. When Honey had been murdered, everybody believed it was a lightning strike. It could never happen twice.

Then Theresa Nolan had been killed. Then Ginny Chapin and Jody Escobar. And so it had gone. Seven girls in all. Jason's understanding was Kowalski had voluntarily resigned and the village council had promptly filled his shoes with able and ambitious Officer Gervase. Sixteen years later Gervase was a well-preserved sixty, looking forward to his own retirement. He had gray eyes, a tidy Van Dyke beard, and the perpetual tan of someone who spent a lot of time outdoors.

He came toward them, offering his hand. "Good to see you, Kennedy." He added wryly, "Christ, you haven't changed a bit."

"Sorry it's under these circumstances." Kennedy was brisk and unsentimental. Given his investigative specialty, maybe you had to be in order to stay sane. "This is Agent West."

"Agent West." Gervase offered a brief handshake and a courteous nod. "Appreciate the help."

"Chief."

The chief waved away an errant wasp and said to Kennedy, "You can see what we're facing. Eden pond is to the east, and the woods are to the west. We've finished canvassing the neighborhood, and we've completed the search of the immediate perimeter, but there's still a hell of a lot of ground to cover, and there's no sign of the Madigan girl. Nothing. It's like she vanished off the face of the earth." His voice was flat as he added, "Just like before."

It wasn't exactly like before. None of the other victims had been taken from crowded events or peopled areas. Honey had been snatched from Holyoke Pond early in the morning. Theresa Nolan had been grabbed in the high school's deserted parking lot when she'd left swim practice late one evening. All the victims had been taken from equally isolated or private venues where there were no potential witnesses and no one to sound the alarm until it was far too late.

Having made that misstep about the crime scene, Jason was resolved to watch and listen. His antagonism for the situation—and Kennedy—was coloring his reactions, and that was not good. Not good for anyone.

"Can you bring us up to speed?" Kennedy asked.

Gervase nodded, but was interrupted by the approach of the grim-faced State Police commander. Kingsfield was a small police department. No detective unit and less than twenty officers, including the chief. That State would be called in was a given.

More introductions followed.

"I thought we'd put all this behind us," Commander Swenson said. It seemed to Jason there was a hint of accusation in his tone.

Kennedy returned, "We'll soon find out."

Given the implication he might have spearheaded the arrest and incarceration of the wrong man, Jason had to give Kennedy credit for that level of cool under fire.

Or maybe Kennedy didn't realize the whispers had started.

In fairness, the FBI had not been the only law enforcement agency involved in tracking down the Huntsman. True, the Bureau—and Kennedy—had got most of the credit for the apprehension of Martin Pink. Local law enforcement had made the arrest, and a local judge and jury had determined Pink's guilt and ultimate fate.

Gervase was saying, "I've got granddaughters about Rebecca's age. One a little older. One a little younger. If this is starting up again…" He shook his head. "I'm not going to pretend we've got the resources to handle this kind of thing anymore now than we did ten years ago."

"At least you've got plenty of reinforcements," Jason commented as a Worcester County Sheriff's vehicle pulled up alongside one of the Kingsfield cruisers.

Gervase grimaced. "That we do. We've even got cadets from the State Police Academy out here lending a hand. And we had them back then too. Which is why I'm asking for Special Agent Kennedy's help."

Kennedy was studying the undulating brown cloud of insects zigging and zagging over the long, empty expanse of grass and wild flowers that served as a green welcome mat to the woods. "You've got it," he said almost absently. As in...of course they needed his help and of course he would supply it.

It was surprisingly reassuring—or at least Gervase seemed to find it so.

Equally reassuring was the cool, crisp competency with which Kennedy collected and summarized the essential information from the chief.

The party had started at nine thirty the previous evening, and by eleven o'clock every kid in the county was there, draining the Madigan wine cellar dry. At eleven fifteen neighbors had called in a complaint about the noise, and Officer Boxner had swung by and spoken to Rebecca who agreed to "turn down the volume."

At around eleven thirty, Rebecca had some kind of falling out with her bestie, Patricia Douglas, but everyone agreed the squabble meant nothing and had been almost immediately patched up. And in fact, it was Patricia who had first noticed, around one a.m., that Rebecca was missing.

The remaining and none-too-sober partygoers had conducted an immediate and impromptu search for Rebecca which had been abandoned when they decided she had probably left for her boyfriend's house.

In the morning Alice Cornwell, the Madigans' housekeeper, phoned Rebecca's boyfriend who told her he hadn't seen Rebecca since leaving the party at around ten thirty the previous evening. Whereupon Ms. Cornwell had phoned the Kingsfield Police Department.

Kennedy said, "Rebecca intended to party with a few close friends, but word got out and her soiree was crashed by...rough estimate?" There was a perpetually cynical note in his voice that enabled him to use terms like "soiree" without sounding like he was kidding.

Boxner had rejoined them by then. He answered, "Sixty to seventy juveniles. Most but not all of them were from around here."

"Not enough supervision. That's the problem with these kids," Gervase said. "If someone is to blame, it's the parents."

Kennedy said, "If someone's to blame, it's the sociopath who took a teenage girl from her backyard." Still unmoved, still unemotional, he continued, "The boyfriend left at ten thirty. Early in the evening. That sounds like there may have been trouble between them."

Gervase said, "We interviewed Tony McEnroe first thing this morning. He said he never saw Rebecca after he left the party. He denied there being any problems in their relationship."

"He would," Kennedy said. "Officer Boxner said you've already interviewed the housekeeper, the neighbors, and the kids who were originally invited to the party?"

"Standard procedure," Gervase said. There was a hint of hope in his tone as he added, "I guess you'll want to read over their statements?"

"We'll look them over," Kennedy agreed. "Assuming we don't locate Rebecca within the next few hours."

That was going to be one hell of a lot of *he said* and *she said* to sort through. Not that Jason had a problem with paperwork. Tracking stolen artwork was largely done through surfing the web or meticulously following paper trails. Jason was very good at hunting. The difference was no one's life was ever hanging in the balance when he hunted. The stakes here were almost unbearably high.

Jason's thoughts broke off as Kennedy turned to him. "Thoughts, Agent West?" His tone was dry as he waited for disagreement or debate.

"I, er, concur."

Kennedy's brows rose as though this was an unexpected concession from an unlikely source. He turned back to Chief Gervase. "I take it you're still gathering statements from the party crashers?"

Jason let out a long, quiet breath. He had never had to work with anyone who detested him as plainly as Kennedy did. Not that he was a member of Kennedy's fan club either, but you had to respect the guy. In fact, when Kennedy had nailed Martin Pink to the wall, Jason, along with pretty much everyone else, had considered him a hero.

That was a long time ago.

Gervase was answering Kennedy. "It's going to take a while to track everyone down, especially when some of the guests don't want their parents knowing where they were."

Jason said, "Chief, can I ask why you're so sure Rebecca is the victim of a copycat?"

Gervase's smile was world-weary. "You're not familiar with the Kingsfield Killings, are you, son?"

Jason wasn't sure how to answer, and in any case, Gervase wasn't waiting for a response. "Over the course of six years, a local man by the name of Martin Pink abducted and murdered seven young blonde and blue-eyed women from swimming areas around Worcester County. The press dubbed him the Huntsman."

"I remember the case. I—"

"Then you know ten years ago your partner was responsible for catching Pink and putting him behind bars. Except now we've got another blonde and blue-eyed teenage girl missing from a pool party. I don't know about you, but I think that's one hell of a coincidence."

Kennedy said, "It could be a coincidence. It's our job to make sure one way or the other."

It could be a coincidence, and it could be a copycat. Copycat behaviors were more and more common thanks to the way violent crime was sensationalized in the "news" and the increased reach social media had given those various outlets of information. Jason had heard of more than one drug dealer legally changing his name to Walter White in honor of *Breaking Bad*, and the number of assaults and murders inspired by *The Dark Knight's* Joker was frankly depressing. Teens and young adults were especially prone to copycat behavior. It was the nature of the beast. Even so, in the broader scheme of things, copycat crimes were relatively rare.

There remained a third possibility, of course. The possibility that Kennedy had put the wrong man behind bars.

The possibility that the Huntsman was still out there.

Chapter Three

The sun rose higher in the blue sky. The day grew hotter, dryer. The swarm of wasps at last dissipated, and the search for Rebecca recommenced in this key sector. Canine teams raced into the woods ahead of the slow-moving lines of volunteers and seemed to be swallowed whole into vast green silence.

It reminded Jason all too much of the search for Honey. Just because they had not managed to find Honey in time didn't mean they wouldn't find Rebecca. Especially given that Rebecca's abductor was not Martin Pink.

Another hour passed, and the search moved farther afield. The lines of volunteers grew smaller in the distance.

As a kid, he remembered thinking how strange it was that the weather was completely unaffected by human tragedy. In the case of a missing child, it should by rights be raining. But no, it was a beautiful summer day. Not a cloud in the sky. And if the air had not been crackling with voices and radios and assorted engines, it would probably have felt tranquil, peaceful.

Anyway, there wasn't time to stand around feeling whatever he was feeling—mostly uneasy; he had volunteered to help and had been handed the thankless task of coordinating the citizen searcher lists. Minimal responsibility and maximum aggravation. Kennedy, on the other hand, had vanished into the housing development an hour earlier. No doubt he was interviewing the Madigan housekeeper for himself, unhampered by his in-name-only partner.

Unless Jason was prepared to bird-dog Kennedy's every step—which he wasn't—he was going to have to try and develop a sense of humor about the situation.

Around four o'clock, Chief Gervase and Boxner returned to base. Boxner was saying, "*I* think it's suspicious."

Gervase shook his head. "When you've been at this job as long as me, you'll find out that people act guilty for a lot of reasons."

"Including they're guilty," Boxner said.

"Yeah, and sometimes people are guilty about stuff which has nothing to do with our investigation." Gervase said to Jason, "Have you got a Tony McEnroe on any of your lists?"

Jason shuffled quickly through the sheets on his clipboard. "No."

"What's up?" Kennedy's voice inquired.

Jason's heart jumped. He hadn't seen Kennedy, hadn't noticed his approach, not that it should have affected him one way or the other, but he was intensely, uncomfortably conscious of Kennedy. Or more likely of Kennedy's dislike.

Kennedy's pale hair was dark with sweat and rings of underarm perspiration marked his blue FBI polo, so presumably he had been doing something more active than interviewing witnesses. Behind the sunglasses, his face was as impassive as usual as he met Jason's look.

"Everyone in Kingsfield is here looking for Rebecca," Boxner said. "*Except* Tony McEnroe."

"Not everyone," Gervase contradicted.

"Everyone who's free to lend a hand is here."

This time Gervase didn't bother to deny it.

"McEnroe is the boyfriend," Kennedy said. It was not a question. Jason didn't doubt Kennedy had already committed all the players to memory.

"The boyfriend," Boxner agreed. "And what a piece of work that guy is."

Kennedy directed his sunglasses toward Jason, and Jason said, "I've confirmed he's not officially on one of the search teams." Then again a lot of people who were out there looking for Rebecca had not bothered to officially sign up. McEnroe might be one of them. Presumably he would know any places that were special to her or where she might run to in times of stress.

"If McEnroe was also missing, I'd have said they took off together," Gervase said. "But we talked to McEnroe first thing this morning."

"Waste of time on a waste of space," Boxner said.

Gervase said, "The Madigans tried to discourage Rebecca from seeing him, but teenage girls have a mind of their own. Like I said, I don't like him, but I don't have any reason to doubt he's telling the truth about Rebecca."

"Except he's not out here in the noonday sun wasting any time looking for a girl he's supposed to be in love with."

"Maybe we ought to have a chat with Mr. McEnroe," Kennedy said.

Jason had become so used to Kennedy treating him as though he were invisible, it took him a second to realize he was being addressed. "Sure! Yeah!"

Maybe he sounded overly enthusiastic because Kennedy's blond brows rose in what was fast becoming his usual skeptical expression regarding Jason, but not only was Jason happy at the opportunity to hand off his clipboard, he was relieved at the promise of at least some cursory investigation into the possibility Rebecca might *not* be the victim of a copycat killer.

Despite Kingsfield's gruesome past, serial killers really were the least likely scenario in most missing person cases. And so far a missing person was all they really had.

"I'll drive you out there," Gervase said. "Boyd can stand in for me for a little while. Right, Boyd? Nothing you'd like better than to show me up at doing my own job." He was grinning as Boyd began to protest.

Jason bestowed his clipboard on Boxner, who gave him another one of those narrow looks—did he really not remember Jason at all?—and followed Gervase and Kennedy to the chief's SUV.

The chief's radio was buzzing with updates as they climbed inside. The interior of the vehicle smelled of the little fake pine tree deodorizer hanging from the rearview mirror.

"I don't believe we're looking at the end result of a lover's quarrel," Gervase told them as he started the SUV's engine. "I admit I'm curious as to why young McEnroe isn't out here with the rest of us."

Maybe because he knows everyone will be watching him, speculating, whispering. Jason didn't say it aloud. He gazed out the window at the tangle of maple, birch, and oak trees, giant ferns, and flowering vines lining the roadside. You could wander a few steps from the road and lose all sense of direction in no time. However, Rebecca wasn't a small child. She hadn't wandered away from home and gotten lost.

"I saw you finally solved that case in Wisconsin," Gervase said as the SUV bumped off the grass and onto the paved road. "Did you really throw the sheriff out the window?"

Kennedy said, "No. I thought about it plenty."

Gervase laughed. "Well, I guess you'll weather that okay. Your record ought to speak for itself."

Kennedy didn't respond, perhaps because he was conscious of Jason sitting behind them, SAC Manning's eyes and ears. Not so much. Jason wasn't going to let Kennedy throw anyone out a window, but he also didn't plan on reporting back to Manning with a transcript of everything Kennedy said and did.

The towering trees overhanging the rural road diffused the bright sunlight, creating a hazy, almost surreal effect. Tonalism. It reminded him of Whistler's nocturne painting, those dreamy, pensive landscapes. In fact, Whistler had been born in Massachusetts.

Through the fretwork of leaves he spotted the distinctive black hump of a familiar hillside outcropping. Memory slithered down his spine.

"Our boy lives a ways out," Gervase was saying apologetically. "Come to think of it, here we all live a ways out."

"Isn't this near Martin Pink's property?" Jason asked.

Kennedy's head turned his way. Sunglasses met sunglasses.

"I guess you've done your homework," Gervase said. "Yep. Pink lived over that ridge to your right. Lived there with his crazy old mother and his pothead brother. They're all gone now. Even the house is falling down. Of course, it always was."

The car hit a pothole.

"How long has McEnroe lived in the area?" Kennedy asked.

"Four or five years. Unfortunately."

Same length of time as the Madigans, Jason noted. Which meant... probably zilch. Despite the sincere efforts of Hollywood writers to prove otherwise, there were actually a lot of meaningless coincidences in crime investigation.

Kennedy had turned that appraising stare on Gervase. "Trouble?"

Gervase dipped his head from side to side in a sort of noncommittal way. "We've got an ongoing situation regarding a little patch of so-called medicinal marijuana he's cultivating on his property."

At the lack of response from either agent, Gervase said, "McEnroe is twenty-two. Rebecca is seventeen. So yes, there is always going to be trouble in that kind of situation."

They passed a stand of battered mailboxes and turned down another dirt road. The tattered green canopy of trees created the illusion it was much later than it was, that the afternoon was growing darker and chillier as shadows lengthened, reached out. The light had a tired, watery look to it.

Jason became aware Kennedy was watching him in the side mirror. The sunglasses made it hard to be sure, but he could feel that steady regard, even if he couldn't see it.

He was newly, uncomfortably aware of how he must have come across earlier. Brash. Cocky. Contentious. Partly he had been reacting to Kennedy's not even pretending to consult with him. Partly...he had been irritated with himself for not having the gumption to refuse Manning's request. You didn't earn promotions by refusing favors to head honchos—however ill-thought-out those requests might be. His irritation, impatience with the situation, had been acerbated by Kennedy's obvious displeasure at being partnered with him. But why *wouldn't* Kennedy be displeased at being saddled with what amounted to a handler?

A handler with a fraction of his experience with violent crime.

Jason winced inwardly. He didn't like thinking he had been playing the role of company stooge. That was not who he was. Though very likely that was what SAC Manning was looking for from him. And it was probably how he appeared to Kennedy.

Well, you only had one chance to make a first impression and… no. So moving forward, he would try not to be such a prick. And maybe Kennedy, who was almost certainly a congenital prick, would stop treating him like the enemy. It would make the job easier for both of them—and allow them to better serve the people they were there to help.

The road jogged to the left, and they pulled through a gate that looked more like a car had busted a wide hole in the sagging fence. The dwelling was a single-story ranch style painted a dusty red. The doors and shutters were an equally faded blue.

The chief parked next to a white pickup truck, and they climbed out.

It was the kind of place where you expected to be greeted by a barking dog, but there was no dog. No sign of any life. Jason felt an uneasy prickle between his shoulder blades.

He rested his hand lightly on the butt of his Glock, and then noticed Kennedy had unsnapped the thumb-break on his holster. So he wasn't overreacting, wasn't unduly nervous. His response was appropriate to the situation. He found it harder to be sure these days.

They followed Gervase across the mowed weeds and up the wooden steps to a small platform that served as, well, a small platform. It wasn't big enough to be a deck, let alone a porch, but it was wide enough to accommodate the three of them. Gervase banged on the peeling wooden screen. Jason and Kennedy waited.

Jason could hear Kennedy's wristwatch ticking over the pounding of his heart in his ears.

It took several more energetic knocks before a muffled yell from inside the house reached them. At last the front door swung open. A willowy young man leaned against the frame as though he needed the support. His long blond hair was rumpled, his jaw was heavily stubbled, his dark eyes bleary and hollow. He wore a long-sleeve plaid flannel shirt and Joker boxer shorts.

"I already told you she's not here!" he snarled at Gervase. It was a weary snarl though, as if most of McEnroe's energy was going into staying upright.

"Okay," Gervase said evenly. "You already told us. We'd still like to talk to you."

"Who would?" McEnroe took in Jason and Kennedy. His scowl deepened. "Who are *you*?" He turned back to Gervase. "No way. You brought the goddamned *ATF* out here?"

"You're thinking of the goddamned DEA. We're the goddamned FBI," Kennedy said. "And yes. We'd like a word."

"How about fuck off?" McEnroe tried to slam shut the door, but he was neither fast nor steady. Kennedy's hand shot out; he grabbed the edge of the door and gave it a sharp shove. McEnroe staggered and tumbled back, landing on his butt. He blinked up at them in bewilderment from the bare floorboards.

"That's two words," Kennedy said.

"Get up, Tony," Gervase growled. "We're not here about your crop, so don't make a bigger ass of yourself than you have to."

McEnroe climbed ungracefully to his feet and, with several looks of mingled reproach and outrage, led the way into the front room.

The house smelled of cigarettes, bacon, and something vaguely antiseptic. Liniment? Pine-sol? Sea Breeze?

McEnroe flung himself on a sagging sofa upholstered in beige corduroy and glared at them.

"I don't know what the hell you want from me. I don't know where Becky is."

"You do remember she's only seventeen, right?" Gervase said.

"I remember."

"What did you argue about last night?" Kennedy asked. He remained standing as Gervase took the tan recliner chair across from McEnroe.

McEnroe's eyes widened. "I don't—how do you know? We didn't."

Jason positioned himself next to the front door. It afforded a cattycorner view of the kitchen, which was in the process of either being remodeled or sold for parts.

You could tell a lot about a person by the art on their walls, but Tony McEnroe did not have art on his walls. No photos either. The place didn't seem exactly untidy so much as under halfhearted and perpetual construction. There was a layer of dust on the floor sander by the window.

Kennedy asked, "Why did you leave her party early?"

McEnroe dipped his head, running a hand through his long, oily hair. Or maybe his hair wasn't oily. Maybe he just used a lot of product. And not much soap. "I-I just felt like it. It was boring. Too many stupid, snotty kids clogging up the place."

"Aren't those stupid, snotty kids the same age as your girlfriend?" Kennedy inquired.

McEnroe shook his head without looking up.

Kennedy studied him as though deciding on the best angle of approach. "Tell us about the party. Walk us through the evening again."

McEnroe raised his head, glowering. "There isn't anything to tell. I showed up about nine thirty, which was when the party started. Becky was in a bitchy mood. So after an hour of it, I left. That's *it*. That's the entire night right there. I went home and went to bed. The first I heard she was missing was when you knocked on my door this morning."

"Alice Cornwell contacted you before she phoned us," Gervase put in.

"Well, okay. Whatever. I just mean I didn't see her again. She didn't come here."

"You don't seem particularly broken up over your girlfriend going missing," Gervase observed.

"She's not missing." McEnroe's gaze was defiant.

Gervase looked at Kennedy.

"What does that mean?" Kennedy asked.

"She's just doing this for attention. I know Becky. This is her idea of getting back at me."

"Getting back at *you*?" Kennedy repeated thoughtfully. "Why would she want to get back at you?"

McEnroe seemed to struggle to put his thoughts into words. At last he said bitterly, "Because she can't stand it when everything doesn't go her way. When she isn't the center of attention. When she's not the one in control." Absently, nervously, he stroked his arms through the soft material of the flannel shirt.

"I see."

Jason could tell Kennedy wasn't buying it. Personally, he wasn't convinced either way. For sure, McEnroe wasn't telling them everything. Most people didn't tell them everything. Not at first anyway.

McEnroe wiped his pale and sweaty face on his shirtsleeve. "Is that it?"

It was a hot summer day. Too hot for long sleeves. Too hot for flannel.

Jason asked, "How did you get those scratches on your arms?" He felt rather than saw the quick look Kennedy threw him.

It was a shot in the dark, but McEnroe gaped at him, instinctively tugged at his sleeves, although the cuffs were already covering his wrists, and Jason knew he was right.

"What? I don't—I was playing with the cat. Becky's cat. Snowball. She scratched me. The *cat* scratched me." He looked frightened.

"You know what I think," Gervase said suddenly, heavily. He placed his hands on his thighs, as though about to push to his feet. "I think we'd better finish this conversation back at the station."

"*What?*"

As McEnroe jumped off the sofa, Jason tensed, ready for anything. He did not reach for his weapon—he would have been the only one who did—but it was close.

McEnroe was babbling, "You're crazy, old man! I already told you I had nothing to do with Becky running away. I don't know anything about it. I don't *want* to know anything about it."

"Maybe you did, maybe you didn't. There are still questions that have to be answered."

"I don't *know* anything!"

"Son, you can cooperate and come in voluntarily, or I can arrest your ass," Gervase said. "Up to you."

"This is *crazy!*" McEnroe was trembling, wild-eyed as he looked from face to face. "I didn't *do* anything."

Kennedy looked his usual stony self. Gervase looked pained.

"What are you getting so worked up about, McEnroe?" Gervase's tone grew fatherly, almost reassuring. "It's routine. You're the boyfriend, you're going to be questioned. If you're innocent, you've got nothing to worry about. It's a couple of hours out of your life."

McEnroe stared at the police chief and seemed to calm at whatever he read in his expression. He stopped trembling. The wild-eyed look faded.

"I'm not under arrest?"

"Not so far."

His Adam's apple jerked. "Can I at least put my pants on?"

"Please do," Gervase said cheerfully. "Please do."

McEnroe shuffled out of the room and down the hallway. A door creaked open. They heard the scrape of drawers opening and shutting. The back and forth of footsteps. The slide of a closet door.

"You won't need your toothbrush," Gervase said to the ceiling.

Jason said, "I'm going to cover the back entrance."

Kennedy nodded. Gervase smiled, leaning back in his chair. "Don't worry. He's not going anywhere."

The chief was probably right. He'd lasted a long time at his job, so he probably knew his constituency pretty well, but this go-put-your-pants-on-and-come-with-us method seemed a haphazard way to bring in a suspect. Jason could tell by Kennedy's expression that he too was listening closely to the sounds of McEnroe moving around his room, so maybe they were on the same page here.

He opened the front door and slipped outside, jumping from the steps and moving quietly along the side of the house, carrying his pistol at low ready.

The mowed weeds ran right up to the foundation of the building. They whispered beneath his feet as he passed the living room window and turned the corner of the house.

No screens on any of the windows.

The back of the house faced the woods. There was a half-constructed deck that looked like someone had got bored playing with giant Lincoln Logs, and a brand new hot tub still in its plastic wrappings. Reassuringly prosaic. The back door screen leaned against the red siding, and the door itself was boarded up.

Nobody was leaving that way. Maybe Gervase knew that.

Those windows without screens made him uneasy. Jason crossed the back of the residence, heading for the east side again—in a minute he'd be going in circles—and turned the rear corner in time to see black curtains gusting in the breeze and McEnroe crawling headfirst out the bedroom window.

At the same instant, McEnroe spotted Jason and brought up his arm.

Jason found himself staring down the barrel of a semi-automatic pistol.

CHAPTER FOUR

Time stopped.

"Drop your gun," McEnroe whispered.

Jason did not move a muscle. He could not have moved if his life depended on it, and there was a good chance it did. A perfect and boundless stillness washed through him as he waited for the shot. That terrifying bang that always came a split second after the worst had already happened.

"*Drop it*," McEnroe hissed. His hand was rock steady.

It wasn't even fear Jason felt so much as numb inevitability. He knew he needed to think past the pistol aimed at him, but he could not tear his gaze from the black hole of the barrel pointed at his face. A suicide special. A cheap, compact, small-caliber weapon. Equally special when used for homicide.

Getting shot in the chest with a .22 or a .25 was almost always fatal. That high velocity bullet would ricochet around tearing up organs and everything else in its path like a murderous pinball machine. Getting shot in the head...

Jason let his Glock slip from his fingers. It hit the ground in front of him with a dull thud.

McEnroe slid gracelessly the rest of the way out the window, pistol trained on Jason. There was no more than three feet between them. Too far—and not far enough.

"Don't move," McEnroe whispered. "I'll blow your head off if you even twitch."

Jason said nothing. There were no coherent thoughts in his brain to speak. He had already done the unthinkable by dropping his weapon.

McEnroe began to walk backward, still leveling his pistol at Jason. Jason stayed motionless, hands at his sides. McEnroe should have made him lock his hands behind his head. Like this, he could tackle McEnroe, wrestle him for the gun.

He didn't move.

McEnroe turned and sprinted for the trees.

Jason bent and scooped up his Glock. He could take McEnroe out right now. An easy shot. A clean shot. *Bam*. Right between the shoulders.

You can't think about what it feels like to get shot.

He raised his weapon. Opened his mouth to shout a warning. The words didn't come.

McEnroe vanished into the trees.

What the fuck did you just do?

He *had* to go after McEnroe. It was his job. His duty. He could not continue to stand there like a statue. But he could not seem to...unstick his limbs. He felt paralyzed. His right shoulder was throbbing painfully as though he'd reinjured it. The reality was he was unhurt, and Rebecca's murderer was getting away.

Metal rings scraped on a metal rod. The curtains next to him suddenly fluttered open, and Kennedy leaned out the window. "Where is he? Where did he go?"

Jason's lips parted as he stared at Kennedy's tense, hard features.

He could lie. He could say he didn't know. That McEnroe had escaped before Jason made it to the back of the house.

The fact he even considered this lie for however brief a moment shocked him. Like it wasn't already bad enough?

He said through stiff lips, "He ran for the woods. He pulled a gun on me."

Kennedy shouted, *"Then what the hell are you standing there for?"*

That broke the spell. Jason launched himself after McEnroe as Kennedy—with a lightness surprising in a man his size—jumped down from the window ledge.

As Jason's feet pounded the soft, uneven ground, he scanned the treeline for motion or color. He saw nothing.

It was a relief to run. Dodging bullets was preferable to facing Kennedy. Or his own thoughts.

What the fuck? What the fuck?

How could you have done that?

He could hear Kennedy shouting to Gervase, but he didn't hear the words. He didn't need to. No time to think about any of it now. Somehow he had to make this right. All his focus needed to be on locating and apprehending McEnroe.

In thirty seconds Jason was across the firebreak. He plunged into the shadowy cool of the woods.

It was like passing through the door into a different world. The tall army of trees seemed to absorb all sound. The temperature dropped an instant few degrees, and visibility grew uncertain. He slowed, listening. From a few yards ahead he could hear crashing sounds as McEnroe piled through bushes and brush in his headlong flight. He was making no effort to be quiet, no effort to conceal his passage. He was desperate.

So was Jason. He charged after him.

High overhead a startled flock of birds took flight.

Twigs snapped to his right. Jason brought his weapon up. Several yards down Kennedy was moving on a parallel line with him.

Wouldn't that be brilliant? Shoot Senior Special Agent Sam Kennedy by mistake?

You should not be here. You are a danger to yourself and everyone on your team.

The unbidden thought frightened him, made him angry. It wasn't true. He had made a mistake, but he would fix it.

He paused.

Behind him came the crackle of a radio, instantly muffled. That would be Gervase coming up from the rear. And ahead of him...more sounds of cracking wood. Quieter now, more surreptitious. McEnroe had stopped panicking and was using his brain.

Where are you?

Jason listened, tuning out Gervase's muted voice speaking softly into his shoulder mic, Kennedy's careful progress through prehistoric-sized ferns...

There. The brush and splinter of something large moving swiftly through dense overgrowth.

Jason charged after, abandoning stealth and relying on sheer speed.

His oncoming rush must have startled McEnroe who suddenly popped up about a yard ahead, red and yellow shirt a sudden flash of color in the blue-green gloom. McEnroe's pale face turned briefly toward him, eyes wide in alarm.

Kennedy was shouting a warning, moving into firing stance.

Christ, don't shoot me. Please don't shoot me...

Jason barreled on, bursting through bushes and tackling McEnroe. His arms locked around a skinny waist—McEnroe wriggled frantically, kicked at him—and they both plunged over the side of an embankment.

There was a sickening dip in Jason's belly as the earth fell away and gravity took hold.

They landed on the hillside, rolled, kicking up dead leaves, pine needles, and loose soil, McEnroe sputtering obscenities all the way down. It seemed a ways, but fortunately it was not a steep drop.

They tumbled to the bottom, Jason on top. He scrambled up, planting his knee in the small of McEnroe's back and pressing the muzzle of his Glock against McEnroe's skull. He was shaking with adrenaline and fury as he fumbled McEnroe's pistol from his back waistband.

"Move again and I'll blow your head off."

McEnroe cried, "You broke my fucking leg, man!"

"Good. I wish it was your neck." McEnroe's legs seemed to be moving just fine, however, and Jason dug his knee in harder. "Quit kicking. I'm warning you."

Kennedy came down the embankment at a quick easy jog, holstering his weapon at the sight of Jason atop McEnroe.

He reached the flatland at the same time Gervase appeared over the crest.

"Tony, you dumbass." Gervase gave the all-clear into his mic.

"You have no right! I didn't do anything!" McEnroe howled.

"Then why'd you run?" Kennedy asked. He helped Jason haul McEnroe to his feet. McEnroe's jeans were torn, and there was a long gash in his leg, but it was not life-threatening or even apparently incapacitating. He made another clumsy kick toward Jason.

Gervase pulled his handcuffs out as he reached the bottom of the hill. He snapped them around McEnroe's skinny wrists. *"Now* you're under arrest," he said.

The satisfaction in his voice made Jason wonder if this was what Gervase had hoped would happen. He hadn't had more than the most circumstantial of evidence against McEnroe, unlikely enough for a warrant to search, let alone arrest. McEnroe trying to make a run for it definitely strengthened the case against him.

Except...what case? All they had so far was a missing girl, and maybe McEnroe was right. Maybe Rebecca had taken off for reasons of her own.

Why was everyone so eager to believe something worse had happened to the girl?

Gervase hauled his prisoner back up the embankment, McEnroe protesting the injustice and his innocence every step of the way.

Jason started to follow but was halted by Kennedy's voice.

"You want to tell me what happened back there?" Kennedy's eyes were like blue steel.

"I told you what happened," Jason said curtly. "He pulled a gun on me."

"You hadn't already pulled your own weapon?"

He wasn't going to lie about it. Even if he'd wanted to lie, not having pulled his own weapon in that situation would not put him in a much better light. "Yes. I had."

"You're saying McEnroe got the drop on you?"

Had he? Jason was no longer sure who'd had those precious few seconds of advance warning. Had he frozen, or had McEnroe raised his weapon first? He couldn't remember. There was only one appropriate answer.

He nodded curtly.

Kennedy continued to watch Jason, granite-faced and unbelieving. To Jason's relief, he did not pursue it.

They followed Gervase up the hill in silence.

* * * * *

"I don't know," McEnroe said.

He had been saying the same thing for nearly thirty minutes.

They had already covered the basics. McEnroe was twenty-two, had been born in Dudley, Massachusetts, and had graduated from Shepherd Hill high school. Following high school he had applied to and been rejected by the air force. A stint in junior college had followed, but he had dropped out after his first year. He had held a succession of low-paying jobs and was currently employed part-time in the local feed store. His income was bolstered by some kind of disability pay. He was unmarried and had no children. Two years ago he had been diagnosed with Lupus which was how he had come by a hardship cultivation registration to grow his own medical marijuana.

"You don't know what you argued with Rebecca about?" Kennedy inquired. "How much had you had to drink?"

McEnroe shook his head and rested his face in his hands. It was clear to Jason they were not going to get anything useful out of McEnroe, that this was tantamount to trying to squeeze blood from a stone. But it was Kennedy's party, and Gervase seemed to be enjoying the game of Pin the Tail on the Donkey, so Jason kept quiet.

If the day had illustrated anything, it was that he and Kennedy could have been working for two entirely different law enforcement organizations, so unalike were both the scope and focus of their investigations. It wasn't just what they investigated, it was how they investigated.

"We argue all the time," McEnroe said. "It didn't mean anything. I was tired of it, that's all."

"What kind of things do you argue about?"

McEnroe moaned. And Jason could have echoed him.

"Okay," Kennedy said with suspicious affableness. He knew they had McEnroe for as long as they needed him. There was the little matter of pulling an unlicensed, unregistered Raven Arms MP-25 on a federal officer, not to mention disarming that law enforcement officer, resisting arrest...there were any number of charges with which to hold McEnroe. "What's going on between Rebecca and Patricia?"

"Huh? How would I know?" McEnroe said with what seemed genuine astonishment.

"They were arguing the night of the party. Were they arguing about you?"

"*Me?*"

The alarm was genuine.

"How long have you been partnered with him?" Chief Gervase asked, jolting Jason out of his thoughts.

"*Me?*" Jason said with almost the same emphasis as McEnroe on the other side of the two-way mirror. "I've never worked with him before today. This is temporary."

"Ah," Gervase said, "that'll be Wisconsin."

What exactly had happened in Wisconsin? Jason only knew what SAC Manning had told him, which was that Kennedy had so antagonized the other members of the taskforce through his overbearing and bullying tactics, it had affected the course of the investigation. Kennedy—and the Bureau—had been called out on the evening news by the governor. Jason would have liked to pump Gervase for information, but gossiping about a colleague was out of bounds, so he'd have to do some web reconnaissance that evening. At the very least he needed to know what he'd got himself into.

He made a meaningless sound of acknowledgment.

"You'll learn a lot," Gervase said. "Just don't get in his way. It's his show and his show alone. He doesn't like the bit players."

What the hell did that mean? Did Gervase feel like Kennedy was overstepping his authority? It had been Gervase's choice—his suggestion, in fact—to leave the interrogation to Kennedy. Just as it had been his decision to bring in Kennedy in the first place. Jason turned to study the older man's profile. Gervase's smile was bleak. He continued to watch the interrogation room.

"We'll be out of your hair before you know it," Jason said. "I'm supposed to be back in Los Angeles in a day or two."

Three days, Manning had told him. A week at the most. Just enough time for Kennedy to reassure and advise the locals. Reassure them no mistakes had been made last time. Advise them on how to proceed this time.

"A day or two? I hope that's true. I don't mind admitting I'd prefer thinking McEnroe is our perp to the possibility of a copycat killer. Or..."

Jason nodded. Understandable. Also a lot more likely.

On the other side of the glass, Kennedy was silently reading—or rather pretending to read—through the file on the table before him. He closed the file and said, "Tell me about your relationship with Martin Pink."

"Here we go," Gervase said with quiet satisfaction. "He was just playing with him. Now he'll go in for the kill."

McEnroe looked stunned. "My...what? I never knew him!"

"You're neighbors."

"No, we're not! Pink's been in prison for years. Way before I ever moved out here."

"Are you trying to tell me you aren't aware the house you're living in formerly belonged to Susan Parvel's parents?"

"Is that true?" Jason asked the chief.

"Yep." Gervase's face was grim.

"No," protested McEnroe. And then, defensively, "Well, so what if it did? The property was cheap. That was all years ago. The Pinks are all gone now. Why shouldn't I live there?"

"I bet a lot of people could tell you why."

McEnroe blinked at Kennedy's stern face. He looked increasingly confused and scared.

Kennedy said, "The Parvels used to have one of those big above-ground pools. Susan used to go for long night swims during the summer. And one evening when she was out there floating in the water, staring up at the stars, Martin Pink came along and dragged her out of that pool. Her parents were out having dinner with friends. There was no one to hear her screams except Pink's mother and brother over the hill. Pink dragged Susan into the woods where he raped and murdered her."

McEnroe was gazing at Kennedy like a rabbit hypnotized by a cobra.

Kennedy said, "After their daughter was murdered, the Parvels had that pool taken down and planted a bed of roses in its place. Are you telling me you didn't know any of this?"

McEnroe shook his head, but whether he meant *no* or *you're out of your mind* was unclear.

Where was this line of questioning going? It made no sense to Jason. It was a horrible story, yes, but what was the point? He glanced at Gervase, and Gervase was smiling with sour satisfaction.

Kennedy said, "And then along comes you, Tony. You rip that rose garden right out without a second thought. And of all things, you replace it with a hot tub. A hot tub. How many young girls did you plan on luring into that hot tub?"

Gervase laughed quietly. He glanced at Jason. "Don't worry, Agent West. You'll be back in L.A. with plenty of time to spare."

CHAPTER FIVE

"He's not our guy," Kennedy said twenty minutes later, rejoining Jason and Chief Gervase in the observation room.

"What?" Gervase's jaw dropped. "But-but what about the hot tub? What about buying the Parvels' old house?" He turned to the two-way mirror where they could see Tony McEnroe sitting at the table, crying.

"It's not even circumstantial," Kennedy said. "We've got nothing on him."

The chief's disappointment was approximate to Jason's relief. He had been increasingly alarmed by the direction of Kennedy's interrogation. It was comforting to know Kennedy had only been bluffing—it had been a frighteningly convincing performance given the craziness of Kennedy's line of attack. *How many young girls did you plan on luring into that hot tub?* In other circumstances it would have been funny, but McEnroe had sure bought it. He believed that any minute now he was going to be arrested for Rebecca's murder.

Gervase persisted. "He's the boyfriend of the victim. He fought with her before she disappeared. He doesn't have an alibi. He's a doper. That's plenty right there!"

"It sounds like Madigan fought with half the guests at her party," Kennedy said. "She was alive and arguing after McEnroe went home."

"She got mouthy with Officer Boxner when he arrived to tell her to turn down the music," Jason said. "She was alive and well and still arguing with her guests until one in the morning."

Kennedy gave him one of those unreadable glances.

Gervase shook his head. His disappointment and disgust were obvious.

"He's lying about something," Kennedy said. "But I don't think he's lying when he says he doesn't know what happened to Rebecca. I think he believes she took off for reasons of her own."

"No, I don't buy it," the chief said. "Why would she? It makes no sense."

"I agree. I'm not telling you what I think. I'm telling you what McEnroe thinks."

Gervase glared at McEnroe and then turned his hostile gaze on Kennedy. "He's our only suspect. If it's not him...you know what that means."

Back to the theory of the copycat killer.

Kennedy shook his head. "It's way too early to draw that conclusion. To draw any conclusion. There are plenty of possibilities as far as what might have happened to Rebecca."

"They haven't even finished today's search," Jason said.

"All right." Gervase sighed, a long weary sound of exasperation. "All right then. You're the expert. Maybe we *will* find her today. Although we're running out of daylight."

"In the meantime, we've got plenty to hold McEnroe on," Kennedy said. His gaze flicked toward Jason, and Jason knew he was thinking about the fact McEnroe had managed to get the drop on him. His face warmed.

"Okay. I'm heading back to the search site," Gervase said. "If you want to start reading over statements, I'll instruct Officer Courtney to make sure you have whatever you need."

Officer Courtney set them up in an unused office and brought them coffee and a stack of papers.

As usual there was no instruction or information from Kennedy. Not that Jason didn't know how to read a witness statement, but he was used to being able to bounce ideas and theories off one of the fifteen other members of the Art Crime Team. His current situation had all the disadvantages of working alone and none of the advantages, because every time he looked up, there was Kennedy frowning over his own reading or directing one of those penetrating stares at Jason.

Let Kennedy think what he wanted. He couldn't prove it. And it wouldn't happen again. Today had been...a fluke. The very natural surprise of coming face-to-face with a loaded weapon. That would give anybody pause.

Getting shot, even in the shoulder, wasn't like on TV. A .22 round tearing through muscles and nerves and ligaments was one very special episode indeed, and as challenging as the physical recovery was, that was nothing compared to the psychological recovery. Having been shot once, the normal human reaction was to wish passionately never to repeat the experience. To do anything to avoid repeating the experience.

Which unfortunately did not necessarily square with the duties and responsibilities of an FBI special agent. Even an agent on the FBI's Art Crime Team. It wasn't all lecturing museums and galleries on how to protect their priceless collections. Sometimes it came down to bad guys with guns, bad guys who were ready and willing to blow a hole in your chest to stop you from interfering with their multimillion-dollar business.

No shame in a healthy fear of being shot. It didn't mean Jason couldn't still do his job. The shrinks at the Bureau believed Jason could still do his job. And they should know.

His shoulder twinged, and he rubbed it. He was okay. He was fine. Next time he would not be caught off guard. Next time he would not hesitate.

He reached for another file, flipped it open, and began to read.

Patricia Douglas's statement was as unhelpful as all the previous statements.

According to Patricia, there had been no argument. She and Rebecca had been joking the whole time. She loved Rebecca like a sister. Everyone liked Rebecca. No, she knew no one who would wish Rebecca harm, knew of no one Rebecca had any kind of serious falling out with, knew no reason Rebecca would leave her own party, knew of no one else who had left the party around the same time as Rebecca.

And if she *did* know, she wouldn't be telling Officer Boxner. *That* came through loud and clear even in Boxner's nearly illegible handwriting.

The problem with adolescents was they believed they were honor bound to tell adults as little as possible regardless of the situation.

The other problem was they thought they knew everything.

Reading between the lines, yeah, there was a good chance Rebecca had left the party of her own free will. Or at least that was the most likely scenario in the opinion of her friends. And if that was the case, the last thing they were going to do was *anything* that might mess things up for Rebecca.

It was pretty much the same story as all the others. Everyone had had way too much to drink. No one had seen anything out of the ordinary.

"There has to be something here."

He didn't realize he'd spoken aloud until Kennedy said, "There always is. Sometimes you know it's there by its very absence."

Very Yoda-esque. *Wise in the ways of aberrant psychology are you, Senior Special Agent Kennedy.*

Then again Kennedy *was* wise in the ways of aberrant psychology. That's why he was so very good at his job. Reportedly he could read over a profile and tell you whether the suspect had a speech impediment or visited the graves of his victims or had financial problems.

What the hell must his dreams be like?

Not that Jason's dreams were so wonderful. He dreamed about getting shot. A lot.

The next time Jason surfaced it was to the sight of the police chief ushering Rebecca's parents into his office. It was obvious who they were. A strained and affluent- looking forty-something male with his arm around an attractive blonde woman with red and swollen eyes. They both wore resort wear and looked like they had come straight from the airport.

You didn't typically have to deal with grieving parents in ACT. Granted, the way some people carried on about a stolen Picasso, you might think they were grieving the loss of a child, but no. The Madigans were terrified. Desperate for any shred of hope.

"She's still alive?" Mrs. Madigan was asking as the door to Gervase's office swung shut. "You do think she's still alive?"

Jason glanced over, but Kennedy didn't look up from the report he was reading. Maybe he didn't hear it. Maybe after this many years of hunting monsters he had learned to tune it out. Turn off the receptors to other people's pain.

Maybe you had to in order to do the job.

For once Kennedy didn't seem to feel Jason's stare, and Jason let his gaze linger. Kennedy wore gold wire reading glasses—exactly how old was he?—his thighs in blue jeans looked muscular, his shoulders powerful. The scent of his cologne had faded, replaced by clean sweat and laundered cotton.

Kennedy knew his stuff. No question there. Whatever had gone wrong in Wisconsin, it didn't make Kennedy the screw-up Manning had implied. Sometimes cases blew up in your face, and sometimes you ended up the scapegoat for local politics. And yes, sometimes maybe you *did* mess up. But should one case, one mistake, define a man's career—especially an agent with Kennedy's impressive record?

Jason forced his attention back to the witness statement before him. Which was the same as all the other witness statements. One minute Rebecca had been there, the next she was gone.

After a time, Gervase ushered the Madigans out of his office. He was kind and comforting, but Jason noticed he was not overly reassuring; Gervase had a lot of experience at this and had learned not to give out false hope.

After the chief saw the Madigans out, he returned to the office where Jason and Kennedy were still cross-checking eyewitness accounts. If you could call see-no-evil-hear-no-evil-speak-no-evil an eyewitness account.

"We've called the search off for the night." His face was bleak. "The light's gone, and those woods are too dangerous to ask people to wander around in the dark."

Kennedy nodded.

"There's no sign of her," Gervase said. "None. The dogs lost the trail a couple of feet beyond the back of the property line. It's like she stepped out of her backyard and vanished into thin air."

"Or she stepped out of her front yard," Jason said.

Kennedy gave him a curious look.

"We tried that too," Gervase said wearily. "Front or back, the dogs never picked up her scent more than a foot or so from the Madigan property."

Jason began, "There's no possibility—"

"No. None. Every inch of that house has been checked. Basement to attic. Tool shed to pool house. Rebecca is not on the premises."

The chief seemed to be waiting for something from Kennedy. Kennedy said, "You'll resume the search at first light?"

"Hell, yes." Gervase's mouth twisted. "By the way, your boy McEnroe is asking to take a lie-detector test."

Kennedy's brows rose. "Is he? Interesting."

"You know as well as I do, the results are unreliable."

"They are. Don't you think his willingness to take the test is noteworthy?"

"Noteworthy?" Gervase snorted. "I guess. So what do you think?"

"I think we give him a polygraph."

Gervase nodded, but he said, "I guess he believes he can beat the machine. I still think he knows where she is."

Jason said. "I'm not so sure. I think he's telling the truth."

Kennedy's mouth curved in that humorless smile.

Gervase said, "Did you find another viable suspect in those reports?"

"No," Jason admitted. "Nothing yet."

Gervase sighed. He looked very weary. "Well, she could still be alive," he said with what sounded like forced cheer. "There's always hope until there isn't. We might find her tomorrow."

Kennedy nodded, but it seemed to be at his own thoughts and not the police chief's words.

Jason said, "If we *are* dealing with a copycat..."

He didn't finish it. He didn't have to. They all knew that if they were dealing with a copycat, Rebecca was already dead.

CHAPTER SIX

"**W**e hope you'll be very comfortable here at the General Warren Inn. Just ask for Charlotte—that's me—if you need anything." The lanky blonde at the motel front desk slid a keycard across the scratched maple counter.

"Thanks." Jason picked up the plastic card and glanced back at Kennedy, who had already finished checking in and was walking out the sliding lobby doors into the dark courtyard.

It was eight o'clock on Saturday night. After the search for Rebecca had been placed on hold, he and Kennedy had continued to work their way through the remaining statements. They had come up as empty-handed as the volunteers scouring the woods and hills.

Sometimes no news was good news.

The search—both on foot and on paper—would start again at first light.

Charlotte was watching Kennedy too, and as the doors slid shut behind him, she said, "I remember him from the last time. He stayed here then too."

She looked to be about eighteen, which would have put her around age eight when Kennedy had been in Kingsfield working the Huntsman case. Jason didn't doubt her though. Kennedy would always leave an impression.

"Did he leave a nice tip?"

Charlotte looked surprised. "He did, yeah."

Jason winked at her and started to turn away, but she said quickly, "Do you—do you think you'll find her? Rebecca?"

"Is she a good friend?"

Charlotte shook her head but then nodded. So which was it? Yes or no? Maybe Charlotte wasn't sure. "I know her. We hang out sometimes. A bunch of us, I mean. What I wanted to tell you—"

When she didn't continue, Jason asked, "What?"

"You're wrong about Tony. He didn't do anything to Rebecca. He wouldn't have any reason."

"No?"

"It's over between them. On both sides; Rebecca just doesn't want to admit it yet because she likes using Tony to piss her parents off."

Charlotte was a cute girl. She had wide blue eyes, expertly lined in black, and shiny hair bound in two braids. Not *Little House on the Prairie* braids, but chic fashion-magazine-style braids. Jason said, "And you know this because you and Tony...?"

She blushed. Nodded.

"I see." Good news for Rebecca's parents and bad news for Charlotte's, in Jason's opinion.

She raised her chin. "Everyone knows what's going on here. Nobody wants to say it out loud, but everyone knows."

"What do they know?"

Charlotte's voice dropped. "The Huntsman is back."

"No." Jason wanted to be very clear about this. He knew only too well how fast rumor spread in a small town. "Martin Pink is sitting in solitary confinement in a supermax prison right this minute."

Charlotte was not impressed. "Everyone knows there was more than one Huntsma—" She broke off as a tall, sandy-haired man of about fifty stepped out of the back office. He wore glasses and a mustache so bushy it looked fake.

"Charlotte, can I see you in here?"

"Yes, Daddy." Charlotte left the front desk at once, throwing Jason an apologetic look.

The man studied Jason, nodded politely, and turned away.

The General Warren Inn was not actually an inn. It was a motel and a pretty basic one. The Bureau did not typically spring for five star accommodations. Jason's room appeared clean and functional, and there was a shiny, solid deadbolt on the door—which was not something he'd used to think a lot about, but appreciated these days.

Everyone knows there was more than one Huntsma—

Great. Thanks for that thought, Charlotte.

A pair of Homer Winslow watercolor marine prints adorned the walls—nice choice—and the queen-size bed was covered by a navy chintz bedspread that had lost its sheen a few years back. So long as there was a mattress under the chintz, he didn't care.

As tired as he was, he was even hungrier. He'd skipped breakfast, intending to grab something at the airport, and then there had never been another opportunity to eat. It all felt like a million years ago—which was probably the last time he'd had a real meal. You didn't join the FBI if you were looking for eight hours a night and regular meal times.

He unpacked his carryall, stared at the ball of wrinkled shirts, and realized he'd have to see about finding a laundromat, assuming this case didn't wind up tomorrow. What were the chances of that?

Everyone knows there was more than one Huntsma—

What the hell had she meant?

He washed up in the tiny bathroom, splashing cold water on his face until he was gasping for air. Drying off with one of the bleach-scented towels, he eyed his reflection. Unsurprisingly, he looked haggard: green eyes shadowed, face drawn. Too many memories—and the good memories were just as painful as the bad memories. Which is why he had never wanted to come back to Kingsfield.

Anyway. He was here, and he'd have to make the best of it. He had bigger problems to worry about. Like his reaction to finding himself at the wrong end of a semi-automatic. Just remembering turned him cold and then hot with humiliation.

Jesus Christ. What a total, fucking disaster that had nearly been. What had *happened* to him?

The eyes staring back from the mirror were wide with horror.

It was okay. McEnroe was safely behind bars, and Jason's weapon was safely stowed in its holster. Everything was okay. Everything was fine. He would never make that mistake again.

He changed his shirt—only noticing for the first time the bruises and scratches he'd collected in his tussle with McEnroe—shoved his wallet in his jeans, and stepped outside his room.

Two doors down, Kennedy, a tall shadow in the gloom, was locking his own door. Jason's heart sank.

Kennedy glanced over at Jason. "You want to grab something to eat?" he asked after a couple of beats.

He was clearly as thrilled about the idea of breaking bread with Jason as Jason was at the thought of spending another hour in Kennedy's dour presence, but since they were both obviously on their way out to eat, it would be too pointed to refuse.

"Sure," Jason said politely.

"There's a Chinese place within walking distance. It's pretty good. They stay open late."

Staying open late being one of the main things LEO looked for in a restaurant.

"I like Chinese." Jason fell into step with Kennedy as they walked down the exterior hallway.

Most of the rooms were dark. Below them, the brightly lit pool was an empty aqua rectangle. Kingsfield held few if any tourist attractions. The kind of clientele interested in what Kingsfield was best known for—a series of grisly killings—were not people you wanted to attract.

Kennedy smelled of shampoo and aftershave, so he must have taken time for a quick shower and shave. In contrast, and despite the clean shirt, Jason felt grubby and rumpled.

He followed Kennedy down the open stairs to the courtyard, and they went out through the white iron arches.

Jason didn't feel like talking about the case, and he couldn't seem to think of anything neutral to say. Kennedy, seemingly immune to social pressures, strode briskly, aloof as usual.

The streets of Kingsfield were quiet. There was no traffic and very few pedestrians. Lights glowed behind curtained windows and old-fashioned streetlamps were haloed in golden haze. The spearpoint tips of wrought iron railing fences cast militant silhouettes on the pavement as Jason and Kennedy walked past the tidy rose gardens and venerable houses. This did not look like a town where anything bad could ever happen, and yet behind all those shining Kinkadeian windows the topic of conversation tonight would be the latest terrible thing to befall them.

"Now that's a full moon," Jason said. "It almost looks like…" He was going to say it looked like Julius Grimm's 1888 study in oil of the moon and its surface, but realized in time how that would sound to Kennedy, and finished with, "unreal."

Kennedy glanced at the silver ball slowly rising behind the church steeple, as though verifying for himself that Jason had not got this wrong too.

He grunted.

What *had* happened in Wisconsin? Kennedy didn't wear a ring. Was there a Mrs. Kennedy? Did he have kids? A cat? A home? Or did he just live on the road, traveling from scene of horror to scene of horror, trying to make sense of the senseless?

He seemed so completely and coldly self-contained. Had he always been like that, or had the job made him so?

"Charlotte Simpson, the girl who checked us in at the motel, says she and Tony McEnroe are seeing each other."

Kennedy stared at him. "Now there's a piece of information. Did she offer to alibi him?"

"No. Was she at the party? Her statement wasn't in my stack."

"Mine neither. But we don't have statements from everyone at the party yet. Here we are." Kennedy abruptly turned down a small alleyway. It smelled dank. Moss grew along the walls. They went up a short flight of stone steps, and there sat the Jade Empress.

Despite its grand name, the Jade Empress was a modest establishment. In fact, it was downright tiny. It hadn't existed sixteen years ago; that, Jason was sure of.

There were no more than six linen-covered tables in the dining room, two of them filled with Asian patrons enjoying deliciously aromatic meals.

Jason's stomach growled so loudly the petite hostess leading them to their table laughed.

They were seated by a window overlooking the dark alley. Kennedy's chair squeaked loudly as he lowered his weight onto it, but that was as much about the fragility of the old furniture as Kennedy's size. The table seemed small too, and Jason wondered if he and his dinner companion would spend their meal knocking knees. He had to swallow a smile at the thought.

He picked up the menu and studied it. The Good Fortune Special. The Little Empress Special. The Laughing Samurai Special. Safe to say there would be no genial sharing of plates and exotic flavors with Kennedy. That idea also struck Jason as funny, and he decided he must be suffering from low blood sugar.

Kennedy laid his menu aside and gazed out the window.

Jason made his selection—how could you resist something called Bang Bang Chicken?—and put his own menu down.

Kennedy's profile did not invite conversation, so Jason studied the restaurant décor. Jewel-colored paper lanterns, oversized folding fans, and subtly tinted *Sansebiao* hanging scrolls that looked like they might actually be contemporary originals.

Asian art was not his area of expertise—that would be twentieth century California Impressionism—but he knew a little. Everybody on the ACT knew a little about a lot of art. And they were always learning more. With only sixteen agents to cover the entire country, they could never possibly know enough.

The waiter—short, chubby, and jovial—arrived, and they placed their orders. Jason also ordered a Tsingtao—he felt sure he was going to need a drink to get through this meal—and Kennedy ordered something called Naale Stoutbeer.

The waiter departed, and Kennedy went back to staring out the window.

It began to irk Jason.

They were never going to be pals, but did that mean they couldn't be polite? It wasn't like Jason had begged to be put on this case. He had been tired after Boston—his first real investigation since returning from sick leave—and had been looking forward to a few days off. It was taking him longer than he'd expected to get back to full speed, and he wasn't sure why. He was trying to be a team player.

A concept clearly foreign to Kennedy.

Jason said, "Gervase wants to believe McEnroe is his guy. I just don't buy it."

Kennedy glanced his way, and Jason once again had the impression he'd been all but forgotten. Kennedy seemed to consider. "He pulled a gun on you."

"Yes." Jason was not likely to forget it. "I could see McEnroe killing someone by accident or lashing out with fatal consequences. I have trouble picturing him premeditating murder."

He was surprised when Kennedy said, "I agree. If he's our unsub, Madigan's murder was not premeditated. It would have been an accident or a violent impulse aggravated by drugs and alcohol."

"Gervase views McEnroe as an undesirable. That might be behind his push to have McEnroe go down for this. He'd like to get rid of McEnroe on general principles."

"Nobody's a model citizen one hundred percent of the time."

The waiter brought their beers. Jason picked his glass up. "Cheers." Kennedy eyes flickered. Jason continued, "I don't see McEnroe as someone capable of successfully concealing his crime for any length of time. I think he'd panic. I think he'd make one dumb mistake after another."

Kennedy's lips curved in a wintry smile. "Probably."

"You don't think he's guilty either."

Kennedy did not agree or disagree. "I'm having trouble with the timeline. McEnroe left the Madigans' around ten thirty. Witnesses corroborate that. And we've got it on record Rebecca continued to party for the next two and a half hours as though she hadn't a care in the world. That doesn't mean she wasn't fuming inside and that she didn't eventually storm over to have it out with McEnroe, but there are no calls to him on her cell phone, and there wouldn't have been time for him to return her car to the garage before people noticed she was missing. One of the first things her friends did was check whether her car was still there."

"Assuming the witnesses are telling the truth."

"There's always that."

"It's also hard to picture somebody snatching her out of her own backyard in front of how many witnesses without someone seeing something. There are about two cleared acres separating the Madigan property line from the woods. Not a single tree in that stretch of land. There wouldn't be any place to hide."

"I agree it would be nearly impossible to drag someone kicking and screaming across that distance without attracting notice. But someone walking quietly on her own might make it to the woods unnoticed."

"You think Rebecca slipped out to meet someone?"

"I think it's one possibility."

"I think she'd have taken her phone. Girls her age always have their phones."

"You know a lot about teenage girls?" Kennedy raised a skeptical eyebrow.

"I have a thirteen-year-old niece. She never goes anywhere without her phone."

Kennedy made a sound of acknowledgment. Or maybe that was as close as he got to amusement.

Their meals arrived. Hot and fragrant food on oversized blue and orange plates that looked like Qing Dynasty knock-offs. Jason was surprised when Kennedy tore open the paper-wrapped chopsticks and attacked his dinner with efficient dexterity.

Jason said tentatively, "The Simpson kid said something to the effect that everyone knows the Huntsman didn't act alone."

"That was one theory for a time," Kennedy replied. "We never found any evidence to support it."

"Was anyone suspected of being Pink's accomplice?"

"Pink's brother Dwayne. Deceased." Kennedy expertly manipulated his chopsticks and popped a shrimp into his mouth. Golden sauce wetted his full lower lip.

"Why do you think the rumors of Pink having an accomplice have persisted?"

"Because it took us—law enforcement—way too long to figure out what was happening, and then to catch the offender. People want to convince themselves that wasn't a failure on the part of the law, but that law enforcement was up against multiple villains."

"Hm." Jason didn't buy it. He wasn't sure even Kennedy bought it, but it seemed to be Kennedy's last word on the topic.

They continued their meal in silence. The food was good, and Jason was very hungry. He had no complaints.

When their chopsticks finally scraped porcelain, Kennedy pulled his credit card out and signaled for the check. "This will go on my expense report."

Jason nodded. Obviously their meals were going on one expense report or the other. Was Kennedy afraid Jason might view dinner as a friendly overture? No fear of that.

"How long have you been with the Bureau?" he asked as the portly waiter departed after returning Kennedy's card and the leather guest-bill presenter.

Kennedy signed the receipt and gave Jason one of those direct blue glances. "Seventeen years."

"That's…"

"A long time."

"Did you start out in law enforcement?"

"No." Kennedy reached for his wallet. His smile was sardonic. "I started out with the Bureau. Why the sudden curiosity? I thought you were the guy with all the answers."

Which meant what?

"No. I don't think I have all the answers."

"I know damn well you don't have all the answers, Agent West." Kennedy gave him a slightly derisive smile. He pushed back his chair with a force that rocked the small table and rose. "I'm going to turn in. See you in the a.m."

That was clear enough. For a second or two Jason toyed with the comedic possibilities of walking a respectful two paces behind Kennedy all the way back to their motel, but Kennedy would not be amused, and anyway, Jason wasn't quite ready for bed.

He watched Kennedy, a long, pale shadow, descend the narrow stairs to the alley and then stride through the gloom until he vanished from sight. Jason ate the two fortune cookies that had arrived with the bill.

One fortune read: *Love for a person must extend to the crows on his roof.*

That would be Kennedy's, clearly. If ever a guy had a permanent case of crows on the roof, it was he.

The other slip of paper read: *The happiest life ends before death.*

Great.

Jason drained the last of his beer and left the restaurant, retracing his steps through the alley and heading back toward the General Warren Inn. As tired as he was, he was also restless, uneasy. Partly it was just the weirdness of being back in Kingsfield after all this time and under these circumstances. Partly...he wasn't sure.

When he reached the motel, he glanced through the arches and saw the lamp shining behind the curtains in Kennedy's hotel room. Maybe Kennedy was working late—or maybe he slept with the lights on.

Jason kept walking.

A block up the street he came to the Blue Mermaid pub. He recognized the flirtatiously smiling mermaid on the retro-style hand-painted sign, grinned inwardly, and pushed open the heavy door.

To his surprise the bar was busy. Not packed, but definitely doing a brisk trade.

Jason went to the bar. "What have you got on tap?" he asked the pretty blonde bartender. She had long, pale hair rippling in waves to her shoulders and glittery blue eye shadow. Her lipstick was a neutral color with a hint of gold. It was startling but effective.

She rattled off, "Anchor, Bell's, Blue Moon, Budweiser, Bud Light, Coors Light, Corona, Miller Lite, Sam Adams—"

"Sam Adams."

"You got it."

Jason leaned back against the bar. Talk about memories. Back in the day they had served a decent lunch, and his parents had occasionally come for the burgers and kitschy charm. He had loved this place as a kid.

In fact, he couldn't wait to turn twenty-one so he could come in here and drink.

The motif was pure ahoy-thar-be-a-shipwreck! relying heavily on clunky wrought iron, broken trunks, and splintered kegs filled with sand and topped with paste junk jewelry. The walls were adorned with pirate flags, fiberglass fish, and kitschy 1950s mermaid memorabilia. The main attraction for his younger self—the pièce de résistance—had been the retro mermaid "tank" complete with plastic seaweed and a giant conch shell.

In actuality the tank was just an ornately framed plate glass window set into the wall and covered with blue cellophane. Once upon a time a succession of scantily clad mermaids had reclined on the glittering blue sand in the room behind the glass, entertaining patrons by genteelly waving their giant rubber fish tails while sipping drinks and reading fashion magazines.

The mermaids had fallen out of favor in the eighties, which Jason always thought was a shame although at seventeen his own taste had run more to mermen.

The black curtains drawn across the front of the tank window cast a slightly funereal air over the former exhibit.

The bartender set his moisture-beaded glass on a fish-shaped coaster. "Did you want to run a tab?"

Jason shook his head. "What do I owe you?"

She told him, and he pulled a couple of bills out of his wallet. "Keep the change."

"Thanks." She smiled. "You're with the FBI, right?"

He smiled. "Is it my haircut?"

She laughed. "No. It's your suit."

"I'm not wearing a suit."

"Yes you are. Only it doesn't have anything to do with your clothes."

It was Jason's turn to laugh.

She offered a hand. "Candy Davies."

"Jason West." They shook.

"You think you're going to find her? Rebecca?"

Jason said, "I think we're all going to do our best. Were you at the party at the Madigans'?"

"Me?" Candy looked taken aback. "How old do you think I am? No, I wasn't at that party. Getting drunk with a bunch of high-schoolers isn't my idea of how to spend a Friday night."

"Right. Sorry."

She tossed her hair in a dismissive gesture. "It's terrible for her family. Terrible for the whole town. I hope whatever happened, it's not like..."

"The last time?" Jason finished.

She nodded.

"Do you know Rebecca well?" He sipped his Sam Adams.

Candy's smile was dry. "I know her. Not well. If you want the truth, I think she's a spoiled brat. Or at least I sure don't remember feeling that sense of entitlement at that age. Of course, my parents weren't rich. Anyway. I'm sorry about what's happened. She doesn't deserve to be kidnapped. Or whatever."

Not kidnapped. There would have been a ransom demand by now. Rebecca had either walked away under her own steam or she had been taken. If she had been abducted, it wasn't for money.

"I mean, you guys *did* get the right guy last time?" Candy was only half-joking. A lot of people in Kingsfield were probably asking the same question.

Don't look at me.

"Yes," Jason said firmly. "We got the right guy. Whatever has happened to Rebecca, the Huntsman is behind bars."

One of the patrons at the other end of the bar waved to Candy, and she smiled apologetically to Jason and moved off.

Jason studied the room and revised his original impression. The bar was busy, but the mood was not convivial. In fact, it was a little somber.

The front door swung open, and Boyd Boxner walked in.

Jason considered turning his back to the room, but Boxner would spot him eventually, and what did it matter anyway? He wasn't afraid to face Boyd. Whatever he had felt, it was a long time ago.

Sure enough, Boxner's tawny gaze scanned the room and lit on Jason. A weird expression crossed his face. He sauntered over to the bar.

"Jason West," Boxner said. "Did you think I wouldn't recognize you?"

"I assumed you did recognize me. I recognized you."

This momentarily nonplussed Boxner. He recovered quickly. "So you're in the FBI."

"I am."

"That's a surprise."

"It's a surprising kind of world."

Boxner was a handsome enough guy, but not the young god he'd been at eighteen. His face was fuller, his waist thicker, his shoulders burly. There was a touch of premature gray in his sideburns. His aftershave was nice though. Something light and herbal and overtly masculine.

He was studying Jason with equal curiosity. His lip curled. "I thought you were going to be the next Jackson Pollock?"

Jackson Pollock? Did Boxner actually know who Jackson Pollock was?

"Nope," Jason said. "It turns out I wasn't good enough."

If he thought self-deprecation would divert Boxner, he was wrong.

"No shit. Somehow the girls always fell for it." Boxner's expression screwed up into what he maybe imagined was a soulful look. "The sensitive *artiste*. Girls always go for that. Which is pretty funny in your case."

Right. Because Boxner had been one of the first to figure out that Jason was gay. In fact, he'd probably realized the truth before Jason had. Definitely a late bloomer, Jason.

"I gotta confess," Jason said mildly, "you remember a lot more about me than I do about you."

Even in the blue-tinged light, he could see Boxner changed color. *Score.* But it wasn't true. Jason had had a crush on Boxner for several years. Talk about misguided affections. That was adolescence for you. Boxner had had a thing for Honey and Honey had a thing for Jason and Jason had a thing for Boxner.

Anyway.

Ancient history.

Boxner ordered a beer from Candy. He greeted some of the other patrons at the bar and drank his beer.

Jason could feel they weren't done though, and sure enough, after a few minutes, Boxner turned back to him.

"I didn't realize the FBI allowed gays in."

One thing about training for law enforcement. It taught you to control your temper. And your face. Plus, Jason knew a wide smile was more effective with the Boxners of the world than any amount of huffing and puffing. He grinned and, for good measure, gave Boxner a knowing wink. "Yes. They do."

Boxner's face turned red. This time it was irritation, not embarrassment. He wasn't smart enough to be easily embarrassed. "I would think being gay would make it hard to do your job."

"Not that I've noticed." What part of his job did good old Boyd imagine he would have trouble with? He almost asked, but really, he didn't want to hear it. He said, "So, how've you been?"

Boxner, however, would not be distracted by chitchat. He sipped his beer and gave Jason a long, brooding look.

"Are you married?" Jason asked. He figured that question coming from him would probably fluster Boxner.

"No," Boxner said. "Are you?"

Oh, touché.

"No."

Studying Boxner now, Jason felt rueful amusement at how very wrong his younger self had got it. Boxner was still attractive enough in a blunt, blond way—a bit like a budget brand version of Sam Kennedy—but other than his looks, it was difficult to recall what had been so fascinating about him. Maybe in the end it just came down to Boxner's certainty, his assurance. Those were mighty rare commodities on the stock exchange of teenage masculinity. Jason, self-conscious and insecure—however well he managed to conceal it—had greatly admired those qualities in Boxner. As an adult he had learned to appreciate men who didn't assume they were always right or always knew the answer. The adult Jason no longer misread arrogance for confidence.

Boxner said slowly, "It's kind of a weird coincidence you being back here the same time we've got a copycat killer running around."

That took Jason aback. Both that Boxner took it for granted they were dealing with a copycat killer and that he'd have the balls to imply whatever it was he seemed to be implying.

Or maybe he wasn't implying anything. Maybe he was just being his normal jerk self.

Jason said, "Yeah, it's hardly a coincidence since I'm here specifically to investigate."

"Yep. That's what's so weird about it," Boxner said with grim satisfaction.

CHAPTER SEVEN

Jason was just climbing out of the shower on Sunday morning when his cell phone rang.

He glanced at the ID. SAC Manning. He clicked accept. "West."

"Agent West," Manning said. "I'm glad I, erm, caught you."

Since Jason carried a cell phone, it would be difficult for Manning *not* to catch him, by which he deduced that for whatever reason Manning was uncomfortable about making this call. Jason felt an instinctive flash of unease.

"Good morning, sir."

"I received an, erm, rather concerning phone call from Agent Kennedy last night."

Uh-oh. What was this about? What fresh hell—? He clipped out, "Yes?"

He could hear Manning's disquiet all the way from Boston. "Kennedy has raised the, erm, question of your, erm, fitness for field duty."

It was kind of like getting punched in the chest. It took a moment's struggle before Jason had the breath to say, "He said *what*?"

"Kennedy has suggested there may be an issue with your return to active duty status. I understand there was an, erm, incident yesterday."

Jason stuttered with anger and alarm, "Th-the issue is Kennedy doesn't like being partnered. That's the only issue here, and it's a big one."

By some miracle he had hit on exactly the right response. He could hear the instant relief in Manning's voice. "Erm. I see. I suspected that might be the case; however, Kennedy was unaware of your, erm, shooting, so his suggestion you froze under fire—"

"He claims I froze under fire?" Jason's voice did not sound like him.

Whoever it did sound like ruffled Manning into saying, "Erm, he didn't quite say that. He—"

"We were never under fire—you'd certainly have heard if we had been—and I did not freeze. Kennedy can't handle the fact everyone on the planet doesn't think and react like him."

Ah. He was playing Manning's song and hitting all the high notes. Manning fully believed Kennedy was an arrogant sonofabitch who listened to nobody and believed he was the supreme authority on all matters.

His tone was almost conciliatory as he told Jason, "I realize it's a difficult situation and, erm, Kennedy is a difficult, erm, personality. That's one reason you were the first, erm, person I thought of for this assignment."

Yeah. Jason was the first *erm* person Manning had thought of because he was geographically closest, between assignments, and too *erm* hungry for promotion to turn down any request from a superior. *Mostly* because he had been the only agent within driving distance to Kennedy—who would not have been willing to wait around in that parking lot even another five minutes, if Jason was any judge.

Manning was still talking, attempting to schmooze down Jason's hackles, but Jason was no longer listening. He was running through the conversation he and Kennedy were going to have five seconds after Manning hung up.

At last Manning stopped blabbing and disconnected. Jason hauled on his jeans, slammed out of his motel room, and stalked down the walkway to thump on Kennedy's door.

Annoyingly, his hair, wet from the shower, was dripping down his face. Jason brushed the drops from his cheeks just as Kennedy opened the door. Terror he might look like he was weeping spurred Jason into attack.

"What the hell do you think you're doing telling Manning I froze yesterday? You weren't there. You have no idea what happened. I did not freeze."

Kennedy said levelly, as though he was used to being greeted every morning by enraged colleagues, "*I* think you froze."

"*I didn't freeze.* You weren't even th—"

"And I think you should stop yelling the word *froze* where anyone can hear you." To Jason's astonishment, Kennedy wrapped his hand around Jason's bicep and drew him into his motel room.

The effect of Kennedy's large, capable hand drawing him briefly and disconcertingly close was...confusing. Definitely confusing. Coworkers did not breach each other's personal space unless they were very good friends—or possibly about to punch each other.

For damn sure straight male coworkers did not casually manhandle each other. It occurred to Jason to wonder if there had been another reason he had been partnered with Kennedy. Was Kennedy gay?

Ha. Could cyborgs be gay?

Cyborg? Fleetingly, he was aware that Kennedy, though also fresh from the shower, had had time to slap on too much aftershave and drink several cups of motel Brand X coffee. He was wearing those reading glasses that made him look older if not scholarly. His shirt was unbuttoned and open, revealing unexpectedly ripped six-pack abs.

Kennedy shut the door and let go of Jason's arm with an okay-knock-yourself-out salute.

"McEnroe pulled a gun on me," Jason said. Loudly. "That's what happened. He had the drop on me. You weren't there. You don't know what you would have done in the same situation. It's speculation on your part. And this isn't about that anyway. This is about you not wanting to be partnered with anyone."

"I don't want or need a partner," Kennedy agreed. "But if I'm going to have one, he sure as hell needs to be someone I can rely on."

"You can rely on me!" Though maybe shouting wasn't the most reassuring means of delivering the message. "And if you honest to God thought you couldn't, you could have talked to me. You didn't have to go behind my back."

He wasn't sure if he imagined the red tinge that appeared on Kennedy's face. "I didn't realize you'd been shot." Kennedy's tone wasn't exactly apologetic, but there was a note of something that might almost have been regret. His gaze lowered briefly to the puckered scar on Jason's shoulder. "Under the circumstances, I don't blame you for being gun shy, and if I'd known the reason, I'd have spoken to you directly. That doesn't change the fact you shouldn't be out in the field if you're not able to—"

"I'm able," Jason cut in tersely. "I'm not afraid. Unduly. Of being shot. I did not free—"

"And if you can't admit there *was* a problem, how am I supposed to believe you've got it under control?"

"Christ." Jason turned away, raking his hand through his wet hair. He faced Kennedy. "All right. Yes. *Maybe* I did freeze for a few seconds. It was just the surprise, the unexpectedness of finding a gun in my face." As he made the admission, Jason realized he had fallen for one of the oldest interrogation techniques in the world: *let's work together to fix this mess.*

Yeah. Right. Busted!

He finished without hope that there would be any comprehension, "I've been back on the job for a month, and I've been fine the whole time." He tried for a lightness he didn't feel—and Kennedy certainly didn't feel. "I give you my word, if we end up in a firefight this week, I'll have your back."

Kennedy continued to study him, flinty-eyed and unmoved. And then, to Jason's astonishment, the powerful, aggressive line of the older man's shoulders relaxed. He said, "All right. I'll hold you to that."

"You'll..."

Kennedy said, "You're correct. I wasn't there. I didn't witness the incident. You've been cleared for duty. You believe you'll be ready next time. We'll go with that."

They...would? *Kennedy* would?

There was a pause—a strange moment—where neither of them spoke or moved. Jason was acutely aware of an unexpected intimacy created by physical proximity and a cautious lowering of defenses. This was probably the first honest, unguarded conversation he'd had with Kennedy. It was more than that. He was intensely, forcefully aware of Kennedy as a man. A powerful man. An attractive man. A man with shoulders like a bulwark and a full, sensual lower lip at odds with the ascetic planes of his chiseled face.

What was happening? He didn't even *like* Kennedy. Did he?

Kennedy broke the spell with a crisp, "Were you planning to go bare-chested today, Agent West? I'm sure it'll be a treat for the ladies of Kingsfield, but I suggest you grab your shirt and shoes. We need to get moving."

* * * * *

"We've had a couple of developments," Chief Gervase informed Jason and Kennedy when they arrived at the New Dominion housing track.

Jason eyed Boxner who was busily handing out radios to the search team leaders. He and Boxner had parted ways the previous evening right after Jason had finished his beer. Which had been plenty long enough for Boxner to share with Jason what he and everyone else on the Kingsfield PD thought of Kennedy.

Which was interesting given Boxner hadn't been on the force ten years ago. Maybe the idea that Kennedy had yanked the investigation of Martin Pink out of the hands of local law enforcement was the view of Chief Gervase? Chief Gervase had been forthright about needing and wanting Kennedy's help, so more likely that was the opinion of those standing on the sidelines.

It reinforced the perception that Kennedy was a difficult personality. Good at this job—maybe even gifted at his job—but impossible to work with.

"What's up?" Kennedy asked.

"A local girl, Charlotte Simpson of all people, came forward this morning with the story she and McEnroe are an item and therefore he'd have no motive for doing Rebecca harm."

"Can she confirm McEnroe's alibi?"

"No. She wasn't at the party, and she didn't see McEnroe Friday evening." Gervase grimaced. "She doesn't seem to understand juggling two girlfriends actually gives McEnroe *more* of a motive."

Kennedy shrugged.

"You just don't like him for it, do you?" Gervase asked glumly. He glanced at Jason. "What about you?"

"McEnroe's not my favorite person," Jason said. "However, I think there would be easier ways to get rid of an extra girlfriend."

Gervase grinned. "You'd probably have some experience with that, a nice-looking young fella like yourself."

Uh... Jason glanced at Kennedy. He could have sworn Kennedy's gaze was speculative.

Jason said, "Am I right in thinking there are fewer volunteers out here today?"

Chief Gervase confirmed this with the news that a lot of people were now convinced Tony McEnroe had killed the girl. Those who didn't buy into that theory believed Rebecca had taken off of her own free will and for reasons unknown.

"No," Kennedy said. "Absolutely not. That is incorrect."

"*I* know it's incorrect, and *you* know it's incorrect," Gervase said. "That doesn't change the fact it's what people are saying."

"I thought the theory was there might be a copycat out there," Jason said.

"That's *our* theory," Gervase told him. "If the people of this town have a choice, they're going to opt for the Madigan kid running away over another monster."

"It's too early to determine what we're dealing with," Kennedy said. "That girl running away from home is not among the possibilities."

"I'm not arguing with you," Gervase said. "We'll do what we can with the resources we've got." He absently accepted a thermos cup of coffee from a young female officer. "McEnroe passed his lie-detector test. Not that it means much. We're still going to hold him on the firearms charges, assaulting a federal agent...we've got plenty on him."

"He's fine where he is," Kennedy said indifferently. Clearly McEnroe's fate was not a matter of interest or importance to him. He was studying the incident briefing map.

New Geographic Information Software had replaced outdated hard-copy quadrangle maps, transparent Mylars, and erasable markers, once standard tools in any search. In the final analysis, it all came down to boots on the ground. Humans searching for humans.

Today Jason and Kennedy were joining those boots on the ground, though that was as much to gain insight into the other players as to help locate Rebecca. According to Kennedy, there was every chance whoever had taken the girl—and he did not entertain any other scenario—would be among those looking for her now.

It was another beautiful hot summer day, and while the general mood of the searchers could not be called optimistic, the morning had brought a renewed sense of determination to find Rebecca.

News vans were parked along the perimeter, a reminder the outside world was watching.

Mid-morning Chief Gervase gave a couple of interviews, and Jason was designated—by Kennedy—to stand in the background and look suitably grave.

"That's what you're here for, West. Just looking at you will instill confidence in the at-home viewers."

"The hell—"

Kennedy had already gone back to his maps and charts, and Jason gritted his teeth and followed the chief to where the cameras waited.

Around lunchtime word spread that the Madigans were holding their own press conference, and the news vans departed. Rebecca's parents were offering a two-hundred–thousand-dollar reward for Rebecca's safe return—and unwittingly creating huge problems for themselves, as they would no doubt discover once the crank calls started flooding in.

Around two o'clock Gervase called his "focus team" together for a quick meeting.

"It's a long shot, but I think we should try Rexford."

"Rexford?" Boxner was frowning. "*Why?*"

"What's Rexford?" Kennedy asked.

Jason was wondering the same thing. The name was vaguely familiar, but he couldn't place it.

"Rexford is a ghost town," Gervase told them. "It was one of the smaller villages that got flooded when they created the Quabbin Reservoir back in the '30s. Some of the houses were moved or razed, but the cellar holes remain. Some of the buildings were just abandoned as was. The majority of the land is still above water. You can't get to it by car. You have to walk in. You've been there, Boyd. Hell, every kid in this county has explored Rexford at some time or another."

"Not me," Boxner said.

"Me neither," Jason said.

Gervase didn't quite roll his eyes, but the effect was the same. "Don't worry, boys, I'm not planning to arrest you for trespassing."

"I've never been inside there," Boxner repeated. "Not ever."

"What's the plan?" Kennedy said.

"A small team. Strictly LEOs," Gervase replied. "There are too many potential risks to even consider bringing civilians into the area. Some of those buildings are half underwater. All of them are falling down. We've got everything from poison ivy to black-widow spiders."

"Welcome to the neighborhood," Jason said.

"It doesn't seem realistic to me Rebecca would be there," Boxner said. "For sure not of her own free will. And why would anyone take her there?"

"You just answered your own question," Gervase said. "Because it's guaranteed no one would look for her in Rexford."

Boxner continued to frown.

Kennedy said briskly, "All right. Let's do it."

"Okay. You, me, West, Boyd, Simpson—"

"George? How does George Simpson fit into this?" Boxner asked.

The chief said with exaggerated patience, "George Simpson used to be a State Trooper."

"About a million years ago."

"He's got the training, and he knows the area. Which would be useful since the rest of you are claiming you've never been there."

"Up to you," Boxner said.

"I know it's up to me," Gervase said shortly. "And our final man—person—will be Officer Dale."

"The little kiss-ass should love that," Boxner said.

"Boyd, you are starting to piss me off," Gervase said. "What's gotten into you?"

Boxner scowled, muttered something, and walked away.

"Thinks he knows better than the old man," Gervase said wryly.

Kennedy said, "They always do."

* * * * *

"Remember the time we opened that old icebox and found that nest of snakes?" George Simpson was saying. "I'm surprised they didn't hear us all the way in Boston."

Gervase snorted. Catching Jason's expression in the rearview mirror, he said, "They weren't poisonous snakes."

Jason and Kennedy were riding with the chief and George Simpson in the chief's SUV while Boxner and the personable and efficient Officer Dale followed in a second vehicle.

"Oh," Jason said. "Great." He glanced sideways at Kennedy. Kennedy was staring out the window at the woodland flashing by as they headed down the highway toward Rexford, but there was the tiniest of quirks to his mouth.

"We don't have many poisonous snakes out here," Gervase said. "You find timber rattlers and copperheads in Hampshire and Hampden. Sometimes Norfolk. Which is not to say Rexford doesn't have its dangers."

"You just have to exercise common sense," Simpson said.

Gervase laughed. "Which we never did."

Simpson looked to be a few years younger than the chief, which still made him rather old to be Charlotte's father, but Jason knew a bit about that. No one could have been more surprised than his own parents finding themselves pregnant again after having raised their family. Though technically the youngest of three, in practice Jason had been an only child.

He gathered Simpson was a widower and a little overprotective when it came to Charlotte. Not that Jason could blame a guy for being overprotective in a town where it had once been open season on teenage girls.

"I thank God I didn't let Charlie go to that party," Simpson said.

Gervase said, "We're going to have to talk to her again about McEnroe. You know that."

Simpson nodded. "She's got nothing to hide."

"Kids always think they have something to hide. We did."

Simpson's frown faded. He grinned at some long-ago memory.

Jason asked, "Were the remains of any of the other victims found in the vicinity of Rexford?"

Kennedy answered. "No. But that's irrelevant. We're dealing with a completely different offender. Pink didn't care whether his victims were found or not. He didn't stage them, but he was an exhibitionist in his own way. He liked the idea that people would be shocked and horrified by what he'd done. That said, once he was finished with them...out of sight, out of mind. Our unsub may be counting on Rebecca not being found."

That put a chill on the discussion.

In silence Gervase exited the highway. They followed the road a mile or two until it turned to dirt and gravel. Gervase pulled off to the side and parked in a small clearing surrounded by oaks.

"From here we have to hike in," Gervase said.

They were testing their radios as Boxner and Dale pulled up behind them and got out.

Gervase pointed to a trail leading through the trees. "We follow this path for two miles until we come to the highway overpass. At that point we're going to have to crawl through the brambles and brush in order to scale the embankment. That's the toughest part of this hike. Then it's another couple hundred yards up on the left. The first thing you'll see is what remains of the old stone mill. The trail forks there. If you go to the left, the path leads down to the old cemetery. If you stay to the right and follow the trail, it leads to the old road and what's left of the village. I'd say we head straight for the village. Assuming we don't find anything, we'll canvass the cemetery on our way out."

"Confirmed." Kennedy pulled back the slide on his Glock and inspected the chamber.

Jason watched him perform the routine weapon check with a rising sense of tension. He couldn't help noting the dryness of his mouth, the tightness of his chest, the knots in his stomach. *What the hell was the matter with him?* Did he imagine they were going to get into a shootout?

No, it was nothing that specific, nothing that comprehensible, and this general and irrational anxiety was infuriating.

He pulled his own weapon and checked it briskly, glad his hands seemed steady even if his heart was knocking around in his chest. He reholstered his pistol.

Boxner had already started down the trail, moving quickly as though determined to get this over with. Dale looked after him, looked at Gervase, shrugged, and followed.

"Ready?" Gervase asked.

"Let's go," Kennedy said, leading the way.

It took a little over an hour to make the trek, and that was due more to the caution that had to be exercised crawling through the Sleeping Beauty wall of thorns growing under the underpass.

The sun was warm on Jason's head and shoulders and welcome after the gloomy shade of the woods. The air was pungently sweet with the scent of dead blossoms and baked earth. He could hear the hum of bees, the faraway rush of the main highway, and the crunch—and occasional slide—of Kennedy's boots ahead of him.

Jason made sure to keep right on Kennedy's tail, lest Kennedy, now aware of the shooting, get it into his head that Jason wasn't physically fit either.

Jason had to give him credit. Kennedy was in terrific shape, and Jason was working to keep up with him. Mandatory retirement age for a special agent was fifty-seven, so Kennedy was probably ultra-conscious of maintaining his level of fitness.

Gervase and Simpson followed at a slower pace.

At last Jason topped the rise and spotted the mill below. A long stone building with a red roof—now half caved in—sat on what appeared to be a sand bar. To the side of the building a giant water wheel lying half in and half out of the trickle of water was all that was left of the former river that had powered the mill for a hundred years.

Boxner was right. This was one hell of a distance from the main drag.

And still farther to go. Through a wall of trees Jason could see rooftops and chimneys...a church spire. Rexford.

Jason wiped his forehead and took a couple of swigs from his water bottle.

Kennedy was already halfway down the right fork in the trail. Jason glanced back. Gervase and Simpson were coming up fast.

"That's the cemetery to your left," Gervase called.

Jason scanned what looked like a swampy meadow and spotted the overgrown cemetery, headstones like scattered teeth and bones.

"They didn't bother to move the graves?"

Gervase shook his head.

"That can't have gone over well."

"No. People were pretty bitter. Course it was a long time ago."

Jason continued the rest of the way with the chief and Simpson, listening absently to their conversation, his gaze on Kennedy striding briskly ahead.

At last they reached Rexford, which had been reduced to the long line of its former Main Street. Everything to the east was now at least partially under water. And to the west, the woodland was hungrily reclaiming its own. There were houses all but engulfed in trees—branches bursting through windows and doors and spilling out chimneys like green smoke.

At first glance, Main Street looked almost normal—until you realized in several cases only the front façade of the building was still standing. Most of the roofs were punctured with large holes. The black and gaping eyes and mouths of broken windows formed a line of shocked faces staring at the ruins of what had once been a small but thriving town.

Boxner and Dale waited with Kennedy, who was checking his phone.

Jason asked, "Are you getting a signal out here?"

"No."

Gervase said, "George, me and you will take the houses down by the water. Boyd, you and Officer Dale go south, and Agents West and Kennedy can take the north part of town."

"Got it," Jason said.

"I can't emphasize enough the need for caution. And if you do find anything…"

No need to spell that out.

Jason and Kennedy started north, going from building to building.

It was not a fast process. Each building had to be checked, room by room. In some cases that could be managed with a glance. In other cases, it meant walking up rickety stairs or crossing loudly creaking floors.

"Why would people just leave everything?" Jason studied a faded horsehair sofa that was now home to a family of rats.

"They'd wait too long, hoping for a reprieve," Kennedy answered. "It's what people do. And then some of them couldn't afford to move everything. Some of them just gave up and walked away."

It was a relief to step outside into fresh air and sunshine. The air inside the buildings was hot and humid and fetid.

Kennedy unscrewed the lid to his water bottle and took a drink. Jason did the same. His gaze fell on a white one-story building with pseudoclassical architectural elements.

"What is that? A theater?"

"I don't think it's large enough."

They crossed the street. A faded sign read Lyceum of the Aquatic.

"A lyceum? In a village this size?" Jason asked.

"What's the right size village for a lyceum?"

"I just mean, why would this be here?"

"Why would anything be anywhere?"

Uh. Okay, that was one way to look at it.

Kennedy went through the open square entrance framed between Ionic entablature and columns. A crumbling and weathered frieze offered images of sea creatures which would never have appeared in genuine classical architecture.

Jason followed.

A small entry hall with a boarded-up ticket kiosk opened onto a larger central room. In the wide doorway with its fake and chipped pillars sat an old-fashioned diving helmet perched on a pedestal as though someone had forgotten it on their way out of the lyceum.

Which was probably about right. Rexford had certainly experienced its share of looting and vandalism. The mystery was that it hadn't been picked to its bones.

And speaking of bones…

"What the hell?" Jason murmured.

The lighter squares and rectangles on the floor spoke to exhibit cases safely removed to new and dryer locations. Embedded within the walls were what was left of four natural-history dioramas that must have been too complicated or too expensive to be relocated. Unfortunately, time, weather, and other predators had all but demolished the cases.

All that remained of the creatures within were bones and feathers scattered across peeling seascapes.

There was a sharp cracking sound as Kennedy put his foot through the floor. "*Damn.*" He called over his shoulder, "Watch where you're walking. The floor is rotten in places."

That was an understatement. In some places the floor was gone or was only represented by a few remaining floorboards. Through the gaps Jason could see only shining darkness. Water?

Their radios gave a burst of static as Gervase requested their status. Kennedy paused to reply, and Jason—his attention caught by an unnatural pattern in the blanket of dust—cautiously continued into the next room.

Were those boot prints? He wasn't sure.

His nostrils were twitching at new and even stranger scents. Mold and decay and unidentifiable chemicals. Hopefully not some kind of poison gas. At this point, nothing would surprise him.

And a few feet farther on, any hope of confirming his suspicion of footprints was lost. The floor was covered with leaves and twigs and dirt thanks to a giant hole in the roof. In fact, a large tree branch had fallen into the room.

The leaves on the branches were green, so this latest destruction was fairly recent.

He could hear Kennedy talking from across the hall. Jason looked around himself. Not including the giant branch filling the middle of the space, this room was also empty, but the walls were studded with what appeared to be a variety of ferocious-looking jaws. Shark jaws?

All those rows of enormous teeth were disturbing. At least to someone who spent as much time surfing and diving as Jason. Not that he didn't know he was sharing the ocean, but somehow...

"West?" Kennedy called.

"In here."

He realized what he had mistaken for a square shadow on the wall was actually another doorway. Or, more exactly, the square entrance into what appeared to be a small antechamber. Jason walked toward it.

The sickly smell of decay and rot were much stronger in this part of the building. His stomach churned with a mix of unease and distaste.

Without the flood of natural light supplied by the giant hole in the roof, it was harder to see more than a few steps ahead. Jason could just make out what looked like one exhibit case. A long, narrow glass box that reminded him suddenly and unnervingly of a coffin.

He heard Kennedy's footsteps approaching.

He stepped forward, feeling drawn toward the case, unable to tear his gaze from the dark misshapen thing lying inside on folds of blue material.

He gazed down through the grimy glass. Peered more closely, trying to make sense of what he saw. His heart seemed to stop in his chest.

"Kennedy?" His voice sounded weird. He felt almost light-headed, unable to tear his gaze away.

"What have you got?"

"I don't…"

It was probably about six feet long. Most of it was tail. A fish tail with scales. The other half appeared to be human, but something terrible had happened to it—to her. Her flesh had been dried and blackened until it had shriveled like leather. It almost had a fuzzy look to it, but maybe that was dust. Though how could that much dust have collected so quickly? Her hair was waist long and coarse, yellow-gray in color, her arms with those strange misshapen hands were outstretched as though she had died in agony, and the expression on her face—could you call those bared jagged teeth and subhuman features a face really?—supported that impression.

"West?" Kennedy said in a very different voice. "What's the matter?"

"God. *God.*" Jason threw Kennedy a horrified look. "Is that…"

Kennedy was staring at the contents of the case too. He shook his head. As if he didn't know, or it wasn't what Jason thought it was?

Because Jason wasn't sure *what* he thought it was. Something dead. Something mummified. Something ghastly.

"It can't be," he breathed, leaning closer. "But then what *is* that?"

To his astonishment, Kennedy suddenly laughed. Jason straightened, stared at him. Despite the gloom, Kennedy's eyes were glittering points of blue, lit with genuine amusement.

"Unless I miss my guess," he said, "that's a Fiji Mermaid."

CHAPTER EIGHT

"A..."

"Yeah. Look at the head. That's a monkey with what looks like a horse's tail glued to it."

Jason looked again. Really looked this time. Relief washed through him.

"Oh, for Christ's sake," he muttered. Had he not been a thirty-three-year-old man—and an FBI agent to boot—he'd probably have been blushing. What the hell had he thought? That it was a *real* mermaid?

No. He had been hanging around Kennedy too long. He had imagined something much worse, something much more horrific. That this was Rebecca and her killer had mutilated her and somehow transformed her into this monstrosity.

And monstrosity was the right word. Jason had never seen a Fiji or Feejee Mermaid before, but he'd heard of them, knew that they had once been common features in nineteenth century sideshows. The mummified "mermaids" were said to be a traditional art form perfected by fishermen in Japan and the East Indies who constructed faux sea creatures by stitching the upper bodies of juvenile apes onto the bodies of fish. One theory was they were created for use in religious ceremonies, but most likely they were manufactured as curiosities, gruesome souvenirs hocked to western adventurers and explorers to amaze and confound the folks back home.

Most of the tail of this one was only a skeletal outline, the scales eaten by mice, some of their skeletons lying dead in the case too.

"I'm glad I didn't have lunch." Jason couldn't look Kennedy in the face. "I'm not sure I'll have dinner." He finally risked a glance, and Kennedy's eyes met his. "Ever again."

Kennedy grinned. "You're too sensitive for this line of work, West."

Jason was reminded of Boxner's sarcastic "the sensitive *artiste*." The difference here was Kennedy was joking. There was no malice, no underlying insult. Kennedy could tease him like this because he didn't think for a minute Jason was too sensitive for the job. He might have other reservations about Jason, but sensitivity levels—whatever those might mean—were not a factor.

"Yeah, well." Jason was still feeling sheepish.

"I thought you were the expert on museums?"

"Museums. Not…House of Horrors." Jason made a face. Kennedy laughed again. He had a nice laugh, deep and good-natured. Startlingly attractive.

"Houses of what was that?"

Was Kennedy actually joking with him? Jason was so surprised he didn't have a reply.

Kennedy was chuckling softly as he moved away, leaving the ante-chamber. He edged around the fallen branch. "Did you check this other room?"

"I didn't realize there *was* another room." Jason continued to study the mermaid for another second or two.

He turned and left the side chamber. There was no sign of Kennedy in the shark room. Or no. There he was, standing in the shadows of the doorway across the room.

Something about the way he stood there, motionless…

As Jason stared, Kennedy raised his radio and said in a flat voice, "Kennedy to Gervase. Come in."

A metallic voice replied, "Gervase. Go ahead, Kennedy."

"We've got her."

Jason started forward.

"Alive?"

"Negative."

Jason joined Kennedy in the entrance of the second antechamber.

"10-4. What's your location?"

"The aquatic thing. Museum."

"We're on our way. Out."

Jason gazed down at the nude female body dumped to the side of the doorway. Easy enough to miss if you weren't checking inside each and every room.

It was puzzling to him this poor broken doll of a real-life girl seemed somehow less shocking than the Fiji Mermaid. Maybe because the mermaid had been utterly unexpected and this...sadly, this was not unexpected. As much as he had hoped—as they had all hoped—it would not turn out like this, it was what they had all feared from the start.

Rebecca lay on her side. Her yellow-blonde hair was loose and covered her face—which was fine with Jason. He did not want to see her face. The photos would be bad enough and couldn't be avoided. Her skin was gray, and there was darker mottling around her face and shoulders. There was bruising and discoloration on her buttocks and hips.

Kennedy pulled out a pair of thin blue latex gloves and squatted down facing the body. Unhurriedly, he put on the gloves, took his pen and gently lifted the girl's upper jaw.

Jason opened his mouth to ask what Kennedy was doing, but he stopped at an unmistakable sound.

Something had fallen out of the girl's mouth. Dropped out and was rolling on the wooden floor. Jason knew it even if he couldn't see over Rebecca's shoulder.

"*Fuck.*" Kennedy's voice was low and...there was a note. He sounded stricken. Recognition raised the hair on Jason's neck.

"What?"

What the hell could make you—you—look and sound like that? That's what Jason meant.

Kennedy didn't answer. It was doubtful he even heard Jason. His face looked like stone. No, chalk. Even in this poor light, Jason could see Kennedy was white.

He heard the pound of footsteps approaching fast. It sounded like an army. He called out, "Watch the floor! It's giving way in sections."

He heard splintering wood and Boxner swearing. "Shit! You could have warned us!"

More voices and more footsteps. More alarms about the floor. Within a minute or so, Chief Gervase, flanked by his officers and Simpson, entered the shark room and picked his way through the broken branches, making his way toward Jason and Kennedy.

"What kind of freak would leave her in a place like this?" Officer Dale's voice floated from the rear of the procession.

No one answered.

Gervase stopped a foot or so from Kennedy. "What have we got?"

Kennedy held up a small brown ball between his index finger and thumb. At first Jason thought Kennedy was showing them a marble. On closer inspection the small sphere looked detailed, carved.

There was a short silence.

Gervase said thickly, "The same kind of freak as before."

* * * * *

"So we're looking at a copycat," Jason said.

He and Kennedy were back in their makeshift command center with the door closed. They had returned to town ahead of Gervase and most of his team while the crime scene was being processed—a slow and pains-taking operation given the general inaccessibility of that remote location.

Arriving back at the Kingsfield police station, Kennedy had requested all the case files including autopsy reports and crime scene photos from the original Huntsman investigation.

"Possibly." Kennedy, back to his normal taciturn self, was sorting through the files quickly. He was obviously looking for something specific. Something he had not chosen to share with Jason.

"Possibly?" Jason repeated. "What are the other possibilities? Pink wasn't acting alone?" *We didn't get the right guy?*

No. He didn't believe it. And, despite what Gervase had said at the crime scene, Jason didn't think the chief believed it either. The evidence against Pink had been overwhelming.

Kennedy had paused in his search. He didn't answer Jason.

"Okay." Jason repeated, "What about the persisting rumor that Pink wasn't acting alone? Is there any basis for it?"

Kennedy said absently, "I already told you there was no evidence to support that theory."

"Hey," Jason said.

Kennedy looked up, frowning.

"Remember me? We're supposed to be working together." As Kennedy's eyes narrowed, Jason continued, "Was anyone besides Pink's brother identified as a potential accomplice?"

"No. Dwayne Pink primarily came under suspicion because his brother used his van in the commission of his crimes. And because it was hard for anyone to believe that he never had any indication of what Martin was up to."

Maybe. Unless you were a psychopath yourself it would be almost unimaginable that someone you knew, let alone someone you were related to, was a homicidal maniac.

"What did you think?" Jason asked.

Kennedy drawled, "I thought Dwayne did a lot of dope. Which might have been one reason he didn't have an inkling. Or maybe he did a lot of dope because he did have an inkling. It's immaterial because he died two years ago. He's not involved in this case."

"Pink didn't have any other friends or associates who might have taken part in the murders?"

Kennedy had gone back to studying the photos in the file he held. He raised his head, and with an obvious effort at quashing his irritation with yet another interruption, said, "Do you remember Martin Pink at all?"

"A little. He used to fish at Holyoke Pond. Even as a kid I thought there was something not right about him."

Not right. But not *that* wrong. Because *that* wrong was simply inconceivable. Or had been once upon a time.

"Right," said Kennedy. "Not a popular guy. Not a busy social life. Not a wide circle of friends."

Jason had to swallow his own annoyance. "Fair enough. Here's my point. The people of Kingsfield already know that Martin Pink's brother is dead. And yet the rumor that Pink had an accomplice—and that this accomplice is still out there—continues to circulate. How do you explain that?"

Kennedy stared at him, and Jason felt a jab of satisfaction.

"Charlotte Simpson was just a kid when you solved the original case. Yet she said to me 'The Huntsman is back' and 'Everyone knows there was more than one Huntsman.' She wasn't quoting ancient history. She was telling me what she and others currently believe to be true."

"All right," Kennedy said. "Go on."

"You don't have that kind of rumor without suspicion falling on a specific person. There's always going to be a particular suspect."

"That's debatable." Even so Kennedy seemed to be mulling over Jason's words. "This could easily be some kind of urban legend. It wouldn't be at all surprising under the circumstances."

"Something else," Jason said. "When Charlotte was talking to me, her father came out of the back office and shut her up before she could say anything else. It wasn't subtle."

"Now that's not at all surprising." Kennedy's tone was dry. "The only other person who came even briefly under suspicion as Pink's possible accomplice was George Simpson."

"George Simpson?" Jason repeated. "The George Simpson who went out to Rexford with us today?"

"The same."

"The George Simpson who, according to Chief Gervase, knows these woods like the back of his hand?"

"That's right." Meeting Jason's look, Kennedy smiled faintly. "No. Simpson was cleared of all suspicion."

"Why was he under suspicion in the first place?"

"Because Simpson sold the mermaids to Pink."

It was plain English, but the words didn't make sense. Jason said, "You lost me. Sold what mermaids to Pink?"

"Ah. You wouldn't know about that. We kept it out of the press." Kennedy slid the photo he had been scrutinizing across the desktop.

Jason picked it up. It took a second or two to make sense of what he was seeing. A small talisman or charm carved out of what was probably wood and enlarged many times over so the details of the carving were clear. Tiny scales and fins on a small female form that was half human and half fish.

A mermaid.

"What is this?" His throat felt tight. He already knew what it was. Honey had carried one like it that summer. A small mermaid charm on her key ring.

"Nearly every one of Pink's victims was found with one of those," Kennedy said. "A carved mermaid charm. Each one distinct but similar."

"Found with them?" Jason echoed. His stomach gave an unhappy lurch as he remembered Kennedy squatting beside Rebecca, taking his pen out, and leaning over her body.

"In their mouths," Kennedy said. "Each girl had a mermaid in her mouth."

CHAPTER NINE

"**W**ho the hell has been erasing my notes off this board?" Chief Gervase glared at the weary officers seated in what was now being termed the Command Center of the Kingsfield Police Station. "Officer Courtney? How many times have I told you about taking it upon yourself to tidy up after me?"

Officer Courtney looked outraged. "I didn't touch that board, Chief."

No one else responded. Gervase, as tired as everyone else in the room after the long and arduous day that had followed the discovery of Rebecca's body, seemed to give up. He released a long pent-up sigh and nodded at Kennedy, who was seated on the low, wide window sill.

"A couple of you have asked why I'm requesting the FBI to take point on this investigation when we've already got the State Police and other key resources. I'll tell you why. Some of you remember Special Agent Sam Kennedy from ten years ago when he helped us bring Martin Pink to justice. Nobody knows the players in this case better than him. And that's what we need right now. That kind of perspective and that kind of insight."

Gervase sat down in a chair next to the whiteboard. Kennedy rose and took the chief's place at the front of the room.

"First thing to keep in mind is we don't yet know who the players are this time around," Kennedy said.

"We know we're dealing with a copycat," Gervase said.

"It looks that way at this juncture of the investigation." Somehow Kennedy's concession hinted this didn't mean a whole hell of a lot.

A slim, dark-haired woman put her hand up, and Jason recognized Officer Dale. Kennedy nodded at her.

"Is it possible we're not dealing with a copycat so much as a previously unknown accomplice of Martin Pink?"

"We have a critical piece of evidence that would seem to suggest an accomplice," Gervase agreed.

Jason could see Kennedy didn't like the direction this was going, but ironically it was his own fault. He had been the one to show the mermaid charm to Gervase's officers and George Simpson. It was inevitable word was going to spread. In fact, Jason realized, Kennedy must have been fairly shaken to have forgotten his normal inclination to hoard all possible information to himself.

No matter how certain Kennedy was that Martin Pink was the Huntsman, seeing that mermaid charm must have given him a very bad moment.

And on the topic of that critical piece of evidence, Kennedy's antipathy for the idea the Huntsman might have had an accomplice seemed illogical given there was no way a copycat could have learned about the mermaid angle.

Or could he?

It could be someone close to Pink or maybe peripherally involved in the earlier investigation. Someone who had never been noticed or had been safely forgotten.

Or someone who had never appeared on the radar because their relationship with Pink was relatively recent.

Maybe not an accomplice. Maybe an apprentice?

Jason tuned back in. Chief Gervase was saying, "Dwayne Pink passed two years ago. He always maintained he knew nothing about what his baby brother was up to, but that's bullshit. He had to have *some* idea."

Kennedy heard this out before saying briskly, "There are notable similarities to the Huntsman case. But we've also got significant deviations from the previous MO. To begin with, the remains of all other victims were found within twenty-four hours and within ten miles of where they were abducted. Their bodies were left in the woods, and there was no attempt to hide the remains. In fact, Pink enjoyed the idea his victims would eventually be found. He wanted to inflict maximum horror and outrage on this community."

"Just because it took awhile to find Rebecca's body doesn't mean the killer didn't want her found." Boxner had only just arrived. He leaned against the back wall of the room, arms folded.

"Choosing Rexford to dump the body is a definite break with the previous pattern," Kennedy said. "There were significant logistical challenges to transporting her so far from home which indicates her killer either did not want her found or that Rexford itself has some meaning for him. Or both."

"What meaning?" Officer Dale asked. "How would we figure that out?"

"We won't know that until we begin to compile the profile of our unsub. We may not fully understand that piece of the puzzle until we apprehend him."

"It is definitely a him?"

"Yes," Kennedy said. "Our unsub is unquestionably male and in peak physical condition."

"Do we have an actual profile yet?" Gervase asked.

"We're working on it."

"No hurry," Gervase said acridly.

Jason understood the acridness, but until that mermaid charm had turned up, there had been a very good chance they were looking at a completely different crime, unconnected to the earlier killings. The charm changed everything. Now, yes, they were having to move fast to catch up.

Kennedy said, "Frankly, this crime doesn't fit the classic pathology. While there are obvious indications of an organized and methodical offender, the crime itself is disorganized."

"Like Pink," Gervase said.

"Appearances to the contrary, Pink was not a disorganized offender."

Boxner said, "Wouldn't a copycat killer stick right to Pink's playbook?"

"Not necessarily. This offender will want to add his own artistic touches. In fact, he's probably unable to resist adding such touches."

Gervase said, "What are some of these other deviations?"

Kennedy said, "The most obvious? Rebecca Madigan was taken from a crowded event in what amounts to full view of over fifty people."

Jason said, "The initial attack is more bold and aggressive than Pink's. But subsequently there's a much more determined effort to conceal the crime?"

"That's the way it appears," Kennedy agreed.

"Is this his first kill?" Officer Courtney asked.

"Unknown. On the one hand, this was a bold and brutal crime efficiently carried out. On the other hand, the foolhardy nature of it would seem to indicate a neophyte."

Jason said, "It's got to be his first kill in Worcester County."

Kennedy nodded. "Most likely."

Gervase said reluctantly, "It won't be his last. That's for sure."

"No," Kennedy said. His expression was bleak.

"Which brings up another possibility. I don't like it. None of us will like it, but I think we have to consider it. Maybe we're not looking at a copycat. Maybe we never got the Huntsman."

Shock rippled through the room.

"Martin Pink is the Huntsman," Kennedy said. "We got the right guy."

"We can't be sure, not one hundred percent sure, Agent Kennedy. How can we be?" Gervase was regretful but stubborn.

"I'm one hundred percent sure. I'll stake my career on it."

Jason heard the words with a sinking feeling. Of course, Kennedy's career was already at stake. He was just putting into words what everyone already knew.

Still. A guy like Kennedy made enemies. Why give them more ammunition? They were already loaded for bear.

Jason had the unmistakable feeling someone was staring at him. He glanced up, and sure enough, Boxner was regarding him with his usual pugnacious expression.

"Well, here's another possibility." Boxner continued to scowl, and for a confused instant Jason thought he was being personally addressed.

"What if this accomplice of the Huntsman was someone young, someone who didn't live here all the time, someone who didn't come back after the first couple of murders. What if he isn't an accomplice? What if he's a *disciple*?"

Boxner's fierce gaze never wavered. Jason, unable to believe what he was hearing, was so flabbergasted he nearly laughed. It wasn't funny though. In fact, it was so far out of line...

No. Even Boxner *couldn't* be that nuts.

Or could he?

"Did you have someone in mind?" Kennedy asked dryly.

Boxner pointed at Jason like the embodiment of *J'accuse*. Everyone in the room turned to look at Jason. Even Kennedy looked startled.

"You're kidding, right?" Jason said. He tried to keep his voice even, but he was so angry he wanted to leap across the room and throttle Boxner. *What the hell?* What was his *problem*? He couldn't really... Did he *really*...?

Boxner was glaring right back at Jason like yeah, he did really. Boxner said, "He was a suspect when Honey Corrigan was killed."

"*What?*"

"Boyd, what the hell are you talking about?" Gervase demanded.

"Are you out of your mind?" Jason cried. "I wasn't a suspect. I was never a suspect. Are you *crazy*?"

Boxner said to Gervase, "You gave him a lie-detector test."

"I did what?" Gervase continued to look amazed and alarmed. "*I did?*"

Everyone else in the room looked like they were watching an exceptionally good show at the Coliseum. That would be Lions versus Christians, not Springsteen in concert.

Everyone but Kennedy, and even he looked slightly less impassive than usual. He was frowning as he met Jason's appalled gaze.

"It's right there in Honey's file," Boxner said. "The files *they* asked for today."

"Who the hell *are* you?" Gervase asked Jason. And then to Boxner, "Who the hell is he?"

"He's Jason West."

"I *know* he's Jason West!"

"His family used to spend summers here. You have to remember them. They used to own the old Harley place out on Amber Road."

"The Harley place?" Gervase threw Jason a quick, uneasy look. "He's a Harley?"

"Right," Boxner said. "One of *them*. A bunch of rich snobs laughing at the rest of us. And he was there, he was a witness—he *claimed* to be a witness—when Honey disappeared. And now here he is again when another girl is murdered."

It was beyond ridiculous. Boxner was leaving out all the essential parts of the story like how Jason had an ironclad alibi and zero motive for Honey's death, like how he had passed his polygraph, like how after Honey's death Jason's family had never returned to Kingsfield, like how he was *only* here in an official capacity to investigate a murder that had already occurred two days earlier—it was ludicrous, laughable, and yet he could actually see the surprise on people's faces turning to shock and suspicion. This was how rumors got started.

How people's careers and lives were destroyed.

"You crazy sonofabitch," Jason said, and this time he did start after Boxner—only to find Kennedy in his way.

"No," Kennedy said. He spoke with utter finality, like he was delivering a decree, and as Jason stared into Kennedy's stern blue eyes, he realized Kennedy was right. He was about to give Boxner exactly what he wanted.

Which was still bewildering because why would Boxner—did Boxner genuinely hate him this much? Could he seriously suspect Jason of murdering his best friend?

Boxner said, "I don't believe in coincidences. He's here for a reason. He's—"

Kennedy said, "Okay, we're going to take this behind closed doors. *Now.*"

"You're not in charge here," Boxner began, but Gervase cut him off.

"*Now,* Boyd. My office."

Kennedy led the way. Jason followed, numbly listening to Gervase adjourning the rest of the briefing until the following morning.

Gervase's office was on the ground floor. Impressively mounted on the wall behind the desk was the head of a seven-point buck. The rest of the wall space was covered with framed commendations. Short bookshelves held binders and law books. Several family photos sat on a reasonably tidy desk.

"God almighty," Kennedy muttered. "You're just full of surprises."

Jason opened his mouth to answer, but the next minute Gervase had entered the room followed by Boxner who fired a furious look at Jason, as though this was somehow Jason's doing.

Gervase slammed the door shut and took his chair behind the desk.

"All right, let's hear it," he said to Jason.

Jason looked at Boxner. "Be my guest."

This seemed to set Boxner off all over again, and he poured out his tale of damning circumstances that weren't really all that damning once you laid them out end to end. Or at least Jason hoped not. Kennedy's face was back to its normal granite state, and Gervase was getting redder by the minute.

"That's it?" he demanded when Boxner had finally come to a sullen stop. "He was a suspect for few hours during the Corrigan investigation? That's what this is about?"

"He was the prime suspect."

"The hell I—!" Jason broke off, startled, as Kennedy placed a hand on his arm.

"Boyd, for chrissake. He was cleared. He was completely cleared." Gervase scrubbed his face in his hands. He looked up at Jason. "I guess I do remember you now. A scrawny kid with long hair and a mouth full of metal. Why didn't you say right away who you were?"

"I did—I wasn't hiding anything. I had no idea I was ever considered a suspect."

"They dragged you in for questioning," Boxner said.

"They didn't *drag* me. And if they did, they dragged you too. They dragged all of us, everyone who knew Honey."

Boxner recoiled as though this had slipped his mind. Maybe he had grown so used to thinking of himself as a police officer, he had forgotten there ever was a time when he stood on the outside.

"Are we done here?" Kennedy sounded bored.

"Done?" Gervase and Boxner echoed.

"Well?"

Gervase threw Boxner a not-exactly-apologetic glance. "Well, Boyd, it does seem like—"

"We're not even going to question him?"

"Question me about *what*?" Jason demanded.

Boxner started to explain *what*, but Kennedy broke in.

"West is a special agent with the Federal Bureau of Investigation. Which means he's passed the most rigorous physical and psychological testing in the country with flying colors. The Bureau takes only the best. We don't make mistakes."

"You're talking about yourself too, you know," Boxner said.

Kennedy grinned. "That's right. I am."

Boxner gaped at the sweeping arrogance of that. Even Jason was a little impressed.

Gervase said in his steady, even way, "Nobody can be above suspicion. Of course no one's suggesting Agent West—"

"Of course not," Kennedy said. "Because that would be fucking ridiculous. So let's call it a night. We've all had a hell of a long day, and enough time has been wasted on this nonsense."

Gervase's jaw tightened. "Anything you wish, Special Agent Kennedy." The words were tinged with sarcasm.

Kennedy nodded to Jason, and Jason opened the door and walked out. His heart was still pounding with frustrated fury—a tidal wave of adrenaline crashing against the rocks of common sense. You could not punch people for saying outrageous, stupid things. No matter how much you wanted to—and they deserved it.

The door slammed behind them, and he could hear Boxner's raised voice through the wood.

"Well, that was interesting," Kennedy said as they walked out the front doors of the station. His tone was sardonic but also weary. They were all exhausted, all depressed over the outcome of the day's search.

Which made the last half hour all the more surreal.

"Thanks for what you said in there." Jason's voice was tight with the effort of not giving in to his own ranting.

Kennedy threw him a look of disbelief. "Believe me, that wasn't personal. A federal agent under that kind of suspicion? Not acceptable. I can't get over the fact you didn't think this was information you needed to share."

"You already knew I spent summers here as a kid. And the rest of it... I never knew I was a real suspect."

Kennedy's expression was disbelieving. "They gave you a lie-detector test."

"They gave *all* of us, every boy, every man Honey knew, a lie-detector test. Her father. Her brothers. I'm sure Boxner took a lie-detector test too. Every guy Honey ever dated—not that there were that many—took a polygraph. It never occurred to me I was any more of a suspect than anyone else. I'm not sure I was. That could be Boxner's take."

Now, looking back, Jason wondered with a sense of shock whether his parents' sudden decision to sell their vacation home and never return to Kingsfield had something to do with Jason falling under suspicion.

It was not a thought he liked.

The night air was cool. Moonlight reflected off the hoods and roof-tops of the cars still crowding the parking lot. Most of Kingsfield PD would be working through the long night—and more nights to come.

They climbed into the silver sedan. Kennedy started the engine and said, "This is getting messy. I don't like messy."

"I'm not compromised," Jason said. "Gervase said himself I was completely cleared."

"I don't like it."

"You think I like it?" And he was going to like it even less if Kennedy tried to use this as another excuse for getting rid of him.

Kennedy did not put the car into gear. "What about Boxner? What's the situation between the two of you?"

"There is no situation."

"West, pull your head out of your easel. Boxner hates your guts. Why?"

"Because I'm gay."

The silence that followed was as stark as the report of a rifle.

"No." Kennedy shook his head. "It would have to be more than that."

That answered one question. Kennedy had already worked out Jason's sexual orientation. Not that it was a secret, but in the Bureau everybody played it straight. It went with the territory.

"Would it? You didn't know Boxner when he was a kid. Believe me, if he wasn't homophobic, he was pretty damned close."

"Yeah. Well. The adolescent male ego is a fragile and frightened thing." Kennedy sounded almost philosophical. "I don't get the feeling Boxner is a homophobe *per se*. I've known guys like him. He probably even regrets some of the shit he pulled as a kid. But not where you're concerned. His dislike and distrust of you shines like a beacon."

"Then it has to be because Honey and I were best friends."

Kennedy sighed. "West, I don't have time to drag it out of you word by word. Tell me about that summer."

"Boxner had a crush on Honey. Honey...wasn't interested."

After a moment, Kennedy said, "I gather you're being modest. Continue."

"We were kids. Honey was sixteen, I was seventeen. We were both lifeguards at Holyoke Pond that summer. And we were involved in the park theater program. I was just stage crew, painting backdrops and props, but Honey acted in the production. We were doing *Barefoot in the Park*."

Patiently, Kennedy said, "And where does Boxner fit into all this?"

"He was a friend of Honey's older brother Dougie. He was just always around."

"He wasn't a lifeguard?"

"No."

"He wasn't involved in the park theater productions?"

"No." *God no*, Boxner would have said at the very idea.

"Okay. So basically you and Honey were inseparable, and Boxner felt thwarted and jealous."

"Basically, yes. I would guess."

"Hm. Maybe." Kennedy seemed to be thinking aloud. "Maybe if he saw you as an obstacle to Honey's affections."

"No," Jason said. "He knew I was not an obstacle. He knew before I did. And partly he knew because..." It was one thing to privately reflect on the old hurts and humiliations. To have to say it aloud was more painful than Jason had expected.

Kennedy sounded uncharacteristically startled. "God almighty." He threw Jason a quick look, although it was unlikely he could see much in the weird light of the dashboard. "You're serious, aren't you?"

"As a heart attack. Which is about how healthy *that* was."

Kennedy made a terse sound that could have been humor.

"So to add to Boxner's frustrations, he had to worry about the fact he was attracting the wrong kind of interest, which is always going to be an issue for an insecure male. Especially an adolescent. Yeah, it fits. It makes sense. What was Boxner's relationship to the second victim, Theresa Nolan?"

"I have no idea." Jason tried to read Kennedy's face in the dim light. "I didn't know Theresa. You're not thinking Boxner—"

"I think Martin Pink is—was—the Huntsman. But it's our job to keep an open mind."

Jason had to admire that level of open-mindedness. Kennedy must have balls of steel if he could contemplate with equanimity having jailed the wrong man ten years earlier. If that *was* the case, it would be the second and perhaps mortal blow to his career.

Abruptly, Kennedy shifted into gear, and they pulled out of the parking lot.

He said thoughtfully, "I think maybe it's time to pay an old friend a visit."

"What old friend?" Jason was thinking uncomfortably of Honey's family. He had made no effort to see her parents since his arrival in Kingsfield, and he really should at least stop by. See how they were. He had spent an awful lot of time under the Corrigans' roof and at their dining table.

So it was with shock he heard Kennedy say, "I think it's time for a field trip to MCI Cedar Junction. I think we need to talk to Martin Pink. Let's have a chat with the Huntsman."

Chapter Ten

Though both manacled and shackled, the bald and bearded man seated at the stainless-steel table in the prison interrogation room looked like a real and present danger. Pink had bulked up during his years of incarceration. He was not tall, but he was all muscle, and despite the chains and cuffs, he exuded a confidence that was frankly disturbing given how much time he had spent in solitary confinement.

What really disturbed Jason was how much he wanted to walk into that room and bash Pink's head against the table until his brains poured out. He had not expected such a violent reaction to seeing him again. Not expected to feel this level of hatred. He despised violence. He believed he was smarter than that, better than that. A civilized man. After seeing Martin Pink in the flesh again—he knew just how thin the veneer of civilization was.

He let out a slow, calming breath and nodded. The prison guard opened the heavy steel door, and Jason walked into the eight-by-ten well-insulated room.

Pink was smirking. "Long time no se—" He broke off. His smirk vanished. "Who the hell are you?"

"Special Agent West." Jason took the chair across the table from Pink.

"Where's Kennedy?"

Fair question. Kennedy was talking to the prison shrink. For reasons known only to himself, he had decided Jason would be the one to interview Pink. At least, that was the story. Maybe he was on the other side of all that surveillance equipment positioned out of Pink's line of vision, waiting to see some sign Jason actually was, as Boxner had suggested, Pink's disciple.

As ludicrous as the thought was, it bothered Jason. He forced himself to concentrate on Pink, unemotionally taking in the shaved head and silver goatee. Pale, dead eyes and a cupid's bow of a mouth. At least Pink had received proper dental care in prison.

Jason said, "I work with Senior Special Agent Kennedy."

Pink glared. "I don't care if you're Special Agent Fox Mulder. I agreed to talk to Kennedy. Nobody else."

"Kennedy's busy."

Pink's lips parted as though he was stunned. After a second, he said, "He's afraid to face me."

"Yeah. You got him cold," Jason said. "He's terrified." He opened his file.

Pink didn't like that. "I'm not talking to a piss-ant junior G-man. I'll talk to Kennedy and nobody else."

"Then you'll talk to nobody." Jason slapped shut his file, rose, and signaled to the guard.

Pink eyed him in open disbelief.

"Let me know if you change your mind," Jason said.

Please change your mind. I can't walk out of this room without something...anything...you asshole...

Pink's expression grew derisive. He leaned back in his chair and folded his arms. "Bah-bye," he drawled.

Jason walked to the reinforced steel door. The guard buzzed Open.

Shit. It had taken him all of two minutes to blow this opportunity. Kennedy was going to nail his hide to the wall. And Jason didn't blame him.

Maybe Pink would back down?

There was only silence from the other side of the room.

Jason strode out. The door closed behind him with a heavy and final-sounding slam.

Kennedy, finally turning up after his meeting with Dr. Fuchs, took it well.

Surprisingly well, in Jason's opinion. Had he anticipated this outcome?

"All right. Don't sweat it. Let's get something to eat," Kennedy said. "We'll figure it out over lunch."

They found a diner a safe distance from the prison and ordered burgers and soft drinks.

"At least Fuchs isn't a complete bleeding heart," Kennedy said, as they waited for their meals. "He doesn't like solitary confinement on principle, but he's not kicking in Pink's case."

"I can't think of a better place for Pink than isolation," Jason said.

"He seems to have hit a nerve with you."

A nerve? Yeah, Pink had hit a nerve. He had murdered someone Jason loved. But the last thing he wanted to do was confirm any ideas Kennedy might have as to his ability to remain objective and impartial.

The waitress brought their soft drinks. Ginger ale for Kennedy and Coke for Jason. Jason peeled the paper off his straw and said, "So according to Fuchs there isn't any chance Pink might have formed a friendship with another inmate who was subsequently released?"

"No. Not a chance. Pink is in that cell twenty-three hours a day." Kennedy was definite. "The only time he's not is when he's escorted to the shower or to exercise outside in that human kennel with the other lifers. What we can't be equally sure of is how much contact he has with the world beyond the prison gates."

In theory he had zero contact—aside from radio, television, and curated reading material. In practice, guards could be bribed and messages could be secretly transmitted through a variety of methods and mediums.

"Is he allowed visitors?" Jason asked.

"He's permitted two visits a month from family members."

"Does he have family members?"

"No."

They paused while the waitress deposited the thick white plates topped with burgers and fries in front of them. She asked if they needed anything else. Kennedy requested mustard and ketchup. Jason requested ranch dressing for his french fries.

Drinks were refilled, the condiments were delivered, and Kennedy said as though there had been no interruption, "He's also allowed two phone calls a month."

"Does anyone call?"

"Yes. His fiancée, Coral Nunn, and—"

"*His fiancée?*"

Kennedy said through a mouthful of burger, "She was a student involved in one of these Innocence Project organizations."

"Why the hell would they waste their time on someone like Martin Pink?"

Kennedy swallowed hastily, cleared his throat, and said, "Clarification. Her class did not take on Pink's case, but that's how they met. Although *met* is not exactly the right term. They do correspond, and she does phone him."

"He raped and murdered seven teenage girls."

Kennedy's brows drew together. He said, "I know. But everyone in this restaurant doesn't need to."

Jason glanced at the astonished faces in the booth across from their table, and grimaced in apology. "Right. I just can't believe—"

"Yes you can. You had all the psych classes. You know it happens. *Hybristophilia.* Also known as Bonnie and Clyde Syndrome."

Yes, Jason did know. Every serial killer seemed to have some woman who loved him—though usually not the one he was married to before his crimes were discovered.

Kennedy said, "He also gets the occasional call from a doctor in Boston. Doctor Jeremy Kyser."

"Never heard of him. What's his field of medicine?"

"He seems to be a psychologist. He's working on a book about the brains of serial killers."

"Why is he allowed contact with Pink?"

Kennedy said mildly, "Presumably because the more we know about the brains of serial killers, the safer we'll all be." He took another large bite of his burger.

Jason dunked his skinny fries in the ranch dressing and brooded. He admitted finally, "I didn't play it right. I didn't play *him* right. I should have buttered him up, appealed to his worser nature."

Kennedy studied him. "Not necessarily. It's what he'd expect, yes. What he would look for. He's going to want to talk. He's been waiting to talk for ten years. I think he'll take what he can get. Unless he thinks you were bluffing."

"I *was* bluffing."

Kennedy's eyes met his. Kennedy grinned. The effect of that broad white display of perfect teeth was startling. He looked younger and a lot friendlier.

"Everybody bluffs. You were willing to walk away from the table. *That*, he won't have expected."

"We'll see."

Kennedy remained unconcerned. "We couldn't shut him up in the old days. He's spent most of the last decade all by his lonesome. I think we're going to hear from Martin Pink before the day is out."

As it turned out, they heard from Pink—or at least the warden—before they finished eating lunch.

When Kennedy clicked off his cell phone, his smile was his usual sardonic one. "Congratulations. You've been granted another audience."

Jason was relieved. Partly. He hated thinking he'd blown it. At the same time he wasn't looking forward to another meeting with Pink. He wasn't afraid for his personal safety. And he wasn't afraid he was going to lose control and try to strangle Pink. It wasn't anything like that. There was something disturbing, unsettling, about Pink. In simply knowing what the man was capable of. Man? Pink was a monster. A monster in men's clothing. Of course it wasn't the politically correct or psychologically informed view, but it was the truth as far as Jason was concerned. To do what Pink had done to Honey and the others was inhuman. Worse than animal.

A good portion of his unease was knowing Pink was *still* capable of monstrous acts. Age hadn't softened him. Solitude and reflection hadn't redeemed him. You had only to look into those dead eyes to know that if he got the chance, Pink would do it all again. Only he'd try a lot harder not to get caught.

That was not insanity. It was pure evil. There was a difference. A big difference.

You couldn't stand in the presence of that indifferent malevolence and not be affected. Or at least Jason couldn't. Kennedy was clearly made of tougher stuff given he had made the pursuit and capture of creatures like Pink his life's work.

"When?" he asked reluctantly.

"Today. Now," Kennedy said.

"*Now?*"

If Kennedy heard the note of dismay, he didn't acknowledge it. "Right, and this time we're going to try a different angle," he said. "One more suited to your personality."

"*My* personality? What does that mean? What's my personality?"

Kennedy wasn't exactly smiling, but his mouth had a wry curve. "You're curious, imaginative, and have a flair for the dramatic. You like to talk, you're a born smartass, and you get bored following a script."

"The hell," objected Jason. *Flair for the dramatic? Born smartass?* "You've known me all of two days!"

Kennedy shrugged. "It's what I do. Remember?"

"How could I forget, O Oracle of Quantico?"

Kennedy grinned, and Jason, hearing his words, curled his lip.

"You sure you don't want to go yourself?" Jason said after they parked in the visitors' lot. He stared at the long, white, forbidding-looking building. "You'd probably get more out of him."

"It's tempting." Jason realized Kennedy wasn't joking. "I don't want to give him that." His mouth quirked a little. "I have every confidence in you, Agent West."

"Sure you do," Jason said dryly. "But thanks."

He was startled when Kennedy reached over and gave his shoulder a quick, hard squeeze. As gestures of affection went that fell somewhere between *buck up, little buckaroo* and *see you on the other side.*

Which was actually kind of embarrassing because the last thing he wanted Kennedy to think was that he was having trouble with this—or worse, that he was afraid. When he glanced at Kennedy, Kennedy was staring out the windshield, frowning at his own thoughts, and Jason had already been dismissed.

Jason got out of the car and headed for the visitors' entrance.

* * * * *

Pink was smiling as the interview room door closed behind Jason. He looked almost genial although the cold look in his eyes never changed. "What can I do you for, Special Agent Mulder?"

Kennedy had two instructions for round two with Pink: go with your gut, and keep him guessing.

"Let's quit playing games. You know why I'm here," Jason said.

Just for an instant Pink looked confused. That was a good thing, of course. That was what they wanted. Jason had spent the entire walk from the car to this room trying to think of ways to keep Pink off-balance. He just wished he didn't feel equally off-balance.

He said briskly, "What can you tell us about the Huntsman?"

Pink stared at him without blinking.

Again Jason was struck by how unnaturally calm and focused Pink seemed for someone who had spent years with almost no human contact. He displayed none of the behaviors prisoners who spent extended periods in the special segregated units typically exhibited. No trouble meeting Jason's eyes, no trouble sitting still, and certainly no fear. No fear at being out of his cell and no fear of Jason.

"You look familiar," Pink said suddenly. "Do I know you?"

Jason asked coldly, "Do you?"

He remembered Pink. Not well. Remembered watching him fish along the banks of Holyoke Pond. Remembered joking with Honey that he only seemed to turn up on the days she was the scheduled lifeguard, never on Jason's days. An odd guy. A guy you kept your distance from.

Not someone you were afraid of. Not someone you thought about enough to be afraid of.

He could not afford to remember these things now.

Pink narrowed his eyes, considering. "What are you, twenty-nine? Thirty? You're too young to have been on the Huntsman taskforce. Huh. Yeah. I know you." He smiled. "I never forget a face. It'll come to me."

The skin prickled between Jason's shoulder blades. But then that was no doubt intended as intimidation. Image was everything in the serial killer business.

He kept his voice flat and unemotional. "I understand you're allowed television and radio in your cell. You must be aware of the situation in Kingsfield. You're not going to pretend you didn't know the Huntsman—the real Huntsman—has returned?"

"The real..." Pink stopped. He laughed. A high breathy sound that raised the hair on the back of Jason's neck. Pink stopped laughing. "Some little girl's boyfriend breaks her neck, and you think *that's* the work of the Huntsman?"

"This offender has the exact same MO."

"*This offender*," mimicked Pink. "Says who?"

"This offender has knowledge of things no one but the genuine Huntsman and law enforcement could know about those crimes."

"The genuine—" Pink got control. He smiled again. "Maybe I have a-a disciple."

Jason laughed. Maybe Kennedy was right. Maybe he did have a flair for the dramatic. "Yeah, right. Maybe *you* were the disciple."

"No."

Jason shrugged.

Pink's eyes narrowed. "He doesn't know everything. This brand new Huntsman of yours. I'll bet money on that."

Jason looked amused. "What do you think he doesn't know?"

Pink watched him, as though trying to read Jason. He was probably very good at reading people. Jason stared right back. And again, he couldn't help thinking Pink simply did not show the mental wear and tear prolonged solitary confinement typically inflicted. It was kind of depressing. Jason would have liked to know that Pink was suffering.

"It's personal, isn't it?" Pink said suddenly.

Jason felt a flicker of unease. "Yeah, personally I loathe psychopaths."

Pink sat back in his chair, smiling knowledgeably. "Yep. It's personal." He clasped his hands, gently shaking the manacle chains as though he liked the sound of the links clinking. "I'll tell you what this other Huntsman doesn't know: the things *you* don't know. The things that fucker Kennedy and the cops didn't notice."

"Like?"

"You're fishing." Pink's rosebud mouth pursed scornfully.

"You're faking."

Something bright and inimical lit the empty depths of Pink's eyes. "No, you little squirt. I'm not. You tell Kennedy to go over all his reports. All his files. All his notes. All his crime scene photos. *His autopsy reports.* He missed something ten years ago. Something he should have seen from the start. Something they all should have caught. You tell him to look again and look good. And then come and see me himself. I'm not wasting my time with the B Team."

Jason nodded, picked up his file and rose. Pink watched him with cold satisfaction.

"Oh, wait." Jason turned back. As though the idea had just struck him, he said, "Could you be talking about the mermaids?"

There was no clock, but he could hear the moments ticking by in the resounding silence.

Pink seemed genuinely stricken. Still as a statue, he stared at Jason. He didn't seem to be breathing.

Jason smiled. "You don't know what I mean, do you?"

Pink stammered, "Y-you—they—how do *you* know? No one ever—"

It was sort of fascinating to watch Pink's confidence crumble. He'd been clutching that secret to his black and twisted heart all these years. So sure that in the final analysis he had outsmarted everyone even if only on this one point.

To him it would have been a major point.

Jason said, "There was already so much evidence against you. The trophies you took from the victims. The DNA splattered all over that van. All that hard forensic evidence. And the last thing anybody wanted to do was romanticize those homicides. So that piece of information was with-held until such time it was needed. Except it never was needed. It didn't take that jury even eight hours to convict you."

"No one knew," Pink whispered. "No one else could have known."

"Somebody knew. I'm thinking the Huntsman."

"*I* am the Huntsman!" Pink leaped to his feet and nearly overbal-anced. His leg irons were fastened to the floor. He steadied himself on the steel edge of the table, breathing hard. "I am the Huntsman. Me. There is no one else."

The guard had buzzed open the door, but Jason held up a hand. He threw over his shoulder, "We're okay here."

Pink sat down in the chair. He began to rock in a tiny, tight, agitated motion.

"Why mermaids?" Jason inquired.

Pink flicked him a peculiar look but did not answer.

"Well, you probably don't know that either."

This time the look Pink cast suggested Jason would be dead if things were different. They were not different, so there was more rocking back and forth.

"Because you're not the Huntsman," Jason pressed harder.

"I saw a mermaid once." Pink stared down at the table.

"Where?" Jason was thinking of Rexford. Pink, who had extensively hunted and fished the area around Kingsfield, would almost certainly be familiar with Rexford. Maybe he'd seen the Fiji Mermaid. Maybe the sight of that grotesquery had sent him off his rocker.

Or maybe he was born with it.

"She had long blue hair," Pink said. He smiled at the memory. "Down to her waist. And blue and gold scales on her tail. Cute little fins. And her boobs were covered by these two gold shells."

"Where was this?"

"She stuck her tongue out at me." Pink was still smiling. "And I thought...some day I'm going to cut that cute little tongue right out of your big mouth, you fucking fish cunt."

Pink leaned forward to spit out the last three words with unsettling viciousness. Jason didn't move a muscle, didn't let anything show on his face.

What he was thinking was, *they should have put you down when they had the chance.*

"I bet you got that a lot," he said.

Pink tilted his head. "What'd you say your name was again? Agent North? South? East? *West.*"

"That's right," Jason said. "Special Agent West. I'm in the phone book under F.U. So how do you think this copycat found out about your mermaid? You must have told someone."

Pink rolled his eyes. Was he being devious, or was he just trying to look like he was being devious? Mostly he just looked unhinged. Granted, that went with the territory.

"He promised," Pink mumbled. "No one would know. It was our secret. Only the two of us. No one else would ever know."

Jason asked skeptically, "Who would never know?"

"*Him.* My disciple." Pink rose. "Guard!" He thumped the table with his manacled hands. "Guard! We're done here. *Guard!*"

Jason stepped away from the table as the guard entered the room.

As Pink was led away his eyes met Jason's. There was an unholy gleam of laughter in his gaze.

Chapter Eleven

"You think Pink had an accomplice?" Kennedy asked.

They had left the prison and gone for coffee, although by then Jason could have used a real drink. He was glad to sit out on this patio, glad of the open air and sunlight. Even the exhaust of cars circling the small parking lot was refreshing after the gray atmosphere of MCI Cedar Junction.

"I think at the end he was trying to make me think he did," Jason replied.

Kennedy's face was grim, and no wonder. If he had missed this—missed an accomplice to Pink's crimes—there would be no living that down.

Jason was pretty sure that was not the case. He said, "I think, belatedly, he wanted to create the illusion he's the one in control. He's still the mastermind. *He's* the important one."

Kennedy drummed his fingers on the pink melamine surface of the patio table, thinking. "Not bad, West."

Jason scowled. "Don't sound so surprised. I did graduate from the academy."

All at once he seemed to have Kennedy's complete and critical attention. "I know. And you did very well. Top of your class. You're on the fast track to promotion from everything I hear. I'm curious as to why someone with a Masters in Art History would want to go into law enforcement."

"I like to keep busy." Jason crumpled his cup and tossed it into the trash bin.

Kennedy, continuing to eye him, offered one of those humorless smiles.

Jason wasn't sure if he was flattered or alarmed Kennedy had bothered to check up on him. Especially now.

"And a Harley to boot."

Jason narrowed his eyes.

"Don't worry. I have no idea who the Harleys are. Nor do I care."

Now *that* Jason believed. He asked, "What's the real reason you sent me in there to talk to Pink rather than interviewing him yourself?"

Kennedy's blue appraisal grew unexpectedly chilly. "The real reason? I needed an impartial judge."

Jason thought this over. "To determine whether Pink really was the Huntsman?"

"You got it. It's what you're here for, right? To make sure I didn't screw up that earlier investigation—and that I don't screw up this one."

"No one suggested you screwed up the earlier investigation."

Kennedy's gaze grew mocking. "Tactfully put. You'll do well in management."

"Fuck off," Jason said quietly.

Kennedy's pale brows rose.

"Sir," Jason added.

Kennedy laughed. It was a sound of genuine amusement. "Or maybe not. Anyway, don't *sir* me. I'm not your supervisor as you know very well."

Yes, they were both aware of their roles. Even so, Jason was a little startled by his reaction. Kennedy had a way of getting under his skin. But then, Kennedy had a way of getting under everyone's skin. That was part of what made him good at his job.

It was also part of why he didn't have a lot of friends to back him up when he needed it.

Jason said, "If you really were worried, you can relax. I've got no doubt Pink is the Huntsman. I don't believe he ever had an accomplice. I believe he acted alone. And as far as acquiring an apprentice, it was clear to me in the initial part of the interview he was floored at the idea that there could be a successful copycat."

Kennedy said, "That doesn't rule out the possibility that he's got one."

"If he does, it's news to him. And not good news either."

"Maybe." Kennedy seemed unconvinced. Was he genuinely afraid he had missed something crucial in that initial investigation? Self-doubt seemed out of character for him.

Jason said, "I don't think Pink plays well with others. And I don't just mean the homicidal maniac thing, though that's an obvious factor. I don't think he's the type to share the glory or the gory. He's a one-man show."

"Yeah." Kennedy drained his coffee and dropped the cup in the trash. "But someone's waiting in the wings."

As they walked back to their car, Jason said, "He honestly didn't think you were aware of the mermaid connection. I don't know how he imagines every single person on that taskforce could have missed it, but he'd convinced himself you had. I think that was important to him. Believing he'd gotten away with something. Believing there was still something that was his and his alone."

"Very possible. It would be his final shared intimacy with the victims."

At Jason's questioning look, Kennedy said, "That's the real point of taking trophies. Serials like to relive their relationship, if you will, with the victims. Trophies help facilitate that."

"By relationship you mean murder."

"There's more to it, but yes, murder is always the keystone of the relationship. Trophies are like talismans. They're tangible. They're proof it actually happened. In Pink's case he took trophies, but he also left something of his own, of himself, with the victims. It was another way of keeping the connection."

"Delightful," Jason said bitterly.

"In some ways Pink was pretty naïve. It was more luck than cunning that allowed him to run free so long. In an urban environment, he'd have been caught right away."

"What was the significance of the mermaids? He told me some cock-and-bull story about a mermaid sticking her tongue out at him once. I think he must have been talking about one of the girls who used to work at the Blue Mermaid. But nothing ever happened to any of those girls. At least not that I remember hearing."

"No. We were never sure what the significance of the mermaids was."

Jason stared at the highway and the never-ending stream of cars racing into oblivion.

Kennedy glanced at him and said, "You're never going to get a satisfying answer on the why. Serial killers don't kill for the normal reasons of gain or revenge or lust. Their motives don't even qualify as motives as recognized by a rational mind."

"Insanity is a legal definition not a medical diagnosis."

"True. But how else do you classify the brain of a ruthless predator that kills and tortures for pleasure? People want to understand the why and the how, but there are some things there's no understanding."

Yes. Kennedy had this right. Despite his training and education, Jason still wanted to understand, still wanted to be able to make some sense out of...insanity. Because regardless of legal definitions, there was nothing normal about a person who could do the things Pink had done.

Jason forced his thoughts to the practical. "Couldn't you track the manufacturer down?"

"We tried. We didn't get anywhere. George Simpson had only purchased the gift shop that year. The mermaids Pink bought from him were the last of already existing stock. It was a dead end."

Kennedy pressed the key fob unlocking the doors, and they climbed into the sedan. However, Kennedy didn't start the engine. He seemed to be thinking.

"Something wrong?" Jason asked.

"No." Kennedy glanced at him. It was an odd look. A measuring look.

"Are you sure?"

"Yeah. Yeah, I am." Kennedy stared out the windshield. "I think we should stay in Boston tonight."

"Boston? Why?"

"A couple of reasons. I want to go over some things regarding the case, and I'd prefer to do that without any audience."

"Okay."

It was true their presence generated a lot of attention in Kingsfield. Not so much that Jason would have thought they couldn't speak freely, certainly in private, but if Kennedy thought they needed a few hours off-site, okay. Jason was in no rush to return.

His puzzlement must have shown.

Kennedy said, "It hasn't hit you yet, has it?"

Jason said warily, "What hasn't hit me?"

"If Pink is telling the truth, then there's a strong possibility this copycat is someone involved in the original investigation."

Jason said, "You're suggesting local law enforcement? Yes, the thought had occurred."

Kennedy's expression was noncommittal. "That's one possibility and, believe me, I like that thought as little as you do. However, that was a big taskforce. We had hundreds of people including crime scene technicians and state police working to break the case."

"Okay, but we also have to consider Pink may be lying about sharing that information. Or he may have shared the information and not remembered."

"Given the fact he has almost zero contact with the outside world and the contact that he does have is screened…"

Jason said, "Yeah, I think someone should conduct another check into this fiancée of his, for starters."

Kennedy nodded. "Also the doctor. Kyser. The desire to impress a doctor, let alone a doctor writing a book on serial killers, would be exactly the kind of impetus that might lead Pink to share that critical piece of information."

"The fact remains he could have talked prior to his arrest. You said he used his brother's van. Maybe his brother was more involved than anyone realized. Maybe someone else was involved. It's possible Pink has an apprentice without realizing he has an apprentice."

"Pink's brother is dead."

"I know, but he could have talked before he died. People do talk."

"That they do."

Jason said suddenly, "Both Boxner and Pink used the word *disciple*."

"It's not an unusual word. In fact, it's a word that crops up a lot in copycat cases."

"Maybe. Boxner was there that night, and he had access to those old files. He admitted looking through Honey's file. That's how he knew I was considered a suspect."

Kennedy frowned. "Rebecca returned safely back to the party after speaking to Boxner. Are you suggesting…what? Boxner arranged to meet her later? Arranged to meet her in the woods?"

"The case he tried to build against me works just as well for him. You brought up the possibility of local law enforcement being involved. I don't think Chief Gervase is a serial killer."

Kennedy answered seriously, "No. Gervase is not remotely the right psychological profile. Neither does Boxner fit the profile. You don't just suddenly turn into a serial killer because a mermaid sticks her tongue out at you."

"Okay, but does the original profile fit this profile?"

Kennedy frowned. "We're not dealing with the same offender."

"But if we're dealing with an apprentice or a former accomplice… shouldn't the profile dovetail in certain ways?"

"It does in certain ways, and those are the ways that eliminate Gervase and Boxner both."

It probably *was* pretty far-fetched as theories went. Jason said, "How about George Simpson? Was he part of the original investigation?"

"No. He'd been recently injured in the line of duty and had retired on a disability pension. Which is how he came to be running a gift shop and motel."

"I bet he still had plenty of friends on the force. Cops are as chatty as everyone else when they're among friends."

Kennedy leaned forward and started the engine. "Let's talk it over at dinner. I want to make some phone calls."

* * * * *

Travel was a big part of the job. Jason was used to it, though he did not particularly enjoy it. The hotel was small and clean, and the adjacent restaurant had a bar, so he had no complaints with Kennedy's choice.

He took a shower and then stretched out on the bed to do a little of his own reconnaissance. The only thing he was able to find out by browsing the FBI's intranet personnel pages was that Kennedy was originally from Wyoming and he had a Masters in Criminal Psychology. He had a number of commendations, which Jason already knew. Kennedy did not share trivial info such as hobbies, marital status, or professional affiliations. He did not take part in any of the employee forums. His unsmiling profile photo was several years old, but Kennedy looked virtually the same, just a little sharper, harder around the edges.

"Wyoming," Jason said. Which probably explained the occasional hint of a drawl in Kennedy's voice. Also the Lone Ranger attitude.

Kennedy must have had a number of calls to make because it was after eight when he phoned and told Jason to meet him downstairs.

Kennedy had already been seated and was studying the wall décor—vintage advertising recommending cocaine tooth drops, canned milk, and Hudson automobiles—with an ironic eye as Jason walked in.

"How'd your phone calls go?" Jason picked up the menu. The food was old-school coffee shop. Soups, hot and cold sandwiches, and a few classics like pot roast and meat loaf.

"Productive." Kennedy added, "The food's decent. I've stayed here before."

Jason glanced up from his menu. "It sounds like you're on the road a lot. I thought that wasn't standard procedure for the Behavioral Analysis Units."

"It's not." That sounded like a full stop, but Kennedy lowered his menu. Cast Jason a direct look. "I'm a skin-in-the-game kind of guy."

Jason nodded. He could see that. Kennedy was not someone to stand on the sidelines. He would not be content with reading over other people's reports, but being on the scene must make it harder to stay completely impersonal, which was one of the keys to successful behavioral analysis. On the other hand, remaining completely impersonal was the challenge for all law enforcement.

The waitress arrived, and Kennedy ordered a whisky sour and the grilled salmon. Jason ordered the fried chicken salad and a kamikaze.

"Kamikaze?" Kennedy asked as the waitress moved off. "Planning on drowning your troubles tonight?"

"I had a rough day."

He was sort of joking, sort of not, but the level look Kennedy directed at him made Jason feel self-conscious.

He was disconcerted when Kennedy said, "I know you did. That was good work this afternoon."

"That remains to be seen."

Kennedy smiled faintly. He was still studying Jason with that steady blue regard that was just a little...unsettling. Yes, it was unsettling to have Kennedy's complete and unwavering attention.

Jesus, his eyes were blue.

Happily their drinks arrived, and Jason was able to break free of the tractor beam.

"Why the Art Crime Team?" Kennedy asked.

It took Jason a second to collect his thoughts. "Because I had a Masters in Art History and I realized I didn't want to teach. I wanted action and adventure." He grinned with self-mockery. "I wanted to be Indiana Jones."

"I thought Indiana Jones was an archeologist?"

"By then it was too late to change my major."

Kennedy snorted. "So you decided to join the FBI."

"Hey, people come to the FBI from all kinds of professional and academic backgrounds. It's not just law enforcement or military."

"I know."

"Did you know the original FBI agents were all accountants and bookkeepers?"

"Yes. Everyone who's made it through the academy knows that." Kennedy gave Jason another of those concentrated stares. "You're the youngest member of the Art Crimes Team. Agents have to have at least five years field experience to be considered for ACT. You had three when you were assigned."

Jason shrugged. "Maybe I have connections."

Kennedy's eyes narrowed. "Do you?"

Once again it was almost impossible to drag his gaze away from Kennedy's. Why did he feel like Kennedy was probing for more than just the obvious answer?

Jason replied, "I earned my position on the team."

"Hm." Kennedy said with a hint of mockery, "People certainly seem to hold high hopes for you."

"And I have every intention of living up to those expectations."

Kennedy raised his brows but did not comment. Instead he beckoned to the waitress for another round.

Their meals came before the drinks, which was probably a good thing, though Jason realized he should have ordered more than salad. It was hard to eat right on the road. Too many skipped meals or eating late at night or ransacking vending machines because that was all that was handy. So he ate salads for dinner when he could, but he usually wasn't drinking more than a beer or two.

Kennedy lived out of his suitcase though, and he sure as hell seemed fit, so whatever he was doing seemed to be paying off.

"Something wrong?" Kennedy asked.

"Why?"

"You're scowling at me."

"Er, no. I was just thinking."

"I could tell from the look of pain." Kennedy grinned. Jason had been treated to that very white, dangerous flash of teeth before. It still made him blink. "So what do you like best about ACT?"

Jason digested the fact that Kennedy was joking with him. He was bothering to make normal conversation with him. In fact, he was actually showing an interest in Jason. Interest in Jason personally. It was flattering. Hell, it was liable to go to his head. Or maybe that was the second kamikaze.

"Like best? Well, I like the feeling I'm doing something that might have long-term, lasting ramifications. There's a lot of misconceptions about what we do. We don't only recover stolen art or lecture museums on how to protect their collections. Not that that wouldn't be important enough. You solve a murder, and there's another murder tomorrow. You save the Mona Lisa, and you've saved something that will move and inspire and delight generations of people."

"You don't think it's important to solve homicides?" Kennedy said.

"Of course I think it's important. That's not what I'm saying. It's just that…people keep killing other people. That's the worst of humanity. Art is the other side of the coin. It represents the best of humanity. And what I'm here for is to try and protect that…legacy. Our cultural heritage. And by *our*, I mean everybody. Our global cultural heritage. I mean the world. Art *is* the world. It's history. It's culture. It's spirituality. It's…everything that sets us apart from animals."

"It's the other side of the coin," Kennedy quoted gravely.

Jason mentally replayed the last fifty-eight seconds of their conversation and winced. "I think two kamikazes on an empty stomach was not such a great idea. Did I just imply I believe what I do is somehow more important than human life? Because that's not what I mean. What I mean is, I couldn't do what you do. I would…lose hope."

Kennedy's brows drew together. He said after a moment, "I meant what I said a little while ago. You did good work today."

Jason looked up in surprise.

"I know you didn't want to go in there. I know it wasn't easy for you. We needed to know what we were dealing with, and you got that intel." Kennedy was making an observation not offering sympathy.

"He's in better shape than I expected from someone kept in solitary confinement for that long." Jason couldn't hide his bitterness.

"He's a survivor."

"I never believed in the death penalty until I joined the Bureau. Even after Honey, I used to think there was probably something salvageable in everyone." Jason's smile was twisted. He hid it behind his glass.

"No," Kennedy said. "Unfortunately not."

"Is it true the number of serial killings have increased over the years?"

Kennedy took his time answering. "What has increased is the number of random acts of violence. Once upon a time you could almost guarantee that in most homicides the victim knew or was at least acquainted with his or her killer. That's been changing for a while now."

"And *that's* what I like best about the ACT," Jason said.

Kennedy raised his glass in salute.

After that the conversation moved into neutral channels. They talked about generalities. Not about the case so much, though ostensibly that was the reason for staying in Boston and meeting for dinner. And Kennedy, as expected, did not reveal much of himself.

Music was always a safe topic of conversation though, and Kennedy admitted he was partial to Mendelssohn.

"Mendelssohn? I thought the serial killers were the ones who were supposed to listen to classical music and swill Chianti."

"You couldn't pay me to swill Chianti. Swill is the right word. But I like classical music. Also George Winston. I've heard him in concert a few times."

"George Winston? My parents love George Winston." What Jason was actually thinking was *you go to concerts*? He couldn't picture it.

Maybe some of that showed because Kennedy said dryly, "Yes, I listen to music. And, I know this will amaze you, the pictures hanging on the walls of my apartment are not crime scene photos."

Jason marveled, "You have an apartment?"

"Smartass."

Jason laughed. "What kind of art do you like?"

Kennedy looked briefly and uncharacteristically self-conscious. "I'm sure my taste isn't up to your standards. I collect paintings by an artist by the name of Redmond Granville."

Jason stared. "Redmond Granville?"

"Yes?"

"Are you kidding?"

"Uh, no."

"Redmond Granville is a key figure in California Impressionism. I did my thesis on Redmond Granville. I *love* that guy. In fact, I helped LAPD recover *Seascape at Twilight*."

Kennedy looked taken aback. His expression changed to amusement after Jason had babbled on for about twenty minutes about California Impressionism and Granville's role in establishing the movement, but the fact was Kennedy was very easy to talk to.

Or—Jason remembered the dinner at the Jade Empress—at least he was when he wanted to be. When he wasn't in the mood to be civil, a glacier was more congenial.

It was getting late and the restaurant had emptied out when Jason, emboldened by a night of locked gazes and quiet conversation—not to mention a couple more drinks—said, "Can I ask you something?"

"Go on."

"Why is the governor of Wisconsin so mad at you?"

Kennedy smiled, but it was not the smile Jason had been seeing over the past few hours. It was the kind of smile that made your scalp prickle.

"I don't like incompetence," Kennedy said. "I especially don't like it from someone who's in a position of authority."

"Right."

"As you've noticed, I don't get called out to the cases where a happy ending is possible. Not everyone understands that. Including some of the people who ask for my help."

It was not exactly an answer, but Jason thought maybe he understood what Kennedy was really saying.

"You're still the one they call for."

Kennedy gave him a strange look. "Yes," he said. "However, I can't afford another Wisconsin. I can't afford anything but success here."

The overhead lights flashed once, twice, picking out platinum glints in Kennedy's pale hair and an enigmatic gleam in his blue eyes.

The waitress appeared. "Last call, gentlemen."

Kennedy gave Jason an inquiring look. Jason shook his head. "I'm good."

"I'll have another," Kennedy said.

Once again, he had guessed wrong where Kennedy was concerned. Jason had figured Kennedy was too controlled to risk going over the legal limit—even if they were only walking back to their hotel. Maybe drinking was a necessity when you had seen the things Kennedy had.

When you gaze long into the abyss...the abyss asks you out for cocktails?

With the arrival of Kennedy's final whisky sour, the conversation abruptly shriveled and died. Kennedy downed his drink in a couple of grim swallows and looked unsmilingly across the table.

"Ready?"

"Yep."

They walked out of the restaurant in silence, crossed the parking lot. The night was humid and scented with cooling car engines and warm rubber. In continuing silence, they stepped into the hotel elevator. But then their rooms were on the same floor, so what was there to say?

The elevator rose, and Kennedy stared bleakly at the closed doors. Jason stared at the ceiling. He was going to have a headache in the morning. In fact, he was probably going to have a headache before he finished brushing his teeth. Assuming he bothered to brush his teeth.

The elevator lurched to a stop, the doors slid open, and they started down the hall.

And seriously. What the hell with that black, red, grape, and lime green swirl-pattern carpeting? Maybe art did represent the best of humanity, but the people who came up with hotel décor belonged on Kennedy's side of the crimes-against-mankind spectrum.

"So are you married or involved or what?" Kennedy asked suddenly, brusquely.

Jason threw him a quick look. Was Kennedy...? Not possible.

He'd asked though. Was it general curiosity, or was he really, truly about to suggest sex?

Now *that* would be funny, right? Hard-ass Senior Special Agent Sam Kennedy was so drunk he'd propositioned *Jason.*

Except Jason didn't feel like laughing. He was ridiculously nervous, his heart pounding so hard he felt like he was going to smother. There was no way Kennedy would—but why else had they both stopped at Kennedy's room door?

Why else would Kennedy be watching him—his eyes gleaming in the shadows—waiting for Jason to answer?

"Uh, no," Jason said. "None of the above."

"You want to come in?"

Bewilderingly, yes. Jason did. So much so it actually hurt. He wanted Kennedy's arms around him, Kennedy's mouth on him, Kennedy's cock inside him. Or his cock inside Kennedy. Either was almost too exciting to contemplate. In fact, he wanted Kennedy so much he was in danger of saying it aloud.

Instead he managed a terse, "Why not?"

CHAPTER TWELVE

Of course there were plenty of excellent reasons why not.

Jason managed to block them all out as Kennedy unlocked his door and let them both inside his room.

The lights were out. The room smelled like all hotel rooms. The only landmark was Kennedy.

The door swung shut, the deadbolt slid home, Kennedy's arms closed around Jason.

Jason was conscious of Kennedy's muscular length backing him into the door, the alcohol-scented heat of Kennedy's breath on his face, the speedy expertise with which Kennedy's long fingers unbuckled Jason's holster—clearly he had plenty of practice in disarming lovers—before turning his attention to Jason's shirt buttons.

"Good," Kennedy muttered. "This is good."

Which…the jury was still out, but yes, it was looking promising so far. Jason arched his neck and found Kennedy's mouth. Hot and tasting like booze with an undernote of stinging sweetness. Kennedy neither rejected nor reciprocated the kiss, his attention focused on undoing the last buttons of Jason's shirt.

Jason's shoulders were wide, and his shirt was tailored, so it took a few seconds, but at last Kennedy laid bare Jason's chest. He let out a sigh of satisfaction, fingertips skating lightly, slowly, over the flat planes of Jason's abs, tracing a line between his pecs, and circling round to graze the nipples that pricked to attention at that tingling touch. Jason's breath caught in his throat.

Kennedy lowered his head, touched a nipple with his tongue, and Jason gasped and jumped, his head hitting the door with a noisy thump.

"Easy," Kennedy murmured. His voice was unfamiliar in its huskiness, even sexy. "Don't knock yourself out." He sounded amused.

Just as well Kennedy hadn't turned on the light. The darkness was a lot of what made this possible. Jason was uncomfortable with his own intense response to this man. Not like he didn't have any experience with casual sex, but for some reason the fact it was *Kennedy* touching him, rasping his hot wet tongue against Jason's nipple, was exciting almost beyond belief.

There was a little moan trapped deep in his throat, a naked sound he'd have died rather than release, and it was nearly strangling him as Kennedy turned his attention to Jason's other nipple. He reached out blindly for Kennedy's belt buckle, and Kennedy leaned into him, offering easier access.

"Yeah, whatever you want," Kennedy whispered before his lips closed on the sensitive point of Jason's nipple. Kennedy sucked, and Jason's entire body seemed to throb with pleasure. It was crazy what this was doing to him. Had anyone touched him like this before? He couldn't remember another guy spending this much time on his breast—not something Jason would have ever asked for or imagined enjoying—but thrills of sensation shuddered up and down his spine as Kennedy licked and nibbled.

Jason's cock was straining painfully at his trousers, so it was a desperate relief when Kennedy's hands dropped to his fly, eased his zipper down, mindful of all that fragile skin and blindly thrusting muscle. His own hands rested motionless on Kennedy's lean hips—he kept getting distracted by Kennedy's relentlessly pleasurable assault—but he made the effort now, fingers fumbling with the buckle tongue, yanking the trousers open with no regard for tailoring. He wanted more of everything. Of that weight and warmth...and wholeness. And he wanted it now.

Kennedy's dick sprang free, crowding Jason in the darkness that pressed closer, smelling of faded aftershave, musk, and imminent sex.

"Beautiful," Kennedy said, reaching for him, and Jason's cock nestled into his curled palm. "This is beautiful."

Yes, it was. After a day devoted to death and dying, sex was a beautiful, life-affirming thing. An art form all its own.

Kennedy's thumb stroked along Jason's achingly hard length in a sensual brailing, and the moan Jason had tried to swallow tore out of his throat. Raw and honest with need.

Kennedy's laugh was quiet, knowing. He slid an arm around Jason's waist, hitching him up against the door—one hell of a lot of upper body strength there—and Jason grabbed for Kennedy's shoulders, instinctively wrapping his legs around Kennedy's hips—also no small effort. Kennedy's hold slipped, and they half fell against the door.

Jason swallowed a half-yelp half-laugh, but Kennedy stayed on his feet. Jason wriggled for leverage against the slick surface, hiking himself up again, and with that gyration initiating more pleasurable motion. Yes to naked friction from any angle.

"Yeah. There. That's..."

"Good," Kennedy urged. "That's so..."

Jason ground his hips against Kennedy's, and Kennedy thrust back hard. Push and pull rapidly shifting into pound and pummel.

Jason arched, and Kennedy's arms tightened around his waist. The door handle lever hit Jason in the back, but he barely noticed. Even if they fell over, he wasn't sure it would make a difference. They were locked in a kind of sexual mortal combat now, hips rocking, cocks plunging against each other, awkward and occasionally painful, but mostly, crazily good.

This is Kennedy. This is Kennedy's dick shoving into my groin. That is Kennedy's dick leaking slickness...

Kennedy's mouth was against Jason's ear, and he was grunting with each thrust, a rough, aggressive sound that was unbearably exciting.

They were both breathing hard, sweat breaking over their bodies as they struggled and strained their way to the prize—and Jesus, this looked easier on television than it was in practice. Jason slid down a couple of centimeters, and he swore in frustration. Kennedy's arms refastened around his back, keeping him pinned, and Jason clamped his thighs, rocking against that eager pulsing hardness.

"Christ, yes," Jason urged. *"Yes. YES."*

"Shhh. God." Kennedy was laughing unsteadily.

They bumped and banged their way into a semblance of rhythm. The door rattled alarmingly in its frame beneath their onslaught. It didn't matter.

You didn't have to be in sync to make this work, and they were making it work.

Anything that felt this good would work. Jason let his head fall back again...*ouch*...this time Kennedy didn't laugh at the thump, he probably didn't hear it—Jason barely felt it as he launched himself into Kennedy's thrusts which were coming now in short, fast bursts.

So good. So sweet. Yes. Yes. Good. I can't believe this is Kennedy— no, don't think about that—

Jason's balls drew tight. Little lights danced behind his eyes. He surged up against the door one final time and went barreling down a luminous blue-green tunnel until he felt orgasm lift him like a wave scooping up his surfboard and casting him into sunlight and spray.

Brilliant...sparkling...blinding...delight. He was transported, flying high as shafts of bright and secret pleasure lanced through him, trans-fixing him...*oh, don't let it stop.* Carried along on that sweet, sweet ride...

He had the presence of mind to shout his reaction into Kennedy's broad and powerful shoulder—it had been way too fucking long since he'd had this relief.

He landed on the shore, wet, weak-kneed, and shaking—and didn't object when he was gathered to his feet and guided to the bed. He didn't recall undressing, only tumbling into cool cotton and warm arms. A sheet drifted down as light as a summer breeze and conscious thought scattered like grains of sand.

He woke to the sound of the shower.

And one hell of a headache.

Jason winced at the steady thump of blood in his temples. Where was he that there was someone using his shower? Wasn't he supposed to be back in L.A.?

The bathroom door swung wide, and Jason's eyes jerked open as a wave of warm, soapy air—and a blast of familiar aftershave—dispelled the mental fog.

"Up and at 'em, Agent West," Kennedy said. "We're not on vacation."

Holy. Shit.

Had he—?

Had they—?

Well, yes. Because Jason distinctly—well, some of it was pretty fuzzy—but Jason definitely remembered...a lot. Too much. The size of Kennedy's cock among other things. The feel of his hands digging into Jason's ass, the rasp of his tongue on Jason's nipples, the taste of his mouth.

Chriiiiiist.

Jason sat up and swung his legs off the mattress. The angry little man in his cerebellum pounded his cane against the ceiling. *You young whippersnappers!*

Jason felt around for his...what the hell was he searching for? He risked a quick look at Kennedy.

Kennedy's face was impassive. He was combing his wet hair and watching Jason feebly paw the rug.

Jason found his shorts—and who didn't enjoy having to pull up his pants in front of someone who looked like he was about to issue a citation. And not one for bravery. Although Jason must have been feeling pretty brave, if not actually foolhardy, to have done what he did.

Really, he would prefer not to think of all he had done. And at the top of his lungs if memory served.

"Uh, I think I'll..." Jason dragged on his jeans. "Shower next door."

"Suit yourself." Kennedy turned back into the bathroom.

Jason grabbed his shirt, socks, shoes and departed Kennedy's room. As he stepped into the hallway with its delirium tremens-themed carpeting and murky lighting, the door to #156 clicked shut behind him, and he realized he'd left his holster and weapon.

No small thing losing—leaving—your holster and *gun.*

"Are you *fucking* kidding me?" he murmured in anguish.

He thumped briskly on the door.

Kennedy opened the door and handed him his holster, weapon still neatly fastened.

"Thanks."

Highly unlikely the gleam in Kennedy's eyes was amusement, but if Kennedy thought this was funny, good. That made one of them.

"I'm going downstairs to grab a bagel," Kennedy said.

"Right. I'll be down in ten."

He was down in eight, not that anyone was counting. Kennedy was reading the newspaper as he enjoyed his continental breakfast in the corner of the dining room.

A cold shower had done Jason a world of good. He talked the girl at the reception desk into giving him a couple of aspirins while watching Kennedy out of the corner of his eye.

I tapped that. The unbidden memory startled him. Or maybe what startled him was that the memory made him feel sort of warm and tingly.

Because no. If he should be feeling anything, it was concern this didn't confuse the issue. The issue being that he wasn't just Kennedy's partner—temporary partner—he had been brought on to make sure Kennedy didn't cross any double lines or swerve into the wrong lane. He had to keep some kind of impartial distance here. For everyone's sake.

Plus, he wasn't even sure he liked Kennedy. And he made it a rule not to have sex with people he didn't like.

He washed the aspirin down with scalding sips of black coffee and made his way over to Kennedy, who was folding up his newspaper.

"We've got time if you want to grab something to eat," Kennedy said.

"I'm fine."

Kennedy nodded and rose.

They squeezed past a couple of families in shorts and T-shirts crowding through the sliding lobby doors. Weekday or not, this was summer vacation for a lot of people.

Kennedy unlocked the car doors, and Jason slid in and buckled up. He felt the need for restraint after the night before.

"You seem a little rattled this morning," Kennedy remarked, once they were on the road and headed back toward Kingsfield.

"Nope. I'm good." Jason adjusted the sun visor. Way too much sun for this early in the morning.

"Gervase phoned to let me know they've got the ME's report. He wanted to wait and discuss in person."

"Okay."

A couple more miles of ruthless illumination, both internal and external.

Jason said abruptly, "I'm not rattled. I just..." He shook his head. "I don't usually do this. That. Last night. In fact, I've never done that."

"*Never?*"

Jason glanced at Kennedy. Was Kennedy *teasing* him? Impossible. Kennedy had no sense of humor.

"Not with a colleague. I don't believe in mixing work with play. Pleasure. Sex. I *mean*, I like to keep my professional life professional."

Kennedy, eyes on the road, said, "You do know the Bureau doesn't have a non-fraternization policy?"

"Yes. I know." Jason repeated—and even he could hear it sounded like it was by rote, "I like to keep my professional life professional."

Really, why was he making such a point about this? It's not like he had a hard-and-fast rule about getting involved with coworkers—although he'd have expected Kennedy to. Jason occasionally dated other agents, and he'd never had any particular problem. Granted, none of those dates had led to relationships. Relationships were stickier.

Also not a factor here.

"Fine by me," Kennedy said. "I follow the catch-and-release rule. By exigency and by inclination."

Exigency and inclination. Wow.

And, oh yeah. *That's* why he'd felt the need for a preemptive strike. Jason had known Kennedy would say something like that, something to make it clear last night had been a one-off and not the start of anything. Because what the hell would they be starting? They had absolutely nothing in common beyond being gay. And horny.

So Jason felt relieved he had clarified his position first. Status and sex. They went hand in hand. Or hand and something.

"So we're good, then," Jason said.

"Yep."

Jason took another swallow of coffee. It seemed to have grown noticeably more bitter over the past mile.

CHAPTER THIRTEEN

"**D**éjà vu," Chief Gervase said. He held up a plastic evidence bag containing a cherry red two-piece swimsuit. "She was strangled with the top of her bikini. Just like before."

"Was she raped?" Kennedy asked.

"No. The autopsy revealed that despite bruising of the genital area, Rebecca was not raped. No discernable DNA evidence was found."

"So there's a good chance he's impotent," Jason said. He glanced over his shoulder at Boxner, who was sitting by the door of Gervase's office.

Boxner changed color and sat up. He didn't speak—as much as he clearly wanted to.

Gervase agreed, "Unlike Pink."

"I don't believe Pink is a player in this," Kennedy said. His tone was polite, but it was obvious he was getting tired of saying it.

"He's not running around the countryside abducting young females," owned Gervase. "I don't know that he's not a player. He's certainly an inspiration to someone."

"You've been wrong before," Boxner said.

"Really?" Kennedy asked. "When?"

Boxner began to splutter, and Jason decided that if Kennedy chose to throw good old Boyd out the window, he wouldn't interfere.

Gervase ignored their exchange. "Time of death is listed between one and three o'clock on Saturday morning. Here's one other point of interest," he said. "Rebecca was already dead before she was strangled." He stared at Kennedy, waiting for his reaction.

"How did she die?" Kennedy asked after a moment.

"Blunt force trauma to the head."

Jason asked, "Is it possible the killer was unaware the victim was deceased?"

"That's a good point," Gervase said. "The ME thinks the strangling took place less than thirty minutes after death. So our guy could have been in a real frenzy and still otherwise preoccupied. He may not have known the girl was dead. He might have thought she was just unconscious."

That would have to be someone supremely unobservant. Jason waited for Kennedy to make that point. Kennedy said, "Does State's CSI think she died at the scene?"

"I'm not following," Gervase said.

"The Madigan girl was found much farther afield than any of Pink's victims."

Boxner said, "He doesn't want to get caught like Pink. He's smarter than Pink. He's making a real effort to conceal the body."

Kennedy repeated his question to Gervase. "Did Madigan die where her body was discovered?"

Gervase said slowly, "They're not sure. They don't think so. And I can't see her willingly accompanying him to Rexford. He'd have had to fight her every step of the way."

"That's not necessarily true," Jason said. "A ghost town is interesting, especially to kids, who aren't going to think twice about flooding or rotten floors or snakes."

"Maybe at Halloween," Gervase said. "It's hard to imagine Rebecca leaving her own party on the spur of the moment to go check out a ghost town."

Jason remained unconvinced. Spur of the moment was pretty much synonymous with adolescence. And the opinion he'd formed of Rebecca through the statements of friends and family was she was a girl who acted on impulse a lot of the time. If someone attractive, someone she admired and felt safe with invited her to share a private adventure to a spooky old ghost town? Jason glanced at Boxner.

Feeling his gaze, Boxner looked Jason's way. They stared at each other with open and equal dislike.

Jason said, "So we continue to have similarities to the original crimes. And the significant differences are probably inevitable given we're dealing with two separate offenders?"

Kennedy nodded.

"Which brings us back to my theory," Gervase said. "That what we have here is not so much a copycat, as the return of Pink's original accomplice. I always said I didn't believe Pink could have been acting alone."

"Yes, you did always say that," Kennedy agreed. Jason knew him well enough by now to know when Kennedy was being sardonic.

Gervase also recognized Kennedy's sarcasm. His eyes kindled with irritation, but he restrained himself, instead reaching for his coffee cup and drinking from it.

That tensions were running high was understandable. They were now past the initial forty-eight. For local law enforcement forty-eight was the magic number. Most homicides were solved within that initial time span—or at least the information vital to solving the crime was provided within that window. Cases that didn't resolve within the initial forty-eight might drag on for weeks, months, even years...or might never be solved.

From the FBI perspective, they were just getting started. The Bureau usually wasn't even called in until well after the initial forty-eight hours had passed.

The real problem here was they had no idea when the unsub might strike again. Pink had waited years after Honey. And less than two weeks after Ginny. What his accomplice or apprentice might choose to do was anyone's guess.

Kennedy said, "The problem with trying to match this scenario with your pet theory is that it doesn't fit the profile. The Huntsman's accomplice wouldn't be someone who lures his victim into accompanying him. There is no coercion, no coaxing. Part of the pay-off for this offender is the abduction itself. The ability to overpower and take his victim against her will. That's always been a fundamental component of these crimes."

Gervase set his cup down. "We don't know that. You said yourself we've got two different offenders. What worked for one might not work for the other."

Kennedy gave an impatient shake of his head but didn't bother to explain. Jason understood though. The police chief was talking about a leopard changing its spots. In this case the spots were psychological markers, but they were just as indelible.

"So we've got the same basic MO but two different profiles. Makes sense to me," Gervase said.

"It makes sense to me too," Boxner said.

"Our boy is having trouble shooting straight. Or shooting at all."

Jason took that opportunity to look back at Boxner. "Now *that* I can see." When he faced forward, Kennedy was watching him. His expression was unamused.

Gervase said mildly, "Unless this is the return of the Huntsman—and he's really off his game."

Kennedy grinned. It was a sharp, white smile. Dangerous.

Gervase grinned too. "Just sayin'."

It was a long day.

There was a new stack of witness statements to go over as one by one the uninvited guests at Rebecca's party were tracked down. Jason and Kennedy divided them up, but nothing stood out.

"She was a wild kid," Jason said. "Not a bad kid."

"No. Not a bad kid," Kennedy agreed. "Spoiled. And not smart enough to know when to be afraid."

That last would be the fault of Rebecca's parents, who were at that moment down the hall in the chief's office, demanding progress. Rebecca had grown up believing there was nothing money couldn't buy because her parents believed there was nothing money couldn't buy. Including justice.

There were some things no amount of cash or credit could put right.

When the final witness statements proved to be a dead end, Kennedy turned his attention back to tracking down Coral Nunn and Dr. Jeremy Kyser.

Or tried. Nunn was not talking to the FBI, and Kyser's old number was disconnected. He did not appear to have a new number.

"He's written three books," Jason informed Kennedy, studying the iBooks listings. *"Voices in the Dark: One Hundred Interviews with Death Row Inmates, Necrophilic and Necrophagic Serial Killers: Case Study Analyses,* and the ever popular and bestselling *Monsters Among Us: An Introduction to Psychopathy, Perversion, and Lust Homicide."*

"Sex sells," Kennedy said absently.

They worked through the morning without much to show for it, but that was to be expected at this juncture of the investigation.

A little after one, Kennedy said, "You want to grab some lunch?"

Yes. He did. Jason said firmly, "I'll get something later."

"I'll leave you to it," Kennedy said—and left Jason to it.

When Jason did finally step out for lunch about half an hour later, he called SAC Manning and explained the investigation appeared to be progressing, though not quickly, and he felt his own presence was unnecessary.

"I can't agree with that, erm, conclusion, West," Manning said. "I wouldn't have assigned you to this case if I hadn't believed your, erm, presence was necessary."

"Sir, I'm not being falsely modest here. Kennedy has this under control. I'm not exactly sure what happened in Wisconsin—"

"I'll tell you exactly what happened," Manning cried. "That arrogant asshole nearly wrecked the investigation. He threatened to punch a county sheriff in his—and I quote—*fat fool face* on national TV. *National TV,* West. The governor's own son-in-law."

"Ah," Jason said.

"And then he refused to apologize."

"I see."

"He is not a team player. He's..." Words failed SAC Manning. He said, "The only reason I can, erm, sleep at night, West, is because I know you're on the scene, I know I've got some, erm, insight, some intelligence into whatever happens from someone who *is*, erm, a team player."

"Sir, you need someone here from the BAU. You need someone who can really assist Kennedy—not that he needs it—and I need to get back to my own team. My own duties."

"I can't trust anyone from the BAU," Manning said. "No one in the BAU is going to report back to me if Kennedy, erm, steps out of line. No one in the BAU is going to help me build a case for, erm, disciplinary action against Kennedy."

Neither am I.

Jason didn't say it. Part of being a team player was knowing when to keep your mouth shut. In any case, Manning was still talking. As the Mannings of the world were wont to do.

"Besides which, West, you know as well as I do that all members of the, erm, ACT are subject to being, erm, moved to other units when and as needed. It's part of your, erm, brief."

Yes. That was true. As understaffed as the Art Crimes Team was, and as important as their work was, they were widely viewed as desk jockeys who could be shuffled from department to department as needed. Cogs in the wheel.

"How long before the case wraps up?" Manning asked briskly into Jason's silence.

"There's no way of knowing, sir. It could be weeks. The unsub is out there. He could strike again. It's not like we're closing in on him."

"Good," Manning said. "The longer you work with Kennedy, the more potential, erm, documentation. Documentation is everything. Remember that. You're smart, you're ambitious, West. You're going places. And I'm going to owe you a favor after this. Now I'm afraid I'm running late for a, erm, meeting. I thank you for this, erm, update."

And with that, Manning rang off.

Good? Manning considered a serial killer running loose good news because it afforded more opportunity to build a case against one of the Bureau's most effective agents?

Jason tossed the rest of his sandwich in the trash and walked back to the police station.

When he reached the office he was sharing with Kennedy, Kennedy glanced at him and frowned. "Everything okay?"

Three days ago this much indication of interest or even awareness would never have happened.

"Yeah." Jason sat down. "I want to look at the original crime scene photos."

Kennedy's brows rose. "Do you?"

What was that careful tone supposed to mean?

Well, okay, maybe Jason knew what it meant. It meant Kennedy was vaguely aware of Jason's sensibilities. And so what?

Jason said, "The mermaids. I want to see what I can find on them. There's got to be an angle there."

"I agree. We were never able to find it."

"This is what I do. This is my turf."

Kennedy went swiftly through the crime scene photos and handed over a stack. Jason accepted them without comment. He got it—and appreciated that Kennedy was sparing him from seeing what had been done to Honey. It didn't matter how hardened you were, how jaded you grew, it was always different—always going to be terrible—seeing someone you knew as the victim of violence.

He found a magnifying glass in desk drawer and began to go over the photos of Rebecca's crime scene with careful, painstaking attention, focusing on every detail of the mermaid charm.

Round, three-dimensional, highly polished...no more than two inches tall. He reached for one of the older photos.

He felt a jolt as he studied the small, pale, circular carving. He knew this one. Recognized it as the charm that had hung from Honey's key ring. Remembered it so vividly, he could almost feel the delicate cut of the tiny fish scales beneath his fingertips.

He closed his eyes. Opened them. He couldn't afford to be distracted by memory or emotion. He reached for the next photo. This mermaid was a fraction smaller and carved from a darker material. The shape was more oval than round. The style was the same, but the face and the scales on the tail were slightly different from Honey's mermaid *and* slightly different from Rebecca's.

Not mass produced then. Hand carved.

He laid all six photos in a row before him. Yes, they were different, but not that different. And as far as the naked eye could tell, these were by the same artist.

The hair on the back of his neck rose.

Was it possible this artist was still out there?

"Find something?" Kennedy asked.

Jason looked up blankly. "What?"

"You look like you've seen a ghost."

"I'm almost positive it's the same artist."

Kennedy seemed to be waiting for more. "Okay," he said when Jason didn't continue.

"They're all different, but the workmanship is so unique, so distinct. I'd swear it's the same artist."

"So the question is how did the unsub get hold of another mermaid charm?"

"Yes. Or...yes." Was that the question? Probably. It was certainly a good one. How the hell had Rebecca's murderer obtained one of these mermaids ten years after the last killing? Jason said, "I think if we knew who this artist was..."

"You think the artist himself is involved?"

It was sort of unnerving the way Kennedy instantly jumped to where Jason's thoughts were headed even as Jason was deciding on a direction. "I don't know. Why shouldn't he be out there?"

"You tell me."

Jason gazed at Kennedy. "You—the taskforce—never connected him—or her—to the crimes. Maybe this person was unaware her work was linked to a series of homicides. She might live out of state. She might live in another country."

"That's exactly right."

"Or she might not."

Kennedy was still watching, still waiting. For what? Some brilliant deduction? Some sign Jason was going to be of actual use in this investigation?

"Not all the original victims were found with mermaid charms," Kennedy said. "Only five of the girls had them. We couldn't be sure if the other charms were lost or if no charms were left at the scene. The first victim's b—"

"Honey," Jason said.

Kennedy gave him a quick look. "Yes. Honey Corrigan was not found with a mermaid. Correction. Her mermaid was hanging on the keychain in her car. In fact, that particular connection wasn't made until some months after the Bureau joined the taskforce."

"She'd bought that charm a few weeks before she..."

"Right. The others were purchased by Pink. He bought the last four mermaids in Simpson's shop. You see the problem. There's a six-year gap. Honey didn't buy her charm from Simpson because Simpson didn't own the gift shop at that time."

"Who did own the shop?"

"Bethany Douglas. She moved to Oregon after she sold the shop to Simpson."

"Douglas? Is she related to Patricia Douglas? Rebecca's best friend? The girl she quarreled with Friday night?"

Kennedy looked startled. "I don't know. I didn't make that connection." The look of surprised approval in his gaze made Jason feel warm.

And then like an idiot for being flattered.

"Was the Douglas woman questioned?" he asked.

"Yep. She was elderly and in poor health. She believed the charms were made by a local artist. She believed the artist was a woman, but she wasn't sure and couldn't remember the name or any details. She said Simpson had all that information. Simpson insisted there was no information to be had."

"That should have sent up some flags."

"It did." Kennedy's expression was wry. "Until we talked to a bunch of people who corroborated the gift shop's ledgers and records were in complete chaos by the time Simpson stepped in."

"Hm." Jason stacked the photos and began sorting through them. "So Honey has a mermaid on her keychain, but then no mermaid turns up again until Jody. Then no mermaid until victim number six, Susan Parvel. And the remaining victim had a mermaid."

"Correct."

"And now Rebecca."

"Again correct."

"Got it." Jason picked up the magnifying glass and resumed his examination of each and every mermaid.

Very interesting. Not at all typical New England nautical folk art. These almost reminded him of *netsuke*. Japanese miniatures sculpted out of ivory, shells, hardwoods, gemstones, or ceramics.

The subject matter was not typical of traditional *netsuke* though. At least he didn't think mermaids figured largely in Japanese mythology.

Either way, he kept coming back to his conviction this was distinct craftsmanship. This was the work of an artist.

He was jolted out of his thoughts as Kennedy pushed back his chair and rose, saying, "I'm going to check out the original crime scenes."

"Okay." Was Kennedy expecting to pick up psychic vibrations or something? Or did he think it would be possible to pick up some over-looked clue this long after the fact?

Some of what Jason was thinking must have shown on his face because Kennedy added, "Mostly I need to clear my thoughts. Stretch my legs."

"Sure."

"I'll see you tomorrow morning."

"Right."

That was clear enough—and a relief, of course. Jason had not expected that they would spend another night together. Had not been hoping for it. Had, by maintaining a cool distance, tried to convey he would *not* be open to it. So it was weird to feel that jolt of letdown.

He listened to Kennedy's footsteps die out down the hallway and then turned on his laptop and began to search the web.

No joy.

Was it possible that Pink had acquired additional mermaids?

No. They would surely have turned up at his house. They'd have been used as evidence during his trial. They'd have been too important not to use. One reason they hadn't been placed into evidence at Pink's trial was the uncertainty of where they fit in. Not all of the victims had been found with mermaid charms.

You never wanted to enter anything into evidence which might lead in an unpredictable direction.

Anyway, no. The mermaids had been purchased through George Simpson's gift shop. That mysterious old stock Simpson had been unable to match to a vendor.

What if Simpson was lying? He'd come under suspicion for some reason, and it had to be for more than owning the shop where the mermaid trinkets were sold. What if he had carved the mermaids himself and lied about it?

No. If Simpson had that kind of skill, there would be physical evidence of it. Plus, Honey's purchase of the original mermaid messed up the timeline. Right?

Jason made a mental note to check Simpson's file for himself, see how he had first come under suspicion—and why those suspicions had been ultimately dismissed.

In the meantime...he used the office printer to scan a few of the photos and then emailed them to his list of dealer and gallery contacts.

They might get a hit right away or not at all. Probably not at all if these really were the work of a local artist or a gifted amateur.

Again, if that was the case, someone on the original taskforce should have recognized the work of a local craftsman. These carvings were exquisite.

Memorable.

Which gave him hope one of his own contacts might recognize the craftsmanship—or be able to point him in the direction of someone who would.

He felt instinctively that if they could just locate this mysterious artist, they would be one step closer to finding their killer.

CHAPTER FOURTEEN

"**G**oodnight," Officer Courtney called when Jason left the quiet station house that evening.

"Night," Jason returned.

That night the parking lot was nearly empty, an indicator Chief Gervase and his department had resigned themselves to the long haul and were trying to pace themselves.

Jason turned left and headed up Main Street, walking until he came to the General Warren Inn.

"I took your laundry up to your room," Charlotte told him when he stopped by the lobby.

"Thanks."

She looked like she had been crying. Her voice wobbled as she asked, "Do you know where Tony is?"

Proof of his preoccupation, it took Jason a minute to remember Tony McEnroe. "No," he said. "Did he make bail?"

"Yes." Charlotte started to add something, but her father called from the back office, "Charlie, can I see you for a moment?"

She threw Jason a look of frustration, but answered docilely, "Yes, Daddy."

Jason left the lobby.

As usual no one was in the swimming pool, and most of the rooms were dark. Certainly there was no lamp shining behind the curtains in Kennedy's room. Was he still prowling the countryside, visiting old crime scenes?

Jason let himself into his room. He was tired, and his headache was coming back, but he needed to eat and the idea of hanging around his motel room was just depressing. He showered, put on clean jeans and a fresh shirt, and headed over to the Blue Mermaid.

The first person he saw when he opened the door was Senior Special Agent Sam Kennedy eating fish and chips at the bar and watching the TV in the corner.

Jason glanced at the TV screen and caught a glimpse of the Madigans, tear-stained and enraged their daughter's killer had not yet been brought to justice. That was followed by the image of Chief Gervase looking harassed and uncomfortable as he tried to answer the barrage of reporters' questions. Even at that distance and with the television sound muted, Jason could see Gervase's mouth forming the word *copycat*.

Briefly, Jason considered backing out of the bar, but that would be ridiculous. It wasn't like he was trying to avoid Kennedy. He just didn't want to look like he was fol—and right in the middle of that thought, Kennedy glanced Jason's way.

Kennedy did not look overcome with delight. He also didn't look disturbed to see Jason. After a moment—and it was definitely a moment—he nodded in greeting, and Jason walked over to the bar.

"How'd it go?" he asked.

"How did what go?" Kennedy returned.

"Your tour of the old crime scenes."

Kennedy lifted a shoulder in dismissal. "I can't say I was struck by any blinding flashes of fresh insight. How did you make out?"

"Unless you have some objection, I'd like to head back to Boston tomorrow. I've got contacts there. I've worked with a couple of dealers who specialize in folk art. They might be able to help us locate the artist who carved those mermaid charms."

"You think those charms are that distinct?"

"I do. Yeah."

Funny how Kennedy's eyes seemed to light up when he was interested. Like someone threw the switch on an electrical current. "Okay. Sounds good to me."

The slender brunette behind the bar stopped moving long enough to speak to Kennedy, "Was I right? Pretty good?"

Kennedy examined the piece of fried cod he held. "Not bad."

She nodded at his half-empty glass. "Again?"

"Thanks."

She turned to Jason. "Sorry for the wait. Our bartender didn't show up for her shift. What can I get you?"

"Sam Adams."

"Were you going to order food?"

"Do you have some kind of salad?"

She laughed. "Uh, no. No salad. Fish and chips, burgers, or chicken wings."

"Fish and chips."

"Good choice." She smiled and turned away.

Kennedy looked inquiringly at Jason.

"What?" Jason asked.

"Were you going to sit down, or are you planning to make a run for it?"

Jason laughed uncomfortably and sat down on the next stool. After a moment he said, "I talked to SAC Manning today."

Kennedy took a large bite of cod. "Yeah?"

"I asked him to release me from this assignment. He said no."

Kennedy gave a short laugh. "Are you kidding? You're the only reason he can sleep at night."

Funny. Almost the exact phrasing Manning had used.

Kennedy added dryly, "He's pinning all his hopes on you and your little black notebook."

"Do you think I'm keeping notes on you?"

Kennedy's smile was crooked. "If you are, they ought to make for interesting reading."

Jason looked away, his face warm.

"No," Kennedy said. "I don't think you're keeping notes on me." He swallowed the last wedge of fish and wiped his greasy fingers on his paper napkin. "Why don't you tell me what's really bothering you?"

"I just did."

Kennedy finished with his napkin, balled it up, and dropped it on his plate. "No. You didn't. Why did you feel the need to phone Manning?"

"I feel like I'm— I don't feel like I'm—"

Kennedy was watching him with that alert blue gaze.

Profiling me, Jason thought wryly.

When he didn't finish, Kennedy said, "You should have told Manning at the start you were too close to this case. That there was too much of a personal connection for you to be able to do your job."

"*What?*" Jason stared. "That's not true. Yes, there are some painful memories, maybe more than I expected, but I can do my job just fine."

Kennedy gave a small laugh. "Okay. I agree. So what's the problem, Jason?"

Jason.

It gave him a start hearing his first name on Kennedy's tongue.

Really he did not want to think about Kennedy's tongue.

And on that topic, why the hell had he made such a big point about not having sex with coworkers? Because of course he wanted to have sex again. Last night had been good. Really good. His job did not leave a lot of time for…well, anything but his job.

Kennedy was watching him, smiling a little, eyes intent.

"I don't know," Jason muttered. "I don't like this case."

"Who the hell would like this case?" There was a hint of wry amusement in Kennedy's tone. He said softly, "I know what you need…"

Jason threw him a quick, alarmed look. Kennedy's grin widened.

"You need a drink. You need a couple of drinks. And here's Nika to save the day."

Nika deposited a fresh beer in front of Kennedy and a plate of fish and chips sizzling with oil in front of Jason. Opening a bottle, she tilted the Sam Adams with practiced speed into a frosted mug. "Anything else?"

"This is great," Jason said.

She grinned at him and departed.

Kennedy said, "They cut McEnroe loose this afternoon. On bail."

"I heard. Well, I figured that was coming. You don't think there's any chance—"

Kennedy shook his head. "No. He'd have been in pieces by now. We'd have had a full confession. He's not our killer."

They talked about the case while Jason ate. Finally Jason pushed his plate away. He considered ordering another beer. Was Kennedy staying longer, or was he headed back to the motel? If he was staying, Jason would have another beer. Just to be friendly.

"Feeling better?" asked Kennedy.

Jason made a face. "Yeah. A lot."

Kennedy nodded approval. "Good. Are you headed out early tomorrow?"

"Tomorrow?"

"You're going to Boston, right? To talk to your art dealer contacts?"

"Oh. Right. Early-ish." Studying Kennedy's face, Jason realized he was about to miss his cue. He said hastily, "Not *that* early."

"No?" Despite Kennedy's serious expression, Jason had the distinct impression he was being laughed at. "Okay. Well, I know you've got that strict no-fraternization policy, so I don't want to put you in an awkward p—"

"Shut the hell up," Jason said, starting to laugh himself.

This time they were both a lot more sober and not quite as frantic, though hearing the seam of his shirt's left shoulder give way as Kennedy backed him toward the bed, Jason was grateful he'd had his laundry done.

Somewhere in the short distance between the door and the bed he lost not only his shirt, but his shoes and socks. And Kennedy had lost a lot more.

Catching a glimpse of his own face in the mirror over the desk— Kennedy had turned the lights on when they walked in—Jason saw himself sprawled on the bed, hair tumbled and eyes glittering wildly as

Kennedy's hands fastened on his hips and dragged his jeans down to his knees.

"You want to turn the lights off?" Jason asked. Flair for the dramatic or not, he wasn't much of an exhibitionist.

"No. I like looking at you." Kennedy hauled Jason's jeans the rest of the way off and tossed them aside. He leaned over the bed, hands fisting the mattress on either side of Jason's shoulders. "You're a very nice-looking guy."

Jason's laugh was a little self-conscious. "Pretty boy," he mocked.

"Yeah," Kennedy agreed. "But not just a pretty face. You're sharper than you look."

Jason spluttered. "And you may actually have a sense of humor."

"I wouldn't bet on it." Kennedy was grinning, though, as he lowered himself on the mattress.

The next few minutes passed in pleasurable physical contact. Kennedy might not be much for mouth-to-mouth, but he was definitely an orally fixated kind of guy. There was not a sensitive part of Jason's upper body that didn't receive the moist attentions of Kennedy's mouth. Nothing like someone nibbling on your ears or licking your nipples to distract you from your worries—not that it didn't create its own set of uncertainties.

"Yeah, very pretty," Kennedy murmured, nuzzling the inside curve of Jason's elbow. And even that...who would have thought the elbows were an erogenous zone?

Kennedy was kind of a one man sensual onslaught. Jason was flushed and out of breath by the time he rolled onto his belly, trying to give himself a few seconds to get control of his voice and face.

Kennedy kissed the nape of his neck, brushing the curls away, and Jason shivered.

"I'll warm you up," Kennedy promised, and his lips traveled slowly, deliberately down Jason's spine, grazing every link of vertebrae right down to the small of Jason's back where he lingered, nuzzling. Jason swallowed hard. No lie, his skin felt warm everywhere Kennedy's mouth touched.

"That feels really..."

"Yes, it does." There was a smile in Kennedy's voice.

Jason jumped and then closed his eyes, willing himself to relax as something slick and wet on the point of Kennedy's finger invaded his anus.

"That okay?" Kennedy asked, and to his credit it wasn't just rhetorical. He was waiting for a response, very delicately stroking, delivering little shocks of pleasure with each press.

"That's...yeah. Nice." Jason's breath caught as Kennedy's finger changed angle, pressed harder.

"I like doing this to you," Kennedy murmured. "I'll be remembering what it feels like to touch you this way every time I see you tomorrow."

Jason moaned. *I'll be in Boston.* But that wasn't the point. He couldn't hide in Boston forever, and it was going to be hard for him to see Kennedy and not think the same thing.

He risked another glance at the mirror, and Christ almighty, that was just...*wanton*. The way he was moving into Kennedy's touch, his expression of flushed and feverish longing. There was naked and then there was *that*.

He closed his eyes, but not before he saw Kennedy's face.

Kennedy looked as intent and absorbed as a predator about to pounce. Not lost in the moment like Jason, or at least not in the same way. All his attention was on Jason, gauging, judging, so he noticed Jason's moment of distraction, followed Jason's glance, saw their reflection in the mirror, and smiled.

He moved his fingers—*what the hell?*—and Jason arched a little and made a sound he was pretty sure he had never uttered before.

Kennedy obviously spent his off-time doing more than attending George Winston concerts because you did not learn that move by practicing on yourself. Or if you did, Jason wanted to know how.

Kennedy twisted his fingers again and Jason squirmed, feeling that thrill of fierce and pleasurable sensation in his belly.

It was too much. One more of those and he was going to come right now. "Wait," he panted. "Don't..."

Kennedy didn't wait, but his touch instantly changed, soothed, bringing Jason back from the edge, steadying him.

"Whoa. Slow down," he whispered. "Wait for me."

Jason closed his eyes, focusing, shutting his mind to all but prolonging this sweet physical reaction.

Kennedy's weight settled on top of him. He was big, but he was surprisingly lithe, and his cock—*condom, okay that's good*—rudely poked Jason in a couple of vulnerable spots before lodging between Jason's buttocks. A pleasurable compromise if that's what Jason wanted.

Jason's heart seemed to swell. *Take it. Don't risk this; don't get any closer than you are now.* It just wasn't enough. He wanted more. Wanted all of it. Everything.

He breathed slowly and consciously relaxed, lifting up in offer. Kennedy's dick slipped, nudged him eagerly.

"Oh *yeah*," Kennedy groaned. "This is what I want." And just like that, his thick cock pushed inside Jason, stretching him wide with a lush and sensuous ease that felt unexpectedly right, familiar.

Jason cried out in pleasure—he had always been vocal, if not always articulate, and this was just too good to smother—and Kennedy made a low sound of amusement and kissed his shoulder.

Jason pushed up on his elbows and knees, rocking into the roll of Kennedy's hips. They fell right into a natural rhythm, push and pull, back and forth, forehand and backhand...now picking up speed. The mattress springs squeaked loudly, the headboard rapped against the wall.

"Oh God, yes," Jason panted. "Oh my God, I need..."

This. All of it. The warm light, the sharp smell of sex, the slick sounds, the heat of skin and warm breath...the connection. You could not see—experience first-hand—the worst of humanity, as they did all too often, and not crave some proof that there was still something more, something better. Yes. He needed to feel some healthy, happy human connection. And you couldn't get much closer than this.

Kennedy whispered into his ear, "You're something else, West. Something special...really special..." impaling him in easy, rhythmic strokes.

I bet you say that to all your temporary partners...

They were racing toward it now, breathing hard, skin flushed, flesh slapping. Kennedy's cock thrust into Jason's hole with swift, strong strokes, piercing him so deeply, so sweetly, his insides were quivering.

Jason gasped with each thrust. *"Ah..."* A small heartfelt sound of pleasure so acute it was almost pain, his moans in time to the fierce guttural sounds Kennedy made.

"Ah...ah...AHH..."

Kennedy's fingers dug into Jason's hips as he changed the angle of his approach, the broad, blunt tip grazing Jason's prostate.

Oh, Christ. Jason reared back, and Kennedy's arms locked around his waist, holding him upright, clamped tight, tighter, against his own broad torso. Jason's head fell back against Kennedy's shoulder, his back flexed as Kennedy impaled him again and again in that most exquisitely vulnerable of all places.

Jason began to sob. It was just so...insanely sweet...like getting hit by lightning. Yes, little lightning strikes of erotic bliss.

As though he really had been struck by lightning, electricity seemed to crackle at the base of his spine and shoot through him, balls to brain. He came so hard he was afraid he was going to blow apart. This orgasm wasn't a gentle blossoming; it was a time-lapse explosion of color and perfume. He felt the hot splash of his release hit his belly and spatter his chest and Kennedy's hands.

"Yeah, that's it..." Kennedy said with deep satisfaction, slowing his thrusts, seeming to savor Jason's reaction.

Jason threw his head back, panting, felt Kennedy's lips brush his skin, kiss his tears.

Kennedy reached up to Jason's nipples which were almost unbearably sensitive now, but it was okay. He wriggled his ass more snuggly against Kennedy's groin, encouraging him because his own orgasm was spent and drying, and he just wanted it over, just wanted to enjoy the afterglow and sleep.

Kennedy's thrusts picked up speed again; his hips lunged, smacking Jason's butt, and Jason moved to accommodate. Kennedy's fingers traced his lips, and Jason tasted himself. It was shocking and erotic, more so when Kennedy whispered, "Suck."

Suck?

But okay, whatever Kennedy needed, whatever it was going to take to get this done so they could sleep. Jason licked Kennedy's fingers, took the tips into his mouth, began to suck. Why would this be a turn-on? He wasn't sure. He gave it his best effort. Salty-sweet. And surprise, surprise... He felt his own cock starting to stir as Kennedy came powerfully, almost violently, inside him.

When it was over Kennedy crashed down beside Jason and, to his surprise, wrapped a muscular arm around him.

Did Kennedy like a cuddle after sex? Now there was a funny thought. Actually though...it was kind of nice like this. More comfortable than he would have thought.

His skin tingled as Kennedy traced a delicate finger over the whorl of pink scar tissue. The exit wound on the back of Jason's shoulder was larger, uglier.

Jason murmured, "My team went to Miami, and all I got was this lousy bullet hole."

"How did it happen?"

"Equipment malfunction." He opened his eyes and smiled at Kennedy, but Kennedy was not smiling.

Well, it wasn't a funny story. It was a terrifying story. The story of how Jason had nearly been shot to death.

"I was working with the Miami field office on the recovery of almost two hundred ancient pre-Columbian artifacts. We were all pretty excited especially after it turned out these items were in the possession of some very bad actors who needed cash to finance their drug trade. Two birds with one stone."

"Nice."

"Yeah. The takedown was to take place in a downtown hotel room."

"Not ideal."

"No, not by any means, but these guys were shrewd and increasingly suspicious with each passing day. Anyway, the plan was for me to hand over the money and while they were doing the math, slip out and let the tactical team into the room. The door was supposed to be rigged so that it would just swing open. I wouldn't even have to turn the lever. Only...the lock malfunctioned. I couldn't get the door open."

"What the hell," Kennedy said softly.

"Just what I said. Among other things. Anyway, tac couldn't get in, and I couldn't get out. It was only for a couple of seconds but long enough for the Columbians to figure out what was happening. And, as you might expect, they weren't happy. In particular, they weren't happy with me."

Kennedy ran exploratory fingertips along the length of Jason's clavicle. That knowledgeable but disconcertingly gentle touch left Jason's skin tingling. "The bullet cleared your vest."

"Yes, it did. That one did. The other two hit me squarely in the vest." He stopped talking as the memory flooded back. It had been like getting kicked by a horse in the chest. Twice. A couple of ribs had cracked beneath the impact—which was still a whole hell of a lot better than what could have happened.

He could feel the hard thump of his heart as it picked up speed. Better not to think about it too much. Kennedy could probably feel that telltale pulse too and was liable to start thinking again that Jason couldn't handle field duty.

"I remember hearing about the Miami shooting," Kennedy said slowly. "So that was you."

"That was me."

He said gravely, "I'm glad you made it."

"Thanks." Jason smiled. "Me too."

Kennedy let go of him and reached up to turn the light out.

Jason turned onto his side and closed his eyes. Kennedy settled on his back with a deep and contented sigh. Jason smiled faintly and let sleep claim him.

He was alone when he woke up.

It took Jason a second or two to realize he was not in his own room—even in the gloom he could tell the difference between a Homer Winslow print and an Arthur Quartley—and then remember the turn of events that had led to him not being in his own room at...he peered at the clock...six thirty on a Wednesday morning.

He threw a glance at the bathroom, but the door stood open and the room was empty.

So...okay. Maybe Kennedy was making a run for coffee. That would be nice. That would be grounds for genuine affection, in fact.

Then he heard the keycard in the lock, the door swung open, and Jason saw Kennedy had been making a different kind of run.

He wore sweatpants. His navy FBI T-shirt clung to him, a sweat-dark line running centrally down to his midriff. His face was flushed and shining with exertion, pale hair dark with sweat.

"You should have—" Jason began.

Kennedy said, "Good. You're awake. We've got to get down to the station. Another girl is missing."

CHAPTER FIFTEEN

Candy Davies was twenty-two and, though she worked nights as a bartender at the Blue Mermaid, was an Olympic swimming hopeful. On Tuesday morning she had been taken from Holyoke Pond where she worked out every morning, practicing her freestyle.

"As near as we can figure, she's been gone roughly twenty-four hours," Chief Gervase said when they had all gathered in the command center. The chief looked bad. Gray-faced and exhausted. "Her car was sitting in the parking lot overnight. The lifeguard found her gym bag and beach towel right there on the grass where Candy left them."

Holyoke Pond. Jason's heart sank. Just like Honey.

Gervase said, "While we have to consider the worst case scenario, there's always the chance Candy's still alive. Finding her is our number one priority."

Boxner was staring at Jason. Jason said, "I've got an alibi. Do you?" He shouldn't have said it, not even in sarcasm. Trying to head off accusations before they were made was liable to lend credence to Boxner's loony theory.

To his relief, Boxner turned his back on him.

Gervase said, "We'll start the search at Holyoke Pond. I've already got a call into State, and we can always count on a strong showing of volunteers even though it's a weekday. We've got storm clouds moving in, so we all need to exercise extra caution out there. If we do get rain, it's going to turn these roads and trails into a mud bath."

Kennedy said, "West and I will check out Rexford."

Boxner said, "Rexford? He's not going to leave her in the same place twice."

"That ghost town has a lot of potential areas for concealment. He wouldn't have to leave her in the same place. Anyway, it won't hurt to make sure, right?"

"No, it won't," the chief said with a warning look at Boxner. "I think it's as good an idea as any. We don't know how this guy thinks."

"He's got to be smart enough not to hide his victims in the same place every time." Boxner shrugged. Glanced at Kennedy. "It's your funeral."

"Rexford?" Jason asked when he and Kennedy were alone in their office.

"I can't think of a better place to hide her body. Can you? It's the last place anyone would think of searching now."

"True."

Kennedy shrugged into his vest. "I forgot you were heading out to Boston this morning. If you want to follow that trail, I'll see if I can borrow a vehicle from Kingsfield PD."

"I want to follow that trail," Jason said, "but I'm going to Rexford with you."

Kennedy's smile was grim. "Even if she's there, she's not going to be alive, West."

"I know that."

Kennedy watched Jason performing his weapon check. "You've potentially got a good lead to follow up with those art dealers. I don't know that you should waste time on this."

Jason holstered his pistol. "The art dealers will wait. I'm going to Rexford."

Kennedy looked up in surprise. He chuckled. "Do you think I can't take care of myself?"

"I think there's a good reason the Bureau partners agents in the field," Jason said. "I think if I told you I was headed out to Rexford on my own, you'd have a thing or two to say about it."

Kennedy grinned. "Maybe. You're way too smart for a move like that, West."

"I'm way too smart to answer that," Jason said.

* * * * *

A lot of the undergrowth had been chopped back to allow the emergency vehicles closer access, but it was still a good hike back into Rexford.

The air was a little cooler, heavy with moisture, and Jason and Kennedy made good time, reaching the fork by the old mill by noon.

Kennedy took his binoculars out, studying the rooftops and chimneys behind the trees. The heavy cloud cover threw an eerie silver-green light over the wild terrain—did they call that witch light?—but so far the precipitation didn't amount to more than a few drops.

"What do you think?" Jason asked. He took a drink from his water bottle.

"Looks quiet. There are some birds circling to the south."

Jason nodded.

They moved on, their boots scraping rock and dirt. The only other sign of life was a fox trotting across the trail some distance ahead. The breeze blew in the opposite direction today, and even the sounds of the highway were hushed.

The rain began to pepper down harder when they reached Rexford. Fat drops pattered in the dust and darkened the peeling paint on the old buildings.

"North or south?" Kennedy asked. "Take your pick."

Jason said tersely, "North." He would prefer they did not split up, but that was impractical. They needed to split up in order to have even a chance of covering this much territory in an afternoon. Which didn't change the fact that something about Rexford made him uneasy. Really uneasy. In fact, he was probably going to have nightmares about this town for years to come.

"You just want to see your girlfriend the mermaid again," Kennedy said.

"Yeah, baby," Jason replied. "I gots to get me some of *that* tail."

Kennedy laughed. "Watch yourself." He turned away and started down the street in the opposite direction.

Jason watched him, sighed inwardly, and started off.

As before, it was slow going, moving through each building, shining his flashlight beam into every nook or cranny large enough to conceal an adult female.

At least this time he had the advantage of having explored these buildings before. That was more of an edge than Kennedy had.

Jason came at last to the Lyceum of the Aquatic.

Jokes aside, he'd have been delighted to never see the inside of that place again, let alone his girlfriend the mermaid. Following Kennedy's logic, the lyceum was the ideal place to conceal Davies's body given it was the last place a sane person would hide her.

He went through the faux entrance, past the ticket kiosk and the pedestal with the old-fashioned diving helmet. As he reached the entrance to the main hall the assorted weird smells of the place hit him. The rotting taxidermy, the mildew and mold, the general air of swamp gas and malaise, all magnified by the rain.

He paused, pulled his Glock, ejected the magazine, squeezed the trigger, and racked the slide. He let the trigger out slowly, listening for the click of the trigger reset.

Click.

There was no problem with his pistol. There had been no problem four hours earlier when he'd last checked it. There had been no problem in Miami. The problem was not—and had never been—with his weapon.

And in any case, they were not dealing with a shooter.

Just do your fucking job.

He slapped the magazine back in, holstered his weapon, and entered the hall.

Floorboards creaked noisily with every step. Shining drops of rain fell through the ceiling.

He stopped, staring around the long center hall. It took his eyes a moment to adjust to the gloom. The imprint of dozens of footsteps coming and going could be seen in the dust and dirt, a reminder of three days earlier.

Changeable light from the broken slats in the roof wavered over the bleached squares of wooden floor. Something glittered in one of the diorama cases, catching the fitful rays, and Jason moved to check it out.

A glass eye.

A souvenir from one of the long gone taxidermy creations. The single eye seemed to glare at him.

Jason turned away, holding his flashlight aloft. Thanks to the lousy weather, there was even less visibility than the last time.

The rain dripped from the ceiling, whispered outside the entrance. Jason's heart began to thud as the uneasy—and unmistakable—sense he was not alone stole over him.

He threw a quick look over his shoulder.

Nothing. There was no one there. *Of course there's no one there.* With two FBI agents canvassing the town?

For Christ's sake. He was not going to be able to do his job if he couldn't stop jumping at every shadow.

He deliberately turned his back on the entrance, scanning the room, probing the shadows with the ray of bright, white light from his flashlight.

His gaze fell on what looked like...something blue. Something... human. He started forward and a floorboard groaned ominously.

Jason froze.

Not a floorboard. The *floor.* The whole rotten expanse of floor. In fact, it sounded like the entire building was about to go.

He held his breath, waiting. He took a cautious step backward.

A loud and unpleasant squeak, but nothing like the other sound.

A bead of sweat trickled down his temple. He took another step back. Another startling squeak like he'd stepped on a mouse's tail.

But still. So far so good.

He threw a worried look at the body of the girl which lay tumbled a few feet away. If the floor went, they would lose their crime scene.

Wait.

Did she—?

Had she—?

Jason stared. Her eyes were closed. Her face lifeless. No. Not possible. Was she *breathing*? He couldn't tell. For a second he'd thought... No.

Right? He could detect no rise and fall of her chest.

What if she *was* alive?

Shit. He couldn't tell. Not from this distance.

He needed to get closer without killing them both.

Jason took another careful step backward.

Again.

Again.

His flashlight beam picked out something pale lying a few inches from her body. Maybe a twig. Maybe a leaf. Maybe...who knew what the hell.

The floor felt more solid—that was probably wishful thinking—or at least had stopped that alarming splintering noise. Jason tried a tentative step to the side. Nothing happened. He stepped closer to the wall. Yes, the floor felt sturdier here.

Cautious step by step he traveled the length of the room along the wall to where Candy lay. Her body did not appear to be bruised and battered like Rebecca's. She still wore her one piece swimsuit.

Beside her outstretched hand, as though it had fallen from her lifeless fingers, was a pale, round marble.

No. Not a marble. A mermaid.

Jason picked it up—the irregular surface guaranteed no fingerprints would be possible—rolling it gently between his thumb and fingers. It was uncannily familiar to the one Honey had. It even felt familiar to his fingertips.

He glanced at the girl's body and nearly got the shock of his life. Candy's eyes were open. Her lips moved soundlessly.

She's alive.

He dropped the charm in his jeans pocket, bending over her. "Candy? Can you hear me? You're okay now. You're safe now. You're going to be fine."

He swiftly checked her vitals. Not good. Not good at all. She was dehydrated and in deep shock. On the other hand, she should be dead, so compared to that...

No visible wounds. No bruising around her throat. Her swimsuit was intact. How was it even possible they had got this lucky? That *she* had got this lucky?

He brushed her hair back from her face. "Candy, can you hear me? Can you tell me who did this to you? Did you get a look at him?"

Her eyes closed again.

"*Damn it*. Hang on, Candy. We're going to get you out of here." Jason jumped to his feet and raised his radio. "West to Kennedy. Come in."

Kennedy answered at once. "Kennedy. What have you got?"

"She's here. At the lyceum."

"Roger. I'll be there in f—"

"She's alive," Jason broke in.

There was a metallic pause. Kennedy said, "Say again, West?"

"She's alive. I'm radioing for medical assist—"

A floorboard cracked behind him. Jason reached for his pistol. Too late he realized that the danger did not come from an intruder. The danger was the floor itself—it was giving way beneath his feet.

"...can you hear me?"

Wet.

Reeking, slimy wet.

What. The. Fuck.

"God *damn* this day. *Jason*?"

What was he lying in? What was he lying *on*?

Soft but not a good soft. A mushy, wet sponge.

Wait...

"*Jason*? West? Jason, can you hear me?"

Where was he? Jason blinked up at...a hole in the roof...and a white face hard with anxiety...and a hole in the roof over that white face...and the white face of the sun...

Even as he stared, the pallid sun slipped into shadow. Darkness fell across him.

Jason closed his eyes. He did not feel very well. He did not think moving would be a good idea.

The voice overhead was swearing quietly. "I'm coming down," it said.

Coming down.

Jason's eyes flew open.

No.

A still worse idea.

Enough things had already come down.

"Wait," he got out.

"*Jason?*"

Kennedy.

That's who that was.

His heart lifted. He liked Kennedy.

"Goddamn it, you scared the hell out of me," Kennedy yelled. He did sound a little scared, but mostly he sounded angry.

"Here," Jason croaked. "I'm right here."

"I know where the hell you are," Kennedy shouted. "Are you all right?"

"Yeah." Or not. Maybe not so much. Jason tried to sit up, and he thought maybe if he took it slowly he might not throw up or keel over or otherwise embarrass himself. He was confused about where he was and why he was wherever he was. He was pretty sure he'd hit his head—but he couldn't tell if that stickiness was blood or something worse. He was lying—now sitting—in about an inch of worse. He'd lost his flashlight and his radio. He had his pistol. That was something. He could always kill himself if the situation went downhill from here.

"What happened?" he called.

The sun slunk out from behind the rafters and feeble rays illuminated what appeared to be patches of muddy fur floating in the muck around him. Jesus Christ. Had he landed on...what *had* he landed on? Were these bits of rotting upholstery or rotting taxidermy? He looked up, and his stomach gave another queasy roll at the sight of the rusty and twisted nails sticking out of the boards a few inches above his head.

Kennedy was still talking to him. "You fell through the floor. I've radioed for help. Are you sure you're not injured?"

"What the hell did I land on?"

Good question. It had probably saved his life. Or at least his spine.

Jason tried to stand up—taking care not to brain himself on the nail-studded overhanging boards. He stepped down with a splash into water that reached his shins. The water was shockingly cold. Like melted ice.

The hole in the ceiling above him—the floor above him—the whatever-it-was above him—was about twenty feet up. He was not going to be able to jump or climb out that way—even assuming the remaining floor would support such an effort.

"What are you doing?" Kennedy sounded alarmed again.

"I'm just going to..."

"You're out of visual range. Come back to where I can see you. Don't move around down there. The basement is flooded. This entire structure is compromised."

Ya think?

He peered at what he could see of his surroundings and made the discovery that he was sloshing around what had probably been some kind of a storage room. No windows. One wall was lined with shelves crowded with grimy jars containing murky substances. Wooden crates were stacked against the opposite wall. Then more shelves, these stocked with...skulls. Animal skulls, but skulls.

As Jason stared, he noticed a snake crawling its way through the eye of one of the skulls.

Yes. An actual live snake. Not a natural history exhibit.

"Is the girl okay?" he called, never taking his gaze from the snake. He was relieved that he sounded pretty normal. For a guy trapped in a flooded basement full of skulls and snakes.

"She's alive. Jason, move back to where I can see you."

"I think there's a stairway on the east wall."

"Jason, *listen* to me. Help is on the way. You need to remain where I can see you."

Was the flashlight down here somewhere? Jason took a couple of slurpy steps, peering into the cold and slimy water. The sun slid away again and the room plunged back into opacity.

Jason drew a sharp breath. No, he really could not do this.

"Jason—"

"I want to try the stairway. I'll keep yelling Marco, and you yell Polo. So you know I'm okay, and I can tell how far from you I am."

"Are you—? And what if you're *not* okay? How am I supposed to get to you?"

"Marco."

"West, you're beginning to piss me off."

"Marco."

"At the least we should be using radio voice procedure."

"Marco to Kennedy. Over."

Kennedy snapped, "Polo."

Jason grinned and reached out, feeling his way across the room. Even a few feet from the hole in the ceiling it was difficult to make out anything in the room.

Just don't let me reach out and touch a snake.

He didn't like anything about this. Splashing blindly around a half-flooded cellar was a bad idea. But he was worried about Kennedy still crouched up there on top of a floor that was about to come down. Kennedy didn't want to leave his partner, which Jason appreciated, but...

Anyway, although he would never admit this, Jason was simply too freaked out to stay put. This flooded room triggered every primal fear lurking in the back of his brain. The dark, the wet, the smell of death and decay...

"Marco."

"Polo."

Kennedy's voice was farther away now, and Jason was almost entirely in darkness. He reached out and felt the railing of the staircase. It felt reasonably stable, all things being relative.

"Polo?" Kennedy called sharply.

"Sorry. Yep. I found the stairs."

The sun coyly, briefly, slipped into view. Yes, he had found the stairs and just climbing out of the water was a relief. He kept thinking about falling over bodies floating in the water. The graveyard was a mile away, and there were no bodies bobbing in the green water surrounding him. It did look like there might be a couple of shark skeletons lying beneath the surface.

Shark skeletons were definitely better than human skeletons.

Yes, there were definitely bones in the water. Would shark cartilage last as long as human bone?

He squelched up the rickety case.

"I'm at the top of the stairs. Can you hear me?"

"You're at the top of the stairs. Can you get out?"

"The door's locked." Jason jiggled the round doorknob. Definitely locked. He felt over the door's peeling surface, picking up splinters as he went. "I might be able to..."

"What? I can't hear you."

He rammed his shoulder against the door. Which was unbelievably stupid, not least because it was his bad shoulder. He reeled back against the railing, cursing quietly, rubbing his shoulder.

Kennedy was yelling again.

"Okay!" Jason managed.

"What's happening down there?"

"Nothing."

"*Nothing?*"

Jason laughed unsteadily. "I mean, everything's under control." He took two careful steps back, lightly bracing himself against the railing, and launched a kick with all his strength at where he reckoned the door-jamb was. He had a split-second to wonder if he was going to break his foot on the wall.

The wood gave a satisfying crunching sound.

Kennedy was yelling.

Jason ignored him. He stepped back and delivered another strong kick. The door flew back and hit the wall behind it. Watery daylight poured down, revealing a window and another staircase.

"I'm out!"

"What?"

"The door is open. There's a window above, and I can see more stairs. I'm coming up."

This time Kennedy didn't answer, and Jason thought he knew why. He could hear the distant wail of approaching sirens.

CHAPTER SIXTEEN

"**W**hy would he leave her alive?" Jason asked.

Kennedy shook his head. His expression was closed.

They were in the bathroom of Kennedy's motel room. Jason sat uncomfortably on the side of the tub while Kennedy liberally doused him with hydrogen peroxide and antiseptic cream. Jason could have done it himself. He was good at looking after himself. In fact, he had declined the on-scene attentions of the paramedics—until Kennedy had ordered him not to be a complete dumbass. Since Jason prided himself on not being a dumbass, partial or complete, he had submitted to being checked for concussion and, once given a conditional all-clear, had headed back to the motel for a very long, very hot shower.

He'd have fallen into bed at that point, but Kennedy had pounded on his door and insisted on this first-aid routine. The truth was, concussion or not, Jason still felt weirdly shaky and chilled. Shock, according to Kennedy. An idea Jason had brushed off, but he couldn't deny that there was something sort of comforting about relinquishing himself to Kennedy's gruff care.

Actually, Kennedy was surprisingly careful, lightly smearing white antiseptic cream over Jason's knuckles.

He answered Jason's question. "Whatever his reasons, she's out of his hands now."

Candy had been airlifted out of Rexford—it turned out it was easier to fly in than drive in—and transported to a hospital in Boston where she was currently sedated and under guard.

"It doesn't fit the profile, right? We didn't interrupt him. He had her for over twenty-four hours. And during that time he didn't sexually assault her. He didn't harm her in any way. Other than abduct her and leave her in that—" Jason had to pause for another of those huge, nervous yawns that kept interrupting him.

"There may be other time constraints we're not aware of," Kennedy said.

"He actually had more time because no one even knew Candy was missing for nearly twenty-four hours."

"That's a hell of a bruise on your shoulder."

"I walked into the door."

"Hm." Kennedy dabbed a blob of Neosporin on a cut on Jason's neck and neatly applied a Band-Aid. "I hope you're up to date on your tetanus shots."

Jason looked up and smiled. To his astonishment, Kennedy leaned in and covered his mouth with his own.

He hadn't been expecting it, so the kiss landed on Jason's open and startled mouth. It was an odd kiss—maybe Kennedy had surprised himself as much as Jason—not hungry and hard, but not quite as light and sociable as perhaps Kennedy had intended.

Kennedy's lips were warm and firm. He tasted dark and sweet. A complex and masculine flavor, unique to him. Nice. Very nice.

They parted, and Jason thought Sam—no, Kennedy—looked as confused as himself.

"She's older," Jason said at random. "Maybe that's a factor. She's not a teenage girl."

"Maybe," Kennedy said. And that noncommittal comment made it clear to Jason that Kennedy did not for one minute believe it.

So what did he think had motivated Candy's abductor to leave her unharmed?

For once, Jason was too tired to care.

Kennedy finished patching Jason's various cuts and grazes and then stood back to examine his handiwork. "You'll do."

"Thank you, Florence. You'll be glad to know I'm making a generous contribution to the Red Cross this year."

"Are you hungry?"

Jason shook his head. "No. I'm beat. I'm going to bed." He rose from the side of the tub, swaying as another jaw-breaking yawn caught him off guard. "I think I could sleep for a year."

Kennedy began to gather up his tweezers, nail scissors, and bits of Band-Aid wrappers. He said over his shoulder. "Why don't you sleep here?"

Jason shook his head, his smile apologetic. "Thanks, but I'm not going to be much fun tonight."

Kennedy turned to face him. "No. I really do mean sleep." His expression was serious.

"Uh...well, if you..." What? *Don't mind? Want the company?* Jason wasn't sure what his question was. He was too surprised by Kennedy's offer. The truth was, he didn't particularly want to be on his own tonight. Every time he closed his eyes he saw that weird basement with its shifting shadows and skulls and snakes. No. He wouldn't mind sharing a bed with a warm body tonight.

"In that case, yes," he said. "However, I think you should know that I snore."

Kennedy said, "I do know that you snore."

"Oh? Right. Okay. On your head—or next to your head—be it."

Kennedy smiled faintly.

It was a relief to stumble into the next room and flop down on the bed.

He shivered. The temperature in here was like a meat locker. Jason made the supreme effort to kick off his jeans and crawl under the coverlet. He pulled the comforter up, vaguely aware that Kennedy moved around the room, turning off the air conditioner, turning down the lamp, putting stuff away—how much tidying up did he have to do?—Jason's eyelids felt weighted.

With the air conditioner off, he could hear the summer rain hitting the windows, making a soothing, shushing sound. Nice. Funny how rain had a different sound in the summer.

And Kennedy's presence was comforting even if he was taking forever to come to bed.

"Are you checking email?" Jason mumbled.

"I'll be right there," Kennedy replied absently, fingers clicking away on his laptop.

At last the lamp on the desk snapped out. A moment later the mattress dipped. Kennedy's long, solid frame slid between the sheets next to Jason. Jason had slipped into an uneasy doze, but that brought him back to wakefulness.

"Are you warm enough?" Kennedy asked. His voice was low and intimate, a bedroom voice.

"Oh, yeah. Boiling." It wasn't the truth though. There was a cold knot in his core, and every so often a shudder rippled through him. Maybe he *was* suffering a little from shock, as ridiculous as the idea seemed.

Kennedy slid an arm under Jason's shoulders and drew him over. He wrapped his other arm around Jason. Normally Jason didn't care to be held while he was trying to sleep, but tonight Kennedy's heat and bulk was a comfort. Jason closed his eyes and relaxed.

After a time he stopped shivering and fell into a state of comfortable drowsiness. But he could tell that Kennedy was awake, could feel him thinking.

Jason murmured, "Everything all right?"

"Of course." Kennedy kissed Jason's temple. "Just relax."

"If I was any more relaxed, I'd be drooling on your chest."

He felt Kennedy's smile. Kennedy nuzzled him, but it was an absent caress. His mind was a million miles away.

Well, not a million miles away because he was consciously quieting Jason, keeping him warm and comfortable, but the focus of his thoughts was not on Jason.

"How did you get into profiling?" Jason asked sleepily.

He felt Kennedy wrench back to alertness. After a moment, Kennedy said with a strange lack of inflection, "I like to hunt."

"What made you want to hunt serial killers?"

The silence stretched so long he didn't think Kennedy would answer.

"It was a long time ago," Kennedy said finally. "I don't talk about it."

Jason considered that slammed door. "Okay."

Kennedy kissed him with that same out-of-character gentleness. "Maybe sometime I'll tell you about it. It's no bedtime story."

"Sure," Jason said. He kissed Kennedy back. "If you want to."

Until that moment he had not considered that he and Kennedy might continue any kind of relationship beyond their current assignment. Most probably Kennedy did not mean that they would literally discuss his past at a later date, was just softening the rejection. Not that he was overly prone to politeness.

Was there potential for him and Kennedy to...?

What?

They lived in different states, to begin with. Then again they both traveled extensively. It was not inconceivable they might hook up again.

And that was probably all Kennedy meant. The sex was good with them, so why wouldn't they, er, socialize if they happened to find themselves with free time while in the same city. And maybe in that unforeseeable future Kennedy might even be in a more confiding frame of mind. That's what he meant.

Right?

And that would be fine with Jason. Either would be fine. He liked Kennedy, but he wasn't making long-term plans either. He wouldn't mind reconnecting at some future date. And if that were to happen, he wouldn't mind if Kennedy confided in him—but he also didn't mind if Kennedy kept his secrets.

Everybody had secrets.

He woke to fragile sunlight and the knowledge that he was alone. Again.

Jason opened his eyes, peered at the clock and then at the indented pillow on Kennedy's side of the bed.

Five thirty on Thursday morning. Jesus Christ, Kennedy was an early bird. Did he not understand the pleasurable possibilities of waking up with someone in a warm bed when you had a few quiet minutes to greet the day?

No. He probably did not. Given the fact that he had, as far as Jason could tell, barely slept the night before. For Kennedy, the night was more about accommodating the scheduling needs of others than requiring sleep himself.

Inviting Jason to crash here had been kind. Jason recognized now he had been more shaken than he'd realized by his fall. He remembered jerking awake at one point—one of those instinctive, spasmodic reactions to the sensation of plummeting down—and Kennedy's arm had tightened around him.

"You're okay," he'd said softly. Just that, but even half asleep, Jason had heard and believed.

It gave him a weird, wobbly feeling in his belly to think of it. He was either close to falling for Kennedy—or desperately in need of breakfast. Desperately in need of breakfast, hopefully.

And right on cue, the motel room door opened, and Kennedy, in sweats, T-shirt, and sunglasses, carried in coffee and a bag of something that smelled promisingly of breakfast sandwiches. Jason's stomach growled.

"I heard that," Kennedy remarked.

Jason sat up. "I wondered where you'd got to."

Kennedy threw him a quick, faint smile. He set down the paper bag on the desk and handed Jason his coffee. Jason checked under the lid that no pollutants had been added—Kennedy doctored his own coffee with sugar and cream—and took a life-saving swallow.

"Thanks. I needed that."

"How'd you sleep?"

Jason nodded. He said a little self-consciously, "Thank you for that too."

"Sausage and egg or bacon and egg?"

"Sausage."

Kennedy tossed him one of the breakfast sandwiches.

"Did you sleep at all?" Jason asked.

"Me? Sure." Kennedy unwrapped a sandwich and took one of those gigantic bites. He grinned sharkishly at Jason.

"I've been thinking." Jason delicately picked paper out of his mouth. He had been a little too enthusiastic tackling his own sandwich. "Boxner is our guy."

"I see. This again."

"You notice he didn't want us to search Rexford."

"He said it was a waste of time. I didn't get the impression he was trying to stop us."

"He stopped by Rebecca's house that night. Something happened. They arranged to meet later. Something." Jason sipped his coffee.

"You're like a dog with a bone on this. And it's pure speculation."

"It's not pure speculation. He did stop by her house. They did speak. And there are no witnesses as to what was said."

"But there are witnesses to the fact that Rebecca returned to the party afterward." Kennedy, in the process of doctoring his own coffee, didn't even look up.

"And a short time later, she vanished without a word to anyone. That could indicate an attempt at secrecy. Which means mine is a reasonable assumption."

Kennedy laughed. "Is it? I don't agree. I don't find that a very likely scenario."

"You're the one who first suggested it."

Kennedy made a sound. Not quite a growl and not quite a groan, but one hundred percent aggravation.

"All right," he said. "Explain to me the lapse in killings. If your theory is that Boxner was Pink's disciple—"

"I didn't say that. I said I *didn't* think Pink had a disciple."

"Then what *are* you saying? What triggered Boxner's slip into homicidal mania? There hasn't been a murder here in ten years. So what set Boxner off?"

"I don't know. Maybe it was something specific to his relationship to Rebecca."

"Which appears to be largely nonexistent."

Jason said stubbornly, "I know I'm on to something with this."

Kennedy closed his eyes as though in pain. Or in a visible attempt to hang on to his patience. "You don't think maybe you're a little biased when it comes to Officer Boxner?"

"You were the first one to bring up the possibility that our unsub might be someone involved in the original investigation."

"On the *periphery* of the investigation. Not directly involved. I was not accusing a member of Kingsfield PD. And I certainly wasn't accusing Officer Boxner who was only slightly older than you at the time of the first homicide."

Right. Because demographics indicated that the majority of serial offenders were most active between the ages of twenty-seven and forty-five, with first kills originating typically in the early twenties. There were plenty of exceptions. Hell, there were even exceptions in Kennedy's own impressive list of successfully closed cases. Female serial killers, child serial killers, geriatric serial killers. If anyone should be familiar with the colorful varieties of serial killers, it was Kennedy.

So yes, maybe Jason was predisposed to suspect the worst of Boxner, but didn't Kennedy also have a blind spot in being unwilling to even consider the involvement of law enforcement in this case?

"You really think I can't separate my personal feelings from the job?" Jason asked.

"I think you sincerely try."

"Thanks for giving me that much," Jason said shortly.

"It's human nature," Kennedy said. "You have cause for not liking Boxner. There's considerable antipathy between you. It's reasonable that you believe he's capable of these other acts. He believes *you're* capable of these other acts. You're going to have to trust me on this. He's not our guy. He doesn't fit the profile."

"Which profile? The original profile is irrelevant."

"It's not *irrelevant*." That was the old Kennedy. Short and sharp.

"Maybe not irrelevant, but this profile, the profile you're working on now, is largely composed of someone trying to copy the earlier profile. Right?"

Kennedy didn't miss a beat. "That's not Boxner. Right there, that is not in his psychological makeup. And secondly, that's one theory. Yours. I'm not convinced."

Jason stared. "You don't think there's a copycat killer out there?" That was news. When had Kennedy made that deduction? And why wasn't he sharing his theories with his partner? Okay, temporary partner.

As though reading Jason's mind, Kennedy said—his tone almost placating, "I think that it's too soon to draw any conclusions. Look, this kind of investigation takes time. We'll know more after we talk to the Davies girl. Meantime, will you at least try to keep an open mind? You've got a promising line of investigation in tracking down the artist of the mermaid charms. That's what you need to focus on."

In other words, *stay out of my way.*

Oh, but hey. They had definitely made progress in the area of interpersonal relationships because Kennedy didn't say it aloud. In fact, he was making an obvious effort not to say anything offensive or dismissive.

"All right," Jason said curtly.

Kennedy looked relieved, but Jason too had made progress. Kennedy was the senior on this, after all, and the guy Jason was currently sleeping with. Jason could also be courteous and considerate—and keep his own counsel and follow his own line of inquiry.

* * * * *

Manning phoned on the short drive to the police station.

Jason saw the SAC's ID flash up and threw Kennedy a quick look. He let the call go to message. A moment later, Manning phoned again.

"Answer it," Kennedy said. "He's not going to give up."

Jason pressed to accept the call. "West."

"Agent West, I was, erm, expecting to hear from you before now. What is the status?"

Hadn't they only spoken the day before? Jason said cautiously, "The status, sir?"

"Are we or are we not looking for a copycat killer in Kingsfield?"

Copycat killer in Kingsfield. Try saying that three times fast. Jason replied, "It's still too early to draw any conclusions. The last victim isn't able to speak yet. We'll know more when we can interview her."

"Diplomatic," Kennedy commented.

Jason frowned at him.

"I watch the news, Agent West."

"Sir?"

Manning said, "All I want to know is did Kennedy put the wrong, erm, man in prison ten years ago?"

Jason stared at the rows of old houses and tidy gardens gliding past. "No. Absolutely not."

"I'm not looking for an, erm, whitewash job, Agent West. I—*we*— want the truth. We *need* the truth."

No, what Manning wanted was corroboration. Justification for going after Kennedy. This wasn't about "we" or the Bureau. It was about Manning and Kennedy. This was a long-running feud. And Jason was now caught in the middle of it.

"Sir, Martin Pink is the Huntsman. I interviewed Pink myself three days ago, and I'm confident we got the right man."

Manning said shortly, "I'm glad *you're* so certain, West. But as I said, I watch the, erm, news, and it sounds to me like not everyone is, erm, convinced on that point."

"Well, I don't believe it's possible to get unanimous consent on any point, sir."

Kennedy gave a quiet laugh and turned into the parking lot behind the police station.

"Indeed," Manning said. "Keep in mind why you've been assigned to this case, West. I want regular updates. I want *daily* updates." He hung up noisily.

Daily? Why stop there? How about hourly?

Jason clicked off and glanced at Kennedy. Kennedy seemed to have nothing more on his mind than angling the car into one of those too-small painted slots.

They parked and got out of the car without further conversation.

Jason's phone rang as they walked around the side of the building.

"*And* another thing," Kennedy murmured.

Jason threw him a harassed look, but it was not SAC Manning this time. It was one of Jason's dealer contacts. Priya Ort-Rossington ran an upscale folk art gallery in New York specializing in woodcarving and sculpture.

"Agent West, what a nice surprise to hear from you. Gerda and I heard about your being shot. Oh my *God*. *So* awful. We were in shock. We're *so* glad you're back."

Jason relaxed. He had history with Priya and her partner—business and romantic partner—Gerda Ort. Two years ago art thieves had used their gallery to fence stolen Haida argillite artifacts. Jason had managed to apprehend the thieves and recover the carvings, while keeping the gallery's name out of the press—thereby earning Priya and Gerda's undying gratitude.

"Thanks," Jason said. "It's good to be back."

"As it turns out, I actually have information for you on the artist you were inquiring after."

Jason stopped walking. "You know who the artist is?"

"I'm almost positive I do. In fact—this is what's *so* bizarre—Gerda and I were discussing him a few days ago, wondering whatever happened to him."

"What's the name of this artist?"

"Kyser. Jeremy Kyser. What's *so* interesting about him is he was actually a doctor. A psychologist, I think. He did these wonderful, detailed carvings in his spare time."

Kennedy walked back to where Jason stood. He watched Jason closely.

"Dr. Jeremy Kyser," Jason repeated. He nodded at Kennedy.

Kennedy's expression changed.

"Yes. I don't think he had any expectation of becoming a professional artist. He said his work was very stressful, and he found carving a way of relaxing, of centering his mind. You saw the work. If I hadn't known better, I'd have thought they were traditional *netsuke*. A *very* gifted amateur artist."

"Do you have contact information on Kyser?"

"Yes, I do, but it might be out of date. As I said, we haven't heard from him in years. For a while he used to regularly bring us his carvings, and they always sold very well. Then all at once he stopped. He didn't respond to phone calls or emails. That's the artistic temperament for you, though usually when artists are selling they don't wander off without a word."

"No," Jason said. "They don't. What was that contact info?"

Rustling sounds on the other end of the line. "Here we go. Dr. Jeremy Kyser. He's in Massachusetts. Or used to be. I remember he lived in an old farmhouse in the middle of nowhere. A place called Old Mill Pond."

"In Hampden County?" He couldn't believe it.

Priya laughed. "I'm afraid I wouldn't know that." She rattled off the address, and Jason typed it into his notes.

"This is very helpful. Thank you, Priya."

"Oh, our pleasure. We're *so* happy to help. When do you think you'll be in New York again?"

"It's hard to say." Jason chitchatted with Priya for another minute or two, tongue on automatic pilot, eyes on Kennedy. His mind raced ahead. *All this time he was right under our noses.*

At last he was able to disconnect.

"And?" Kennedy demanded.

Jason said, "Dr. Jeremy Kyser lives—or at least used to live—less than thirteen miles from here."

CHAPTER SEVENTEEN

"**Y**ou don't look any the worse for wear, Agent West," Chief Gervase greeted Jason. "Glad to see you back on the job."

"That's youth for you," Kennedy said.

Gervase grinned. "That's exactly what I used to think about you, Agent Kennedy."

Kennedy snorted.

"It's been an interesting twenty-four hours," Gervase said, leading the way back to his office. "We've had some developments you'll want to hear about." He called toward the direction of the front desk, "Could we get coffee, Officer Courtney?"

"Coming, Chief!"

Boxner was already in Gervase's office going through his file cabinet. He jumped guiltily at their arrival, and Gervase said, "How many times have I told you to ask before you start pawing through my files? This isn't your office yet, Boyd." He sounded more resigned than annoyed.

Boxner, face red, leaned against the wall and folded his arms. "I just wanted to double-check something."

"What?"

"It'll keep."

Gervase sighed and shook his head. He took the chair behind his desk. "First things first. Tony McEnroe has *no* alibi for the night Candy Davies was abducted." He directed a challenging look at Kennedy.

"McEnroe is not our unsub." Kennedy was uncompromising as usual.

Gervase's face tightened, his eyes hardened. Jason sighed inwardly. He agreed with Kennedy, but would it kill him to occasionally soften his delivery, at least *pretend* he didn't think he had all the answers?

Gervase leaned back in his chair. "Then *do* enlighten us, Special Agent Kennedy." He nodded in curt thanks to Officer Courtney who had appeared with a tray of steaming coffee mugs.

Kennedy said, "West has developed a promising lead on the artist who carved the original mermaid charms. It turns out he lives locally."

Gervase took a cup from the tray and threw Jason a startled look. "Is that so?"

Jason said, "Yes. Dr. Jeremy Kyser is one of Pink's two permitted outside contacts. He's supposed to be working on a book about serial killers. But as it happens, he's also a talented amateur artist. We—I believe—we've got verification that he carved the mermaid charms."

"That's what I call a big coincidence," Gervase said.

"What are we waiting for?" Boxner stepped away from the wall. "I'll go talk to him right now."

Jason opened his mouth to object. He had uncovered this lead, and this was by rights his line of inquiry.

Except...the FBI was there at the invitation of Kingsfield PD. They couldn't take over the investigation, couldn't even insist on conducting interviews of suspects without the permission of local law enforcement. Technically, they were there to advise and assist.

"Okay, slow down," Gervase said. "We need to understand what we're dealing with. Kyser's name never came up in the original investigation."

"But that's it; that's what this is about," Boxner said, and as much as Jason disliked Boxner, he couldn't help sounding his agreement and approval.

"Now hold on, you two," Gervase said. "If these charms had been produced by Acme Corporation, we wouldn't be considering Acme Corporation a suspect. Let's not confuse cause and effect. The Corrigan girl had that mermaid for months before her death. Pink didn't plant it on her."

"I don't see what you're getting at," Boxner said, and once again Jason was in agreement. The charms were not mass produced. They were the work of a local artist. That personal connection could not be ignored.

Kennedy said, "The Corrigan girl was the first victim. Everything that happened in her case set the pattern for the subsequent killings. It's very possible Pink bought the other charms to match Honey's."

"So what?" Boxner said. "We've got the man who made the charms. That's a lead."

"Yes, it is, and I think you and West should follow it up together," Kennedy said. He ignored Jason's startled look. "I'm not arguing with you. I agree that this is a line of inquiry that needs to be pursued. Before you pursue it, though, we need to keep in mind a couple of facts. The first one being, that as sinister as his emergence in this case might look, so far Kyser's involvement is tangential. Assuming he is the artist—and we've yet to confirm that—" He shot Jason a cool look. "He may have become interested in Pink's case partly because Pink used Kyser's own creations in his crimes. That is certainly going to get someone's attention."

"Yes, but how would Kyser know that when it wasn't publicized in the media?" Jason objected.

"It's possible Pink contacted him after the fact with that information. Actually, for all we know, Pink may have chosen those charms for that very reason: he wanted Kyser's attention. We don't yet know the extent of, or his history with, Kyser."

"Wait a minute," Jason said. "So you're suggesting that Pink may have hit on the mermaid theme because Kyser carved some mermaid charms? And if Kyser had carved rabbit charms or leprechaun charms, Pink would have gone with that?"

Kennedy sighed. "I'm suggesting that we don't know. I'm suggesting that we don't assume. Let's keep an open mind."

"We do know that the mermaid theme is central to this case. Aside from the fact that mermaid charms were found at nearly all the crime scenes—in the victims' mouths—the victims themselves could be viewed as mermaids. They were all taken from aquatic venues, most of them were in bathing suits, and they were all females of a certain physical type and age. So I'm not sure what you're getting at."

Gervase answered before Kennedy could respond. "If the suggestion is that Kyser is still providing someone with mermaid charms, that's not going to work. There was no charm found with Candy."

"Yes, there was," Jason said. "I picked it up and put it in my pocket, but I guess it fell out when the floor gave way. Anyway, somehow I lost it."

"You *lost* it?" Kennedy, Gervase, and Boxner all repeated at the same time.

Jason said with asperity, "Yes. I lost it. While I was plunging fifty feet to the flooded room below."

"Maybe twenty," Kennedy said. "Still. Fair enough."

Gervase sighed. "That's too damn bad. We'll never find it now. That place is a deathtrap. I guess one mermaid more or less doesn't really make a difference."

Jason grimaced. He already felt bad enough about dropping the charm without them trying to be understanding.

Abruptly he remembered that sense of recognition when he'd picked up the charm. The certainty that he knew it.

Well, that he recognized a copy of an original he knew well.

Except...no. For one strange moment, he had believed he was holding the original.

Yes. That was it. He'd felt the shock of recognition. Then the next instant, Candy had opened her eyes, and he'd forgotten all about the charm until he'd searched his pockets for it when he was receiving medical attention some hours later. That had been a sickening moment.

The phone on Gervase's desk suddenly rang, buzzing loudly in the small office, and Jason jumped.

Kennedy threw him a curious look.

Gervase's face changed as he listened to the voice on the other end of the phone. "Is she?" he said. "Well, thank God for that. When can we talk to her?"

More silent listening from the chief. More frowning.

Kennedy continued to study Jason. Jason met his gaze. Kennedy smiled faintly. Was something funny? Jason didn't get the joke.

He glanced at Boxner who was watching him and Kennedy with narrow-eyed suspicion.

Great.

"We're not going to interrogate her," Gervase said into the phone. "We just want to ask her a few questions. We'll be just as quick and careful as we can. It might end up saving someone else's life."

Buzzing on the other end.

"Well—"

"But—"

The chief's eyes lightened. He looked at Kennedy and nodded. "So you think today for sure?"

A few more words were exchanged, and Gervase hung up the phone.

"Candy Davies regained consciousness about half an hour ago. She's pretty groggy, but the doctor thinks she might be able to give her statement as early as this afternoon."

"That's good," Kennedy said. "That's very good news."

Gervase nodded in grim agreement. "What do you think about heading out to Boston now? I don't want to waste any time. That girl won't be really safe until she gives her statement."

"I agree," Kennedy said. "And I'm all for driving to Boston immediately."

Gervase rose. "Boyd, you take West with you and interview this Dr. Kyser. But go easy, for God's sake. We don't need someone else threatening us with a lawsuit."

"Who else is threatening legal action?" Kennedy asked.

"The Madigans. They believe releasing McEnroe was an act of criminal stupidity. They think we're deliberately dragging our feet bringing their daughter's killer to justice."

Kennedy shrugged. "It takes how long it takes."

"It's nice you can get some emotional distance," Gervase said sourly. "Boyd and I don't have that luxury. We have to live with these folks. They're frightened and angry, and they want answers."

"Maybe after we talk to the Davies girl we'll have some for them."

When Kennedy and Jason were alone in their office, Kennedy said, "Watch yourself." His eyes were grave.

"I plan on it." Jason checked his weapon. He popped the magazine, reaffirmed he had plenty of ammo. Which...since he had not fired a single shot since his last session on the target range should not be a surprise. He replaced the magazine.

When he looked at Kennedy, Kennedy was still regarding him intently. There was something odd about his expression. As though he wanted to say more but couldn't decide whether to speak.

"Do you think the unsub is going to go after Candy?" Jason asked.

Kennedy said. "Desperate people are dangerous."

Jason's shoulder twinged at the reminder. "No kidding," he said.

* * * * *

"So," Boxner said. "I guess you and Kennedy are partners in more ways than one."

Jason had been staring out the passenger side window at the green tangle of woodland flashing past. He turned to study Boxner's profile.

Boxner was gazing at the road ahead, smiling faintly. His body was relaxed, one arm draped casually over the steering wheel. The epitome of confident masculinity. It was partly façade, but a lot of it was genuine. Boxner was very pleased with the man he'd become. He probably didn't have a self-doubting cell in his body.

"Sorry. What did you say?"

Great. Just Great. Was there any possibility that SAC Manning would ever have reason to speak to Officer Boyd Boxner?

Boxner said, "You and Kennedy are partners on and off the screen."

"Nope. This is a temporary assignment," Jason said.

Boxner laughed. "Is that so? He was sure clucking over you like a hen with one chick yesterday."

Insulting on so many levels. Also totally stupid. And it would be equally stupid to respond. And yet there had been a moment yesterday when Jason had looked away from the paramedic's checking-for-concussion routine and caught sight of Kennedy talking to Chief Gervase.

Kennedy had glanced over at Jason, and his eyes had blazed electric-blue in his wet and dripping face. There had definitely been emotion there.

Kennedy would take losing—or nearly losing—a partner, even a temporary partner, as a major failure.

Well, who wouldn't?

Jason drawled, "Yeah, that sure sounds like Kennedy."

"Oh, he'd have crawled down into that hole after you," Boxner said. "No question. He doesn't realize you're one of the lucky ones."

"The lucky ones?" Jason asked warily.

"One of those people who always land on their feet. Like a cat. Doesn't matter how far you drop 'em. They always land upright."

"What do you know about what I am?" Jason said. "You knew one thing about me and used it to justify—" He stopped. This was a conversation he did not want to have. Not least because it wouldn't solve anything. He had figured that much out a long time ago.

Boxner tilted his head, considering. Astonishingly, he acknowledged, "Maybe."

He met Jason's eyes. "I probably did bully you. So what? That's what kids do. It made you tougher. It made you tough enough for the FBI."

Jason said dryly, "Remind me to thank you."

"I don't want you to thank me. I don't like you. I wouldn't have liked you even if you hadn't been queer. People always say it's not personal. But it is, believe me."

"Likewise."

"*But,*" Boxner said, "since you *are* still queer, I realize now you didn't kill Honey."

Jason said scornfully, "You know damn well I didn't kill her."

Boxner grinned. "Because you think *I* did? Prove it."

"I plan to."

Boxner laughed. "My money's on good old George Simpson. Chief won't even consider it because he and Simpson go way back, but I think we're going to find the connection we need when we talk to this Kyser character." He glanced at Jason. "Which is going to be very disappointing for you, I know. Since you're hoping Kyser will lead straight to me."

Jason's curiosity got the better of him. "How did Simpson come under suspicion in the first place? Wasn't he a cop?"

"Ex-cop. Ex-state trooper. He was hunting buddies with Pink. His wife was a distant cousin to Pink."

"Simpson's wife was *related* to Pink?"

"A third cousin or something."

"And how was it that Simpson was cleared of suspicion?"

"He had an alibi for all the murders."

"All of them? That's suspicious right there."

Boxner nodded grimly. "Yep."

"What was Simpson's alibi?" Jason groaned as the realization struck him. "Are you kidding me? His *wife* alibied him?"

Boxner's smile was dour. "The light goes on," he said.

CHAPTER EIGHTEEN

Dr. Jeremy Kyser lived in a renovated nineteenth century stone farm-house in the middle of nowhere. The two-story structure sat in a green field surrounded by four acres of neatly trimmed grass. And only grass. Not a tree or a shrub or so much as a wild flower was in sight. A pristine black Porsche was parked in the drive behind the house.

"There's a guy with bucks," Boxner commented. "You have to be rich to be able to afford this much nothing."

They got out of the cruiser and walked up to the front door. Boxner buzzed the doorbell and then thumped on the door.

Jason took a step back to examine the front of the house. The curtains were open, but there was not another sign of life. Not a sound came from inside the house. No dog, no TV, no radio.

"Maybe they're out," Boxner said.

"There's a car parked out back."

Boxner rapped on the door again. Jason was turning to go scope out the back of the house when the front door suddenly, soundlessly swung open.

"May I help you, Officer?" the man in the doorway inquired.

"Dr. Kyser?"

"Yes. That's right." Kyser looked from Boxner to Jason. He was tall—very tall—and rawboned. Despite the warmth of the day he wore jeans and a sweater, but maybe the sweater was due to an air conditioner working overtime. Frigid air wafted out of the house as though a secret door to Antarctica had just popped open.

"I'm Officer Boxner with Kingsfield PD. This is Special Agent West with the FBI. We'd like to ask you a few questions."

"FBI?" Kyser stared at Jason.

Jason held up his ID, staring back. Kyser was not a handsome guy. If anything, he seemed to be rocking the mad-scientist look. His salt-and-pepper hair frizzed out around a long, gaunt face dominated by heavy-lidded eyes with dark circles.

"May we come in, Dr. Kyser?" Jason asked.

After a moment, Kyser stepped back. Boxner and Jason entered the house and, still not speaking, Kyser led them down a dark hallway to a large living room.

"Do you live here on your own, sir?" Jason asked.

"Yes. I live alone. I work from home."

At first glance the room was ordinary enough. A long rectangle lined with walnut bookcases and crowded with antique furniture. The bookcases were crammed with old books. Red and orange *objets d'art* packed the tops of the shelves like an overstocked grocery store.

"Why would the FBI have questions for me?" Kyser asked. He frowned, cracked his knuckles.

Jason kept an eye on those large, bony hands. "We w—"

"Happy Halloween!" Boxner interrupted. He was staring up at the shelves, and following his astonished gaze, Jason realized the spherical autumn-colored objects filling every conceivable inch of flat space were carved jack-o'-lanterns. Not real ones. Wooden ones in all shapes and sizes.

Kyser said stiffly, "I'm not interested in Halloween. I'm interested in jack-o'-lanterns."

That was putting it mildly. This was closer to compulsion than interest. Besides which...

These jack-o'-lanterns were not the typical smiling or scary Halloween fare. Their expressions were tortured, menacing, sinister, agonized—and all too lifelike. Jason liked to think he was capable of evaluating art without interpreting it through the subjective lens of his own background and biases, but the word that formed in his mind was... *troubling.*

He said, "You mean you're interested in jack-o'-lanterns as an art form? Or their significance in folktales and mythology?"

Kyser's black eyes refocused on Jason's face. "I didn't catch your name."

"I'm Special Agent West. This is Officer Boxner with the Kingsfield Police Department. Dr. Kyser, we wanted to ask you about some *netsuke*-style carvings you did several years ago for the Ort & Rossington Primitive Art Gallery in New York."

Kyser's gaze seemed to sharpen. "You're familiar with the art of *netsuke*?"

"I wouldn't say familiar. I know maybe the rudiments."

Kyser's eyes finally moved from Jason's. He glanced at the towering army of wooden jack-o'-lanterns. "I've moved on from miniature sculptures, as you can see."

"Can you tell us about those early sculptures?" Jason asked. "The mermaids?"

"What is there to tell? I no longer work with the Ort & Rossington."

Jason said, "You sold several of those miniature sculptures to the owner of a Worcester County gift shop as well. Can you tell us about your relationship with George Simpson?"

"Who?" Kyser looked confused.

"The owner of the gift shop."

"No. I don't know any Simpson. I sold those miniatures to several gift stores. Only one shop was in Worcester County, and that was owned by a woman. I forget her name. It wasn't Simpson. I suppose I could look it up if it really matters."

"That would be helpful."

Kyser's frown deepened. "That would be inconvenient."

"But helpful," Jason repeated.

"Very well."

Boxner said, "You're in contact with Martin Pink, aren't you? You're one of the only two people approved to phone him up in prison."

Kyser cracked his knuckles again. "I was writing a book on Pink," he said. "I've written several books on the topic of aberrant psychology and crime. I've interviewed any number of convicted killers in their place of incarceration—as I'm sure you're aware, Officers."

"You *were* writing a book?" Jason asked. "Does that mean the book is finished?"

"No. I decided Pink was not a suitable subject for my work. Can we get to the point of your visit? I'm very busy." He started to pop his knuckles, caught Jason's glance, and stopped himself.

Jason said, "Regarding those miniature carvings—"

Kyser burst out, "Agent West, I'm not a fool! It's obvious that someone—presumably you—has finally made the connection between me and the carvings that Pink planted on the bodies of his victims. Ask me what it is you wish to know. I have nothing to hide."

"You have nothing to hide?" Boxner said. "How about the fact that you never came forward to admit you were the one who carved those mermaids?"

"As far as I'm aware," Kyser said, "no effort to find the creator of the mermaids was ever mounted. No such search was advertised in the press. And why would it be of interest or importance? I had nothing to do with those murders, was not aware that my work was used in such an obscene way by Pink until I interviewed him years later."

"You could have come forward then," Jason said. He was considering the use of the word *creator*. It struck him as off. Kennedy would probably have some theories on that.

"No. That would have solved nothing. I would have lost Pink's trust, which I needed for my book. And it would have directed unwelcome publicity and attention my way. Only a fool or a madman would willingly put himself in that spotlight."

Boxner said, "That wasn't your call. You should have—"

"Incorrect and inaccurate," Kyser said flatly. "Pink is already serving several life sentences with no possibility of parole. There was nothing you could have gained, but there was—and is—a great deal I could lose."

Everything Kyser said made a certain amount of sense, and yet Jason had the feeling that they were missing something.

"That's a pretty weird attitude to take, sir," Boxner said. "If you don't mind my saying so."

Kyser glared at him. "As a matter of fact, I do mind you saying so. Who are *you* to judge me?"

Boxner bristled. "I'll tell you who I—"

"Why mermaids?" Jason raised his voice, talking right over Boxner who just wasn't going to let it go even if he antagonized Kyser into lawyering up.

Kyser's strange dark gaze fastened once more on Jason's. "What do you know about mermaids, Agent West?"

"Not a lot," Jason admitted. "Mythological creatures, half-woman and half-fish, that appear in most of the folktales and legends of the world. They're water spirits, right?"

"Mythological." Kyser laughed. "No. The mermaid is as real as you or I. She is an Assyrian demon. There are numerous historical accounts of these creatures. Christopher Columbus reported seeing mermaids during his exploration of the Caribbean. Sightings continue to this day in Scotland, Ireland, Canada, Israel, and Zimbabwe. To encounter one is to encounter disaster."

"An Assyrian demon." Boxner was looking at Jason.

Kyser glared at him. "Yes, Officer Box. And I know what you're thinking. To believe in an angel is perfectly normal. To believe in the Christian devil is reasonable. Yet to believe in an Assyrian demon, the oldest by far of all of these, is to be crazy."

Okaaaaaay.

"Dr. Kyser, did you know Martin Pink previous to interviewing him for your book?" Jason inquired.

For the first time Kyser hesitated. His licked his lips. "I wouldn't say that I knew him. I ran into him on occasion. I'm something of an amateur naturalist, and I used to spend a good deal of time in the woods around Kingsfield. As did Pink, though our objectives were very different."

"I see. Are you familiar with Rexford?"

Kyser stared. "Rexford. What is that?"

"It's a ghost town. On the edge of the Quabbin Reservoir. One of the villages that were flooded during the thirties."

If Kyser was an amateur naturalist spending *a good deal of time* flitting around the woods of Kingsfield, he had to be aware of Rexford. It was the first time during their interview Jason was sure he was being lied to. Lied to in spirit if not in letter.

Kyser frowned at Jason. He cracked his knuckles twice in quick succession.

"Dr. Kyser?" Jason prodded.

Kyser seemed to snap out of whatever preoccupied him. "Excuse me a moment," he said. "I believe my lunch is burning." He turned and left the room.

Boxner, staring up at the rows of grimacing, contorted jack-o'-lanterns, softly whistled the theme to the *Twilight Zone*.

"Shut up," Jason muttered.

"Are you afraid the Assyrian demons will hear me?"

Kyser's footsteps faded away. Jason took a closer look at the some of the books on the shelves. Art books...medical books...*Russian Folk Belief; The Encyclopedia of Spirits: the Ultimate Guide to the Magic of Fairies, Genies, Demons, Ghosts, Gods, and Goddesses; The Mermaid and the Minotaur...Principles of Deformity Correction... Disability, Deformity, and Disease in the Grimms' Fairy Tales...*

"Look at this." Boxner lifted one of the elongated jack-o'-lanterns. "Look at the hole in the bottom. You could wear this. It's like a-a—"

"Headdress," Jason said.

From the rear of the house he heard a car's engine roar into life.

"Oh, hell no."

Boxner looked at him in surprise and then belatedly registered the engine sound too. "Shit!" He set the jack-o'-lantern on the floor, following Jason as he dived out of the room.

They ran through the house, feet pounding the wooden floorboards until they reached the kitchen.

White cupboards, quartz counters, and stainless-steel appliances. Nothing strange. Nothing sinister. Aside from the fact that no one was in there.

Nothing sat on the stove. There was no aroma of cooking food, let alone burning food.

The unlatched back screen banged gently in the summer breeze. The black Porsche parked behind the house was gone. Dust seemed to sparkle golden in the sunlight as it drifted down on the wide, empty dirt road.

"I don't know what spooked him," Jason said. He was standing in front of Kyser's house, speaking to Kennedy on his cell phone. Overhead, silver-edged clouds rolled and tumbled playfully through the wide blue sky. "I will say, I think Kyser's a very weird dude. Even so, nothing happened in the course of that interview that should have made him bolt."

"You and Boxner were together the entire time?"

"Yes."

"Nothing was said to Kyser out of your hearing?"

"No."

"Hm."

Jason had already recounted the entire interview with Kyser in detail, and it continued not to make any sense to him. "His answers were plausible. I can't say that I had a sense that he was lying about anything except maybe knowing of Rexford's existence. And why he would lie about that, or why the question would panic him into flight, I don't know. Rexford's existence isn't a secret. Nor is it illegal to explore the village, despite all those No Trespassing signs. I feel like something's not right here, but I can't..."

Kennedy finished, "Put your finger on anything that gives us legal grounds to pursue Kyser any further."

"Correct. It's not against the law to carve art objects that were later misappropriated and used in homicides. It's not against the law to refuse to speak to the police. It's not against the law to drive off like a bat out of hell."

"All right. Thanks for the update."

"Should we...I don't know. You'll want to see these jack-o'-lanterns though. I'm not sure if they're supposed to be ornamental or ceremonial, but they're pretty unsettling. As was the lecture on Assyrian demons. Anyway, I took a bunch of photos with my phone. Boxner and I had a look around, but we couldn't find anything that would justify an official search of the property."

"No," Kennedy said quickly. "Don't proceed without a warrant. For all we know Kyser is on his way to his lawyer right now. I think we've learned what we needed to."

"We have?" News to Jason, but there was no point trying to get into this on the phone. "How's it going there?"

"The doctors still won't let us in to interview the girl. At least she's stable. I'm sure we'll get a statement before the day is out. You're headed back to Kingsfield?"

"Yes."

"Good. Keep me informed." Kennedy disconnected.

Keep me informed. Jason grimaced. Well, that would be one of them being kept informed.

CHAPTER NINETEEN

The next time Kennedy phoned it was after two in the afternoon.

Jason was in their temporary office, eating a late lunch and once again poring over the crime scene photos from the original Huntsman investigation when his phone rang.

He swallowed a bite of dried-out turkey club and said, "West."

"We're on our way back to Kingsfield," Kennedy said. "The Davies girl isn't going to be able to tell us anything."

"She hasn't regained consciousness yet?"

"She regained consciousness. But she was hit from behind. Boston has a two-man protection detail on her hospital room until she's released tomorrow. Then she's flying out to stay with an aunt in Colorado."

"Damn. She didn't see *anything*? She didn't hear anything? Nothing?"

"No. There's a possibility a stun gun was used to—"

"A stun gun. You mean a *taser*—?"

Kennedy continued, "Before you rush out to read Boxner his rights, if she was tasered, it was through her swimsuit, and there are no discernible marks."

"So somebody knew what he was doing when he zapped her. That's all that means. What about Rebecca? Her swimsuit was skimpier. Marks might have shown on her body."

"I've already checked with the medical examiner, and there were plenty of abrasions but nothing to indicate she was tasered."

"Okay, but then that fits in because I don't think the killer wanted Candy dead."

"West—"

Jason rose and closed the door to the office. He kept his voice down as he said, "I think we were meant to find Candy. That's why she was put back in the same place as Rebecca. Because Boxner was right about that. It didn't make sense to use the same dumping ground twice."

"Let's discuss this when I get back."

"All right. But I've been going over the crime scene photos again. And I agree with you. We're not dealing with a copycat. I think Candy was taken to make it *look* like Rebecca was the victim of a copycat killer. This case is all about Rebecca. She's the key."

"West." Kennedy sounded as cold as he had on the day of their first meeting. "We will discuss this when I get back."

"*Wait.* Will you just hear me out? I know you don't believe Boxner could be involved, but you can't argue with the fact that he was on the scene. He was *there*. And he's got access to those old files and the old evidence."

Kennedy's faraway voice said, "Can we pull over for a minute?" And then in Jason's ear, a terse, "Hold on."

Jason held on. He heard a door slam, heard what sounded like footsteps on gravel, and then Kennedy's voice came on loud and clear.

"What part of *leave it alone* do you not get, West? Goddamn it. I am telling you *leave it alone*."

"Leave what alone? The investigation we're supposed to be working *together*? Aren't you the guy who said we needed to keep open minds?"

"You're not keeping an open mind! You're obsessed with proving Boxner guilty."

That stung. "The hell. I'm not *obsessed*. This isn't personal."

"Oh, for fuck's sake. The hell it isn't. You need to take a step back, Agent West. A *big* step back. Do you realize what's going to happen to this investigation if you start accusing members of Kingsfield PD? Do you comprehend what's going to happen to *both* of us if you make these allegations without—"

"What if I can find physical proof?"

"*What* physical proof?"

"Proof that the mermaid I found next to Candy originally belonged to Honey."

Kennedy said very quietly, "What exactly are you saying?"

"When I picked up that charm, I recognized it."

Why that would make Kennedy all the angrier, Jason wasn't sure, but he could hear the effort he was making to keep his tone even. "How would that be possible?"

"It would be possible for someone who had access to the evidence room."

"No. I mean how could you possibly, after sixteen years, remember a trinket from a keychain?"

"I...just do."

"For the love of God. A hunch is not proo—"

"I'll *get* proof," Jason repeated.

"*How?*"

"I just told you. The evidence room. I can go through Honey's effects. That mermaid charm should still be there. If it's not, then someone took it to plant it on Candy's body in order to make it look like either the Huntsman or an unidentified accomplice had returned. Or that Kingsfield had a copycat on its hands."

There was a silence on the other end.

"Negative," Kennedy said. "Do not request access to the evidence room."

Jason heard it with disbelief. "Why?"

"Because every cop in Worcester County will hear about it within the hour. And every cop in Worcester County will put two and two together and conclude that we're questioning the integrity of this investigation. That we suspect the involvement of local law enforcement."

"That's bullshit, Kennedy. And you know it. I could have any number of reasons for requesting access to the evidence room. No one is going to instantly assume—"

"You think Boxner isn't going to wonder what the hell you're up to? And if he *is* your guy, he'll know immediately what you're looking for. Right?"

"Well, according to you he isn't my guy, so that shouldn't be a worry."

"Goddamn it, West. I am telling you to back off. You are to *wait* to do anything until I get back to Kingsfield, and then we'll decide together on the best course of action. That is an order. The situation there is a lot more delicate than you understand."

"An order?" Jason repeated politely.

"I'm the senior fucking officer on this case and yes, you're goddamn right; I'm *ordering* you to back off. Do you understand?"

"Oh, I understand," Jason said.

I understand that you think an order should be enough and you don't have to explain yourself. I understand that you've treated me like your errand boy—when not a downright nuisance—throughout this entire investigation. I understand that you believe if you're not here to tell me what to do and when to do it, I'll jeopardize both the investigation and your job. I understand that you trust no one. Particularly not me. And, by the way, I understand you're not my boss and can't actually give me orders, you asshole.

"Defy me and I'll break you." Kennedy clicked off.

"And I'll break you?" Jason stared at his phone in disbelief. "Did you just—? Did you—? Who the fuck do you think you are, Kennedy? You'll *break* me?"

Jesus Christ. No wonder Manning wanted Kennedy's head on a platter. The only surprise was that everyone Kennedy had ever met wasn't ordering off that same menu.

It had been a long time since Jason had been this mad. So mad that he was standing in an empty office ranting to himself. In fact, he wasn't sure if he'd ever been this angry in his entire life.

"You'll break me. Wow. You are something else, Kennedy. Just be glad I'm not interested in breaking *you*, you asshole."

He took a couple of calming breaths, plastered a pleasant smile on his face, and went to find Officer Courtney.

"Sorry to interrupt. What's the protocol for the evidence room?"

"Oh! Well, biological samples are stored at State. We don't have the facilities here. Guns, money, and narcotics are kept in a locker, and only the chief has the key. All other physical evidence is kept in the property room."

"You don't have a computer program for inventory control?"

"We've been talking about it, but we're a small department and those programs are pretty expensive."

"Sure," Jason said. "It's the same everywhere. And who has access to the property room?"

She looked confused. "Any officer who needs access."

"Is it procedure to return or purge adjudicated items?"

"Adjudicated? Oh! Well, it depends. We try to return valuable property when we can. We don't really have a firm policy in place. Of course, you're really asking about the physical evidence collected during the Huntsman case. That's all upstairs. We won't ever dispose of that. I think we all feel it would be a kind of...sacrilege."

"Yes," Jason said. "Can I get the keys to the property room?"

"Of course." She opened a drawer and handed him a key on a ring. It was that easy. "We may not be computerized, but everything is organized and labeled. Older cases in the back, new cases in the front. Cases waiting to go to trial on the metal shelf to your left when you walk in."

"Thank you."

He took the stairs fast. He was not hiding what he was up to—and if he had been, hiding in plain sight would be the best way to go—but he was conscious that it was probably better to fly under the radar on this. He hadn't needed Kennedy to tell him that much.

Jason reached the second floor and walked quietly down the empty hallway.

He was still very angry, his heart pounding hard, his hands a bit unsteady as he let himself into the property room, closed the door, and turned on the light.

If Kennedy had not been such a complete bastard, if he hadn't *threatened* him, Jason probably would have waited till he got back to Kingsfield. He wouldn't have liked it, would have continued to think Kennedy was paranoid, would have given Kennedy an earful, but he wouldn't have deliberately launched himself on a collision course.

If Kennedy thought he was going to break Jason career-wise, he was in for a rude awakening. And if he was talking about physical assault, well, *bring it on, old man. Bring it.*

He needed to stop thinking about Kennedy and focus on the job at hand.

He studied the crowded shelves, boxes neatly labeled with case numbers and the last names of the victims. He had to give Kingsfield PD—or maybe Officer Courtney—credit. This was an exceptionally clean and well-organized property room, and Jason had been in a lot of property rooms over the years.

He moved down the aisle of shelves, scanning labels.

There it was. *Corrigan.*

He swallowed. Lifted the box gently down. He carried it to the table in the front.

If he was correct, if the charm he had found with Candy had originally belonged to Honey, someone had removed it from the property room. And even while security measures here were pretty lame, the cast of actors was relatively small.

Jason lifted the lid off the box.

The first thing he saw was Honey's pink sweater, and that initial glimpse seemed to suck the air right out of his lungs. For an instant it was as though she stood right in front of him. He had not expected to remember...so much. Or be so moved by the memories. It took him a second or two to steel himself. He went swiftly, carefully, through the items one by one: sweater, scuffed sneakers, a copy of *The Real Freshman Handbook*, a Big Gulp cup, a yellow beach towel with purple sea horses.

Her swimsuit with her blood and other DNA evidence would be stored at State Police evidentiary lockup.

He tried not to think about what he was doing, tried not to remember. But...

She had been pretty. Not beautiful, but cute. Rosy-cheeked, a little chubby, shorn golden curls, and big blue eyes. "Dancing eyes" was book talk, but yes, Honey's eyes had sparkled with bright interest and lively curiosity.

They had laughed a lot. Told each other everything—almost everything.

All at once he was back there, back at Holyoke Pond...the smell of suntan oil and grass and water. Honey's voice, both their voices— young and confident—ringing out across the water, bouncing back from the dark trees. He could see them sitting on their beach towels, talking, as though he was observing them from the woods.

Which was how Martin Pink had watched them.

"Maybe Boyd will ask you to the dance."

Honey had said archly, *"Me? Maybe you should ask Boyd."*

"Oh yeah, right! You think that Neanderthal can dance?" He had flushed hotly, laughing and looking away. Inside he had not been laughing. Inside he had been embarrassed and hopeful and longing. Young love was really hell. Especially when it was unreciprocated. And his was hopeless. He had known that much even then.

Honey had teased, *"Oh, but he's good enough for me!"*

He had glanced sideways, caught her unguarded gaze, and realized with a pang that he was not the only one suffering—longing for what was never going to be.

He had looked away quickly, and both had pretended they had not seen too much.

No. No, this was not the time for remembrance. He could not afford to feel this right now.

Jason lifted out the last item in the box. An old first-aid kit.

He opened it.

For a minute he mistook a stray cotton ball for what he was looking for, and he felt a zap of...he wasn't sure if it was relief or alarm.

In the end it didn't matter. This white puff would change the course of no one's life.

He went back and checked through every item again.

Nothing.

Her keys were there. The charm was not on the ring.

There was a knocking sensation in his stomach. He felt almost light-headed. Even though this was what he had been looking for—this absence of something that should be there—it was still a shock. Still unbelievable.

The mermaid charm was gone.

He sank down on the long table and tried to think.

Kennedy was right. They could not afford to make any mistakes at this juncture. Jason could not afford to make any mistakes. Having gone against Kennedy, and with so much at stake, he could not get anything wrong.

So think.

Boxner had access to the evidence room and to all the original case files. He was clearly not the only member of Kingsfield PD who had access, though. However, he was the only member who visited Rebecca's home earlier in the evening.

Which, as Kennedy had pointed out numerous times, did not in itself mean anything. It was possible that Boxner could have arranged to meet Rebecca later. But there was absolutely no proof that such a thing had happened.

It was all circumstantial. Which was more than they had on anyone else at the moment.

What bothered Jason most was that none of this addressed the big problem of why. *Why* would Boxner kill Rebecca Madigan?

Why abduct Candy Davies?

Okay, that he could answer. To make it look like Rebecca's murder was part of that larger and earlier pattern. Candy's abduction helped foster the illusion that the Huntsman was back.

Except…if someone really wanted to make it look like the Huntsman was back, Candy should have been killed too.

So the real question was why had Candy not been killed?

No. Skip that for a second. If he was right about Candy's abduction simply being smokescreen…it brought him full circle back to *why kill Rebecca?*

As much as Jason wanted Boxner for this, he knew Kennedy was right about Boxner not fitting the profile—any profile—of a serial killer. Asshole Kennedy might be, but he did know his stuff.

Therefore Rebecca's was not the first death in a new series of copycat slayings.

Rebecca's homicide was a unique and separate crime.

Opening up new avenues of investigation—and a much larger roster of potential suspects.

Rebecca's character was key. Victimology became crucial once more.

So what did they have?

Not a lot really. Rebecca was the daughter of wealthy parents. Wealthy and demanding parents. She was sexually active. She was described by a number of people as smart, sassy, headstrong, spoiled, entitled, bratty... put it together, and they were left with a girl you didn't want to mess with if you were a young ambitious cop on a small-town force.

A girl who could do your career a hell of a lot of damage.

Boxner.

Right?

As hard as it was to believe after the drive to Kyser's that morning, it *had* to be Boxner.

Because if it wasn't Boxner, who was left?

"Everything okay?" Officer Courtney asked when Jason returned the key to the property room.

"Yep."

She studied him sympathetically. "It does get pretty warm up there in the summer, I know."

Jason smiled. "A little. I've got to compliment you. That's a well-organized property room."

She smiled back.

Jason said, "That noise complaint at the Madigans' on Friday night. Was Officer Boxner alone when he responded to that call?"

"Yes."

"Small department, solo patrol?"

"Yes." She gave him a rueful look.

"And that was the only call to the Madigans' that night?"

"Yes."

"Officer Boxner asked Rebecca to turn down the music, and she obeyed, and everything was peaceful and quiet for the rest of the night?"

Officer Courtney gave a dry little laugh. "I wouldn't say *that*. There was a second noise complaint. The chief said he would look into it, but he ended up having to help a stranded motorist."

Jason stared at her. "So Boxner went back to the Madigans' a second time?"

"No. Officer Boxner was off-duty by then. Anyway, it would have taken a team of officers to break up that party. We knew they'd be winding down eventually."

"Right." Jason frowned, nodded, started to turn away—when her words fully sunk in.

"What time was that?"

"What time was what?"

"What time did the second noise complaint come in?"

Courtney said promptly, "Twelve thirty."

"The chief was on his way to the Madigans', but instead stopped to help a stranded motorist?"

She looked puzzled. "Yes. Actually, two girls with a flat tire. They didn't know how to use their jack."

Jason asked carefully, "What time did he call in?"

"Who?"

He didn't need to look at her expression to realize he had to tread very carefully here. Kennedy had been right about that. "At what time did Chief Gervase let you know he was canceling the call to the Madigans' because he was stopping to help the girls with the flat tire?"

Officer Courtney did not look at her computer monitor. She said coolly, "Within a couple of minutes or so. He was in route when he pulled over to aid the girls."

"And after he finished up with the flat tire, he signed off for the evening and went home?"

"Yes. There was no reason not to. There was no indication that Rebecca was missing at that time."

"Right. Of course."

She was frowning, watching him closely.

He wanted to ask her for the license plate number of the car belonging to the girls Gervase had stopped to help. He wanted to run that plate. And, assuming the registration was valid, talk to the driver of the car and verify the exact time Chief Gervase had stopped to lend a hand with that spare tire and jack.

However, he could not ask Officer Courtney for that number. He could not ask her for the very reason that she did not offer it. Because they had both realized at the same instant that here was an overlooked and alarming possibility in someone's movements on the night of Rebecca's murder.

The difference being that Chief Gervase had Officer Courtney's complete and unquestioning loyalty. She was not going to willingly give Jason even one more piece of potentially damaging information—and she was most certainly going to warn Gervase.

She would not think of it as *warning* him because she would reject the idea that he had anything to do with Rebecca's death—Jason was also having trouble picturing that scenario—but Courtney could see how things might look for Chief Gervase.

Yes, she would give her boss a heads-up. And Gervase...already knew that Jason was going over and over the original crime scene photos. He would soon learn that Jason had been looking for evidence in the property room. In fact, he was driving back with Kennedy and might have heard enough of their conversation to guess which direction Jason's suspicions were headed, even if Jason had originally locked sights on the wrong target.

"Thanks for your help," Jason said.

Officer Courtney smiled, her eyes unfriendly.

CHAPTER TWENTY

One problem.

Okay, not one problem. Next problem.

Only Jason had seen the mermaid charm that had been left with Candy.

The fact that Honey's charm was missing sixteen years later, well, a lot of explanations could be offered and arguments made that did not include the Chief of Police murdering a teenage girl and faking the return of a serial killer.

Jason beeped the locks on the Dodge sedan, opened the door, and slipped into the driver's seat.

Now what?

Another problem: the charm found with Rebecca. Where had that come from? Was that also from an earlier case? He should have checked every single one of the murder books while he had the chance. Too late now.

He drummed his fingers on the steering wheel.

Kennedy was not going to be happy about this turn of events. But then Kennedy should have taken the time and trouble to explain to his partner what he was thinking—especially if, as Jason now suspected, Kennedy was on the same track.

But the Kennedys of the world liked to play their own hand. Which left their partners stumbling around in the dark.

So now what?

In order to make his case, Jason needed that mermaid charm back.

And how the hell was he supposed to manage that?

He could have dropped it anywhere in that basement.

Jason listened to the echo of that thought with dismay. No, he wasn't even *considering* going back to Rexford. Was he?

There had to be another way.

He could still make his case without the charm, but it was going to be harder to prove. It left a lot more wiggle room for the defense. The mermaid was the linchpin.

There was a reasonable chance he'd dropped the charm on that pile of rotting whatever the hell he'd landed on. Even if he hadn't... The water was only about a foot deep. Two at the most. He had been able to see down to the bricks when the light was right. And it wasn't like there was a current running through. If he'd dropped the charm in the basement, it was still there.

He swallowed.

Was he really thinking about doing this? Going back to that deathtrap?

He needed to make his mind up one way or the other because Kennedy and Chief Gervase were liable to drive into this parking lot any minute. Unless they stopped for lunch or an early dinner.

No, they'd had to wait around the hospital, so they'd have eaten. They would drive into this lot a little while from now, and Officer Courtney would tip her boss off, and Kennedy would lose the advantage of surprise. Chief Gervase would begin marshalling his witnesses and strengthening his alibi.

Jason started the engine and slowly pulled out of the parking lot.

Jesus. What if he was wrong about this? An hour ago he would have bet money on Boxner being guilty. And now he was convinced it was Chief Gervase even though until this minute it had never crossed his mind that Gervase was anything but one of the good guys.

Even if Gervase had killed Rebecca, why in God's name would he bring Kennedy and the Bureau in?

Or was this all about Kennedy? About making him look bad? Ruining his reputation? But why? As obnoxious as Kennedy could be— *defy me and I'll break you!*—ten years was a long time to hold a grudge.

No, it couldn't be that. Or…it couldn't be *only* that. For sure it was a factor. Bringing Kennedy in had been a huge risk. Yet Gervase had deliberately done that very thing, so part of this did have to do with Kennedy. But it wasn't just about Kennedy.

The fact that Gervase hadn't seriously harmed Candy…what did that mean?

Obviously he wasn't a serial killer.

No, Jason was sure his original theory about Candy was correct. She had been abducted to make it look like Rebecca's murder was part of that larger and earlier pattern. She had been snatched to strengthen the idea the Huntsman—or a previously unknown accomplice—had returned.

It seemed Gervase had been forced by circumstances to improvise. What circumstances?

Whatever had happened, Gervase had been scrambling ever since to cover up. And he'd been abandoning plans nearly as fast as he came up with them. First he'd come up with making Rebecca's death look like part of the earlier pattern; then he'd thought about fobbing the murder off on Tony McEnroe; then he'd directed them to Rexford, again trying to make the Return of the Huntsman scenario work…

Round and round Jason's thoughts went while the sedan's tires ate up the miles.

When his cell phone rang, he was as startled as if the call was coming in from outer space. He glanced down and was unsurprised to see Kennedy's name flash up.

"West."

Kennedy said in a voice markedly unlike the one he'd last used on Jason, "Where are you?"

"Is Chief Gervase with you?"

"No. Listen, West. Jason. I realize I may have been a little abrupt earlier. I apologize. We need to speak as soon as possible."

A little abrupt. That was almost funny.

Jason spotted the turnoff up ahead. "I'm en route to Rexford. I've just reached the overpass."

There was a very loud silence on the other end of the line. "Say again." Kennedy spoke in the tone of one who was determined not to get *a little abrupt* again.

"I'm going back to look for the mermaid charm I dropped when I fell through the floor."

There was a strange noise on the other end. "No," Kennedy said. "No, you're not doing that because everything I've seen so far indicates you're a smart and careful guy. And going back to Rexford on your own would be *fucking insane.*"

"If you thought I was so smart and careful, maybe you should have taken the time to tell me what the hell was going on."

Silence.

"Anyway, I've got to find that charm. It's the only way I can prove my case."

"*Your* case? This is *our* case—"

"Oh, then you *did* notice."

"—and I'm telling you, no. Don't go back there. For God's sake. We can get divers."

"Divers? It's a few inches of water. A foot at most."

"You know what I mean. We have recovery specialists for this kind of thing. You splashing around in the basement of a condemned building is a bad idea. Stop and think. That place is liable to come down on top of you. And I don't know where Gervase is."

"There we go," said Jason with bitter triumph. "That's the part of *our* case you didn't feel like sharing earlier. Chief Gervase is our guy, and you've known it for how long?"

Another of those pauses. Kennedy said, "I had a pretty good idea when we found Davies alive and unhurt. I've known for sure since this morning when you said you'd lost the mermaid charm."

Yes, looking back, Chief Gervase had seemed almost jovial at Jason's admission. In fact, looking back, a lot of his emotional cues had been just plain wrong.

The car bumped down hard in the grass and dirt. Jason had driven as far as he could go. He parked and turned off the engine. He reached down to unlatch the trunk, got out of the car, and went around to the back, still listening to Kennedy who was saying, "We don't need the charm to make our case."

Jason unlocked the lockbox and shrugged into a bullet-proof vest. "That charm is the only piece of evidence that can't be explained or argued away. Everything else is circumstantial. We both know it."

Kennedy's voice dropped.

Jason stopped, listening. Kennedy said with quiet sincerity, "I would rather lose the case than lose you." He added gruffly, "And I don't say that to all my temporary partners."

"I'll bet you don't." Jason sighed. "And thank you. For the record, I'm not doing this because I'm angry or need to prove anything to you. We require that piece of evidence. And we both know this is our sole window of opportunity."

"Have you not heard a single word I've said?"

"Sam, I've heard every word you've said to me since the day we met." A bird warbled, filling the stricken pause that followed. Jason said, "I'm going to have to hike in from here."

Kennedy groaned. "Goddamn it! You stubborn bastard. You've got maybe three hours of good daylight left. That village is going to get very dark, very fast."

"I know."

"I'm hoping Gervase isn't as crazy as you, but if he is, you could have company before I get there."

"Hopefully, he's not that crazy." Jason didn't want to acknowledge how much that *before I get there* cheered him up.

Kennedy's voice grew urgent. "Yeah, but Jason, listen. Gervase went this far. He's not going to go down without a fight. Don't misread the fact he let the Davies girl live. It's a totally different dynamic with you. You're the enemy as far as he's concerned, and if he *is* coming after you, it's to kill you. Whether you find that charm or not, he figures you know too much. He may regret it later, but he's not going to be rational. Stay out of his way."

"Okay."

"*And* he's familiar with the territory. The advantage is all his."

"Got it."

"Jason."

"Yep?"

"He's a good shot. A marksman."

"Roger that." Jason clicked off before Kennedy weakened his resolve any further.

The silence that followed was so complete he felt like he was standing on another continent, millions of miles from everything he knew, everyone he cared about.

He shook off the feeling, found the high-powered flashlight in the lockbox and slammed shut the trunk of the sedan. He did one quick final weapon check—better OCD than sorry—and set off at a jog down the trail leading into the trees.

It took him about twenty minutes to reach the old mill. He was making excellent time, and there was still no sign of pursuit from behind. And no sign of life ahead.

Either way he was past the point of return.

He continued down the trail, still moving fast but now extra alert to his surroundings. The sun was starting to slide, but there was still warmth to the afternoon and plenty of daylight. A few blue swallows swooped down to investigate, then swooped away.

He thought of Jeremy Kyser and wondered suddenly, uncomfortably, whether he might be lurking somewhere nearby. The idea was a bizarre one, but the whole interview with Kyser had been so strange...

However, after returning to Kingsfield, Jason had run Kyser through the system, and nothing alarming had flagged. Kyser seemed to be just what he appeared: a weird but talented guy who had managed to build a lucrative career out of studying people even weirder than himself.

By the time he reached Rexford, Jason had worked up a good sweat and was slightly out of breath. The good news was he'd given himself a healthy lead on any possible pursuit. The bad news was if he got into any trouble in the basement of the lyceum, help would be at least an hour in coming—and it was unlikely help would arrive first.

He walked north, scanning the hollow-eyed, peeling faces of the buildings falling down along Main Street, and came at last to the Lyceum of the Aquatic.

He'd have liked to know what the story was behind this now defunct institution, but then every building in Rexford had a story.

Crime scene tape was stretched across the entryway. Jason went around the building to the back entrance.

More crime scene tape; black and yellow warnings bobbing in the breeze.

He ripped the plastic tape down and pried opened the tall blue door. The hinges screeched a protest that was going to carry for miles. Especially on such a quiet, clear day.

It wasn't like Gervase didn't know where Jason was headed.

He went down the short stairwell, forced open the door to the basement, and turned on his flashlight.

Beyond his range of sight he heard a low, hoarse croaking sound. Something huge and white flew out of the darkness straight at him. Jason yelled and fell back against the wall, grabbing for his weapon, unable to tear his gaze away from great wings...burning eyes...

"Jesus Christ!"

...long orange bill...

Wait.

Long orange bill?

A bird. A goddamned bird. A great white heron. In the goddamned cellar.

"How the hell did you get in here?" He was talking to himself. The bird was long gone. Jason hadn't thought egrets or heron could fly, but this one had exited that cellar posthaste—which was faster than Jason, who'd had the same idea but less presence of mind.

Thank God no one had seen that little interaction. He'd never live it down. What had he imagined? A ghost was coming after him?

Jason knelt, searching for his flashlight, which he'd dropped while grabbing for his pistol.

It was there, a few inches from his feet, the triangle of white light still cutting a swath through the darkness.

Picking up the flashlight, Jason aimed it at the floor below. If he'd been hoping for a miraculous receding of floodwaters, no. Not happening this eon.

He continued down the rickety staircase and splashed into the murky pond. No sign of the snake today, but he thought it might be better not to look at the rafters too closely.

Most likely he had lost the charm when he crashed down on the pile of rugs or skins or whatever the hell it had been. He had been partially submerged, and the charm could have floated out of his pocket, which meant there was a good chance it was resting somewhere near his landing area. He just hoped he hadn't stepped on it and crushed it when he was stumbling around down here. Or the egret hadn't mistaken it for a fish.

The sunlight pouring through the twin holes in the roof and ceiling lanced through the water, illuminating the floor in golden patches. Jason moved slowly through the water, studying the shifting blurs of darkness. Now and then he spotted something small and white, but each time he reached into the water, all he found was a bone or a piece of cartilage.

It took a while to work his way to the pile of rotting hides, and by the time he got there, the light had faded considerably and his hands were numb from reaching into very cold water and grabbing things he'd rather not think about.

The smell was getting to him. That reeking sulfurous stench.

He was starting to feel desperate. There was so much debris on the floor. And, for that matter, so much floor. And with every minute he was losing both time and light.

If Gervase was not already in Rexford, he must be getting near.

Assuming he had not decided to take a leaf from Kyser and bolt.

Where could Gervase run? Canada? His family was here. His life was here. No, Kennedy was right. Gervase would follow Jason because he would believe Jason was the only real obstacle to his safety. Candy couldn't identify her attacker. And Kennedy seemed pretty confident that he had managed to hide his own suspicions from the chief...

Leaving only Jason as a threat to be eliminated.

What was the plan? Following his brief reappearance, this copycat or previously unknown accomplice of the Huntsman would disappear again? Senior Special Agent Kennedy would have failed to capture this new threat—and much doubt would be cast on his diffusing of the old threat. After all, plenty of people in Kingsfield still believed there had been two Huntsmen. This would probably confirm it for them for all time.

Jason got down on his knees in the frigid water and used both hands to sift gently through the rotting materials. His stomach churned with nerves and revulsion as he found and released various squishy and non-squishy items.

You're here. You've got to be here. I'm not leaving without you.

He looked at the hole in the ceiling above. He could no longer see dust motes floating in that wedge of anemic light.

How late was it now? What time was it?

He was starting to shiver with the cold. So much so, that when his fingertips brushed something small and hard and round, he accidentally pushed it farther away. Jason groaned and spread his fingers, feeling gently, lightly...and *there*! There it was. His heart jerked. He closed his hand around the small sphere.

He raised his hand and stared at the pale marble-sized object lying in his palm. The tiny scales, the delicate fins, the arch smile.

Yes. He knew her. He'd have known her anywhere. Honey's mermaid.

CHAPTER TWENTY-ONE

*G*o. *Go now.*

Jason studied the signal bars. Or rather the lack of signal bars. *No service.*

No kidding.

What are you waiting for? Go.

He could wait for darkness to fall, but he didn't think that would gain him much advantage. There was only one way out of the cellar of the lyceum, and by now Gervase must be in position to pick him off when he stepped outside.

Jason could stay put and wait for Kennedy to show up with the cavalry. Except maybe Kennedy wouldn't have the cavalry. Maybe the cavalry was on the other side this time.

And if Kennedy walked into Rexford looking for Jason, he would put himself in the line of fire.

Jason waited by the door of the cellar, watching the panes in the window overhead turn gray with twilight.

Maybe Gervase hadn't made it to Rexford yet? Maybe he was still hiking in? In which case Jason was wasting valuable minutes hovering in this doorway.

No. No, Gervase was in great shape for his age—plus he had desperation to fuel him. No, he would have reached the village by now. And he would know exactly where Jason was.

All he had to do was wait for Jason to stick his head up.

Whac-A-Mole. Only with police issue mallets.

Angrily, Jason realized he was shaking. He told himself it was from the cold water. He was not going to come unglued at the idea Gervase was standing up there waiting to put a bullet in him.

Think.

First of all, if Gervase was going to kill him—kill a federal agent—it was going to be because he believed he could get away with it. He was acting to protect himself, so he could go on living his life as police chief and solid citizen. So he wasn't going to murder Jason outright. That would be idiotic. Aside from having to also and immediately deal with Kennedy—and how the hell would he explain the murder of *two* federal agents?—he'd bring the full investigative resources of the entire federal government down on himself.

No. Gervase was intelligent. And practical.

Even if his original idea had been to shoot Jason on the spot, he'd had the entire hike from the highway to calm down and think.

And what he would think was that if he was going to get rid of Jason, he would need it to look like an accident. Gervase would need to fix it so that even in a worst case scenario, there would be a nice big reasonable doubt in his favor.

Therefore…he was not going to pop Jason when he walked out of this cellar.

He would not want to kill Jason in Rexford at all, if he could help it.

Jason focused on this thought, breathing slow, calming breaths as he continued to reason it out.

An accident. That's what Gervase would be thinking.

Maybe he would sabotage Jason's car? Or maybe he would ambush Jason on the way back to the car. He was not going to shoot Jason when he walked out of the cellar unless Jason didn't give him a choice.

Which meant if Jason could walk out of this cellar looking like he was not expecting trouble…Gervase might give him the benefit of the doubt long enough for Jason to make it to some kind of cover where he wasn't completely pinned down.

Either way, he could *not* continue to stand in this doorway, paralyzed by indecision.

No. Call it what it was.

Paralyzed with terror at the idea of being shot.

He had made it all the way to this point—spent how long in that swamp downstairs?—and now he could not get himself to walk out the fucking door. Just thinking of it was turning his breath fluttery and shallow, making him feel light-headed and unsteady.

Because he could not forget how it felt to have a bullet slam into his chest. Could not forget the sound of metal chewing flesh and bone, the smell of gunpowder and blood, could not forget the sight...

He swallowed down the sickness.

He had promised Kennedy he was fine. Promised him that if Kennedy needed him, he would be there to back him up. And now he couldn't force himself out the door.

Even though he didn't know for a fact Gervase was there, waiting.

And even though he *did* know for a fact Kennedy was on his way. Was he going to just stand here and let Kennedy be shot?

Coward. You useless, gutless coward. His eyes stung with the revelation. He wiped them impatiently.

How long had he already wasted standing here?

Minutes.

Half an hour?

Long enough that his hands had dried.

What are you waiting for?

The idea seemed to come from nowhere. A single thought taking form amidst all the swirling doubt and confusion.

If you let something happen to Kennedy, you're going to shoot yourself anyway.

He listened to the words echo through his brain.

His breathing slowed, calmed. He stopped shaking. Yes. That was the truth. If Gervase opened fire on Kennedy, Jason would be out that door in a heartbeat. So why not move now when there was still a chance everyone could walk away alive?

It was almost comically simple when you looked at it that way. *You don't have a choice.*

Jason took a deep breath, released it, loosened his shoulders, and stepped through the doorway.

His heart thundered in his ears. His vision seemed to blacken around the edges. Nothing happened.

He kept walking.

He could see the half-sunken buildings to his right, like broken puppets peeping out of the water. And to his left, the long and straggling line of derelict buildings he had searched with Kennedy only days earlier.

Where the hell should he go?

His boots were squelching with each step. It was physically painful not to reach for his weapon, not to at least let his hand rest on the butt of his pistol.

Where to take cover? Where to take shelter? Should he just keep heading out of town, making for his vehicle?

Uneasy awareness rippled down his spine. He was being watched. Every step of the way. That feeling was unmistakable. Like a weight on his shoulders.

He was not going to get as far as his car. He was not going to get as far as the edge of town.

Well, he had never claimed to be a profiler.

"All right," Gervase called from behind him. "That's far enough."

Jason kept walking.

"Stop walking, Agent West."

The little blue building to his left... Twin broken windows on either side of a front door half-hanging from the frame. Whatever it was, it was his only option now.

"*Agent West!*"

The dust kicked up beside his boot before he heard the shot. The sound seemed to blow apart the sky. Birds took flight from inside the crumbling buildings like scattershot.

He doesn't want to shoot you in the back.

Jason had no idea where the thought came from, but he knew it was the truth. For whatever reason, Gervase balked at the idea of shooting him in the back.

He leaped for the porch, hitting the ground, rolling, and landing on his haunches. He crashed through the broken front door, knocking it the rest of the way off its hinges.

Jason scuttled over behind what looked like an old soda fountain bar. He pulled his weapon.

His heart was racing, but his mind was actually focused. Not calm, but not panicked. He had not been shot. He was under fire, but he still had his weapon, and he was trained to deal with this.

So deal with it.

He looked around himself. Beneath the dirt and animal droppings and leaves he could see black and white linoleum, curling up in places. No furniture beyond the bar itself, which at least was heavy and solid wood. There was probably a back door somewhere down that shadowy recess to his left. The lack of any light coming from that direction meant that exit might be boarded up.

Okay. He was pinned down again. But at least he had better visibility—and he wasn't standing in wet muck up to his shins.

Kennedy had implied Gervase would have already worked through whatever objections his conscience might make to murdering a fellow law enforcement officer. It couldn't be that easy. Not for a man who had dedicated his life to upholding the law. Gervase might be capable of murder, might feel driven to it, but he wasn't going to enjoy it.

He would need to justify it to himself. He would *want* to justify it to Jason.

You didn't have to be a behavioral specialist to know that much. It was basic human nature. Nobody saw themselves as the villain in their own story.

"Why'd you do it, Chief?" Jason called. "Why'd you kill her?"

The shot came through the broken window and hit the wall low behind the bar where Jason crouched.

Not good. Gervase already knew exactly where he was.

"You must have had a reason. It had to be an accident."

There was something halfhearted about the shot that followed. It was a foot away from Jason's hiding spot.

"You brought us into this. If you're going to kill me, you at least owe me that much."

"I didn't bring you into it," Gervase returned. In a strange way it was a relief to hear his voice. "I didn't ask for you. This isn't on me."

"You brought Kennedy into it. Which makes me think you wanted to get caught."

"Which makes me think *you're* dumber than dirt." Gervase's next shot grazed the top of the bar above Jason's head. Jason stared up at that pale, splintered gouge in the darker wood.

He swallowed. Yelled, "Why the hell did you call for the FBI then?"

"I didn't have a goddamned choice!"

Well, that made no sense. Regardless of the actual words, the fact Gervase was willing to talk meant there was still a chance of reaching him.

Or maybe not; the next bullet plowed a couple of inches lower, and Jason flattened himself to the dusty floor.

Shit. Shit. Shit.

He looked around for a better position. To his right there was a staircase leading up to the second floor, but it looked like it had torn away from the landing. And Gervase, who appeared to be positioned outside the front window also on the right, would have a clean line of fire.

Jason moved to the end of the bar and trained his weapon on the window where he could just see the edge of Gervase's shadow.

"If it was an accident, why didn't you report it right away? Why did you try to cover it up?"

"It doesn't matter what it was. It's too late now."

"It does matter. You kill a federal agent in cold blood, you're done."

"I'm done if I *don't* kill you."

"Kennedy knows. For Christ's sake. Everybody in your station must have figured it out by now."

"I *know* Kennedy knows. The bastard never stopped phoning me the whole way here."

If that was true, Kennedy must have been desperate to stop Gervase. He'd deliberately abandoned any element of surprise.

"Then what the hell is the point of this? You're not going to get the drop on him. It's too late anyway. You have to know that. You're making it worse for yourself."

And me. You asshole.

Maybe he should swallow the charm. That was one way of preserving it, just in case Kennedy didn't arrive in time. Or didn't survive. Chances were good it would be found in the autopsy. It would certainly trigger a few questions. A lot of questions.

A grisly thought, but…kind of hard not to consider it when someone was firing round after round at you. Except Gervase hadn't fired for a few seconds.

Motion on the right. Jason brought his weapon up.

"I'll deal with Kennedy." Gervase stepped into the empty window frame. His weapon was leveled at Jason. He could hardly fail to notice Jason's weapon was also trained on him.

Great. Straight out of Hong Kong Cinema.

Gervase stared coldly down at Jason. Jason stared back.

Were they really going to shoot each other?

There did not appear to be another option. If Jason was going down, he was taking Gervase with him. He was not leaving Gervase to deal with Kennedy. That much he knew for sure.

Three.

This was so stupid. So pointless. So unbelievably…

Two.

Don't think. Don't talk. Squeeze the trigger.

"You've never shot anyone before, have you?" Gervase sounded suddenly weary.

"I have," Kennedy's voice said clearly from behind Gervase.

Kennedy fired.

Chapter Twenty-Two

"**Y**ou could have told me to drop it," Gervase muttered as he was lifted onto the stretcher that would carry him to the waiting helicopter.

"I could have blown your head off too," Kennedy said. "I didn't."

"You should have."

"I probably should have," Kennedy agreed. Always there with the warm and fuzzy.

Or maybe he was doing Gervase the courtesy of being honest with him. Since he had not obliged him by helping him commit suicide.

While they had waited for the state trooper and the med chopper, Gervase had talked. He said it was to keep his mind off the pain of his gunshot wound. Jason believed he had been longing to get the story off his chest since the homicide had happened.

Except it wasn't homicide. Manslaughter at most. And if Gervase had just owned up to it at the start—

"I should have taken early retirement," Gervase said as Kennedy shoved his own jacket against the wound in Gervase's shoulder.

"You should have taken something," Kennedy said.

Gervase winced as Kennedy applied pressure to the wound. "I didn't have the patience to deal with the bullshit anymore."

"What happened that night?" Jason asked.

"It was an accident. I went out there to tell the Madigan kid to turn the goddamned music down or else. She told me to fuck off. Right to my face. Like I was her peer, like I was her *servant*. She told me her parents paid my salary. Paid the salary of all my officers. Spoiled, mouthy little bitch. I slapped her. Which I shouldn't have. I know that. I knew it as it was happening. Big mistake. And then it got worse. She fell and hit her head on a rock."

Gervase stared at them in disbelief. "Just like that. Boom. Lights out. I couldn't believe it. She was *dead*."

"Why the hell did you try to conceal it?" Kennedy asked.

Gervase's eyes were still dark with horror. "My God. What was I supposed to do? You've seen her parents in action. I wouldn't just have lost my job. They'd have taken me for everything I own. And I don't own that much, not after a lifetime of public service. They would have destroyed my family. And it wouldn't have stopped there. I'd have gone to jail. They'd have seen to that. A cop in jail. You know what happens to cops in jail? But they wouldn't have cared. They could afford the best lawyers. I'd have lost everything because of a mouthy little brat."

"Because you struck and killed her," Kennedy said.

Awareness seemed to come back to Gervase's face. He looked away. "Yeah," he said thickly.

Jason said, "Why the hell did you drag Kennedy into this? Why involve the Bureau? You'd probably have got away with making it look like a sex crime or something if you hadn't tried to make it look like the Huntsman was back."

Gervase gave a strange laugh. "I know! I think I lost my mind there for a while. I'd seen you on the news the night before." He was staring at Kennedy. "And I thought what a lucky sonofabitch you were. Everybody else does your grunt work, and you get to be the big hero who saves the day."

"You don't know what you're talking about," Kennedy said.

"A *governor* called you out right there on TV, and you *still* walked away with your job. Anybody else would have been fired. Hell, you were getting credit for solving that case too!"

Jason repeated, "Why did you bring him in?"

"Because I couldn't see how not to. I knew how to stage Rebecca's body, make it look like maybe the Huntsman had a copycat, but then if we really *did* have a copycat, we'd bring in Kennedy. So how could I not bring him in? What would be my excuse?"

Maybe it was true. Jason thought there was more to the story. Resentment? Jealousy? Hatred? On the surface Gervase seemed like a decent, well-balanced guy. As sane as they came. But to harbor such bitter feelings for so many years? Was this because of how good Kennedy was at his job? Or because he didn't bother to pretend he wasn't that good?

Maybe Kennedy felt the same thing, because he rose and walked away from the little ring of light created by their flashlights.

"How did it happen that nobody saw you with Rebecca?" Jason asked, watching Kennedy's straight, motionless silhouette.

"She was on her way into the house when I pulled up. She walked out to meet me. It took...no more than a couple of minutes."

"You goddamned fool." Kennedy's voice was a growl from the darkness. "You should have reported it immediately."

"That's easy to say. You weren't there. You'll never be there because you don't have anything to lose. *This* is your life."

Kennedy didn't answer.

Jason said, "What about the mermaid charm found with Rebecca? Where did that one come from?"

Gervase groaned. "I found it years ago where Ginny's body was discovered. I go out there sometimes, into the woods where we found each of the girls. And one day I spotted it lying there in the grass. Right where we'd searched a dozen times. I carried it on my own keychain ever since because I never wanted to forget."

The low and distant thwack-thwack-thwack of an approaching helicopter reached their ears then. Jason had spotted lights skimming the black tree tops, heading their way.

Chief Gervase's light, pain-filled eyes followed Kennedy. "You don't know what those murders did to us. We're haunted to this day. Those ghosts will follow us until Kingsfield crumbles away like this town. It was just another case for you. Another big career triumph. Not for me. I *knew* those girls. Every one of them. I had to face their parents. I don't ever get to forget. To walk away."

Kennedy turned. His eyes glittered in the glare of the high beams. "You're not walking away from this, that's for sure."

* * * * *

It was much later before Jason had a chance to speak to Kennedy on his own. Chief Gervase had been whisked away to Boston for surgery, and Rexford was crawling with state troopers while most of the deeply shocked and grieving members of Kingsfield PD looked on.

"You can head back to the motel now. In fact, you should head out for L.A. tomorrow," Kennedy told Jason. "Assuming you can get the okay from SAC Manning. I'll finish wrapping things up here."

"You want me to leave?" Jason could have blushed after the startled words left his mouth. He just meant…well, actually he did kind of mean it the way it sounded.

Is that it?

Of course that was it. There wasn't enough of a case left to require two special agents, especially when one of them was on loan from another and greatly understaffed unit. And as for the rest of it…

I follow the catch-and-release rule. By exigency and by inclination.

"You're in a big hurry to get back to L.A. Correct?" Kennedy's appraisal was as cool and direct as the day they'd met.

"Right. Yes."

Kennedy nodded and turned away.

"I would have fired," Jason said to his back.

Kennedy turned to face him, regarding Jason steadily, bleakly.

"Thank you for what you did earlier, but it wasn't necessary."

Kennedy said, "West, the only reason you're not dead is because he didn't want to kill you." He sounded as tired as Gervase had at the end.

"That's not—" Jason stopped. "I would have fired. I was squeezing the trigger."

"You didn't fire. You didn't shoot. He let off five rounds. You didn't return fire once."

"I thought I could talk him down. I *was* talking him down."

Kennedy closed his eyes as though in pain.

"You can think what you want. I didn't freeze. I would have fired if I hadn't had another choice."

Kennedy started to answer, then stopped. He said finally, "You're too smart not to understand the potential consequences—for everyone—of being wrong about this. That's all I'm going to say."

Their gazes remained locked. Jason nodded.

Kennedy didn't believe him, but Jason was telling the truth. He had been about to fire. For him, the nadir had been during those minutes when he *had* been frozen with fear in that cellar doorway. He had hit rock bottom, but he had come back from it. In fact, there was a kind of comfort in knowing no bullet could ever hurt like the pain he had faced in that basement.

"What about Kyser?" he asked.

Kennedy frowned. "What about him? He's not part of this case. If he wants to behave like a freak, that's his business."

Right. It wasn't against the law to be a very weird guy.

"Okay. Well, I guess that's it."

Kennedy nodded and once more turned his back to walk away.

What the hell. You only lived once.

"How often do you get to L.A.?" Jason called.

Kennedy stopped. Turned. He looked at Jason. Impassive and cool. Shook his head. "No."

For the record. All purpose and all encompassing. *In answer to any question you could ever ask...*

No.

Not even a polite and face-saving *sorry to say, not that often.*

Nope. Just a flat and businesslike *no.*

Police line. Do not cross.

"Right. Well, nice working with you." It was kind of amazing Jason got the words out so calmly, given the way his throat closed like a vise on that final *you.*

This time it was Jason who turned away.

* * * * *

By the time he made it back to the motel, Jason was angry.

Also sick with disappointment and hurt.

Which made no sense whatsoever.

He had understood the terms of engagement.

He himself was *not* looking for a relationship, let alone a long-distance relationship with someone as difficult and unpredictable as Sam Kennedy.

His emotional reaction to Kennedy's curt goodbye was...embarrassing, frankly.

Thank God he had managed to hide it. Probably not well enough. And he could have kicked himself for that hopeful, tentative *How often do you get to L.A.?*

Jason swore and threw the last of his clothes in his suitcase.

What he was feeling was probably something akin to leaving summer camp. You bonded with people through adversity, and sometimes it was hard to say goodbye. That was all.

And that was normal. This had been a tough case for him. He'd had to work through a few things. So it was natural to confuse his feelings about the situation with his feelings for Kennedy.

His brief conversation with SAC Manning did not improve his mood.

Manning was *erm* bitterly disappointed at the way things had worked out in Kingsfield. He could not come up with a reason for insisting Jason stay on, but it was clear it killed him to give up without a fight.

"Agent West, do you feel that perhaps, erm, something Kennedy did during that previous investigation might have ultimately, erm, triggered—"

"No, sir. I really don't."

Jason had stuck to that line, and eventually Manning had to accept defeat.

"Your cooperation and diligence have been, erm, duly noted, Agent West."

"Thank you, sir."

He was in bed, not sleeping, when he heard Kennedy's footsteps on the landing. Jason glanced at the clock. Two thirty in the morning. It would be light soon. He would be leaving for the airport soon.

Heart thumping, he listened to that firm tread approach...and then pass his door.

No pause. No hesitation.

He scrunched the pillow over his hot face. What had he thought? That Kennedy was going to change his mind when he remembered all those great times they'd spent together?

Jesus. Christ. *Get over it.*

He closed his eyes. A second later his eyes popped open again—like his eyelids were broken.

He was too tired to sleep. That was the truth. He was wired. He ought to just head out now.

Yes, actually, that was a good idea.

Why was he wasting time lying here when he could be on his way back to Boston? That would save him from the awkward possibility of running into Kennedy in the morning.

He sat up, snapped on the light, and then sat on the edge of his bed, wondering at the wave of depression he felt at the idea of never seeing Senior Special Agent Sam Kennedy again.

Really, Jason? Coz you couldn't stand the guy five days ago. And now you're getting choked up because you'll never again have to put up with that perfumy aftershave and his insistence on always driving everywhere?

There came a soft knock at the door.

His heart nearly jumped out of his chest. Jason rose, hauled on his jeans, and went to the door. He peered out the keyhole.

Kennedy was frowning at the landing.

Jason slid the safety chain, turned the deadbolt, opened the door.

Kennedy transferred the frown to Jason.

"I saw your light was on."

Jason frowned back. "I've got an early flight."

"Right. Look." Kennedy drew a breath. "I'm not good at goodbyes. But I enjoyed working with you too, Agent West."

"Thank you."

"That's all."

Jason nodded curtly.

Kennedy turned away.

Jason very, very gently closed the door. He leaned his forehead against its glossy enameled surface.

He listened for Kennedy's retreating footsteps.

Nothing.

More nothing.

He raised his head.

Was Kennedy still standing outside his door?

Knock. Knock. Knock.

Jason wrenched open the door. "Back so soon?" he asked tersely.

Kennedy's blue eyes seemed to be the only color in the night. His hair looked platinum, his face white in the thin light radiating from the overhang. "Listen," he said. "You don't want to be involved with me."

"You're right."

"If you think I'm an asshole now..."

"You don't have to convince me."

"I'm too old for you, for one thing."

Jason folded his arms. "And getting older by the minute."

"I'm always on the road. Always traveling. I like it that way."

"Sure. Sounds ideal."

Kennedy drew a deep breath. "I made the decision a long time ago that this job did not allow for anything other than...this job."

Jason was silent. "Wow," he said finally.

Kennedy's throat jumped as he swallowed. "And even if I could find the balance of work and relationship—and I don't think that's in me—this isn't the kind of job you want to bring home to someone you care about. I would not want to open this door to someone I cared about. Especially not someone like you."

"*Especially* not someone like me," Jason repeated. "I see."

"No, you don't. But I do. And that's why I think this would be a horrible idea."

"Kennedy, when you retire from the Bureau, you should go into sales. You're a natural."

Kennedy finished quietly, "Because I care about you, Jason. More than I thought I could."

Jason rubbed his eyes. Pinched the bridge of his nose. He opened his eyes. "Okay. Let me get this straight. You like me too much to ever see me again. Is that pretty much it?"

Kennedy stared at him. There was so much pain in his face. He wasn't even trying to hide it. Features set and pale, mouth too firm, eyes dark with naked emotion. Where had all that come from? Four hours ago he had been Mr. Freeze.

"Jesus Christ," Jason said. "I was just asking for a fucking date. But since you're putting it out there, I didn't expect this either. And I can't say it particularly fits in with my plans. I'm not whatever it is you've convinced yourself I am. I'm not a civilian, for one thing. I don't care that you're an asshole—although you are—and I don't care how old you are, or that you travel a lot, or that the job comes first. And I don't even want to know what the rest of it is, though obviously there's something I should probably know about. I would like to..." He was astonished when his voice cut out.

Kennedy stared at him, watching his struggle.

Jason finished steadily, "I would like to try." He amended, "I would at least like to try one date."

Kennedy let out a long breath, like a swimmer who just didn't have the strength to keep fighting current. The moment seemed to float there, and then he reached out, hand locking in Jason's hair, pulling him in for a kiss.

Just before their lips met Kennedy said softly, "When and where?"

THE END

*Watch for the return
of Jason West and Sam Kennedy in*

THE MONET MURDERS
(THE ART OF MURDER BOOK II)

Coming Winter 2017

AUTHOR NOTES

Thank you to the following people: Keren Reed, Marilyn Blimes, Dianne Thies, Susan Sorrentino, and Janet Sidelinger. Have I told you lately that I love you?

Those of you paying attention will remember that Sam Kennedy was a Behavioral Analysis Unit Chief in *Winter Kill*. He has not been demoted. The events of *Winter Kill* coincide with *The Monet Murders*, the second book in the Art of Murder series.

ABOUT THE AUTHOR

Bestselling author of over sixty titles of classic Male/Male fiction featuring twisty mystery, kickass adventure, and unapologetic man-on-man romance, Josh Lanyon has been called "arguably the single most influential voice in m/m romance today." Granted, that was yesterday.

Today Josh's work has been translated into nine languages. The FBI thriller *Fair Game* was the first Male/Male title to be published by Harlequin Mondadori, the largest romance publisher in Italy. The Adrien English series was awarded the All Time Favorite Couple by the Goodreads M/M Romance Group. Josh is an Eppie Award winner, a four-time Lambda Literary Award finalist for Gay Mystery, and the first ever recipient of the Goodreads All Time Favorite M/M Author award.

Josh is married and lives in Southern California.

Find other Josh Lanyon titles at www.joshlanyon.com
Follow Josh on Twitter, Facebook, and Goodreads.

ALSO BY THE AUTHOR

NOVELS

THE ADRIEN ENGLISH MYSTERIES

Fatal Shadows

A Dangerous Thing

The Hell You Say

Death of a Pirate King

The Dark Tide

Stranger Things Have Happened

THE HOLMES & MORIARITY MYSTERIES

Somebody Killed His Editor

All She Wrote

The Boy with the Painful Tattoo

OTHER NOVELS

THE ALL'S FAIR SERIES

Fair Game

Fair Play

THE SHOT IN THE DARK SERIES

This Rough Magic

The Ghost Wore Yellow Socks

Mexican Heat (with Laura Baumbach)

Strange Fortune

Come Unto These Yellow Sands

Stranger on the Shore

Winter Kill

Jefferson Blythe, Esquire

Murder in Pastel

NOVELLAS

THE DANGEROUS GROUND SERIES

Dangerous Ground

Old Poison

Blood Heat

Dead Run

Kick Start

THE I SPY SERIES
I Spy Something Bloody
I Spy Something Wicked
I Spy Something Christmas

THE IN A DARK WOOD SERIES
In a Dark Wood
The Parting Glass

THE DARK HORSE SERIES
The Dark Horse
The White Knight
The DOYLE & SPAIN Series
Snowball in Hell

THE HAUNTED HEART SERIES
Haunted Heart: Winter
The XOXO FILES Series
Mummy Dearest

OTHER NOVELLAS
Cards on the Table
The Dark Farewell
The Darkling Thrush
The Dickens with Love
Don't Look Back
A Ghost of a Chance
Lovers and Other Strangers
Out of the Blue
A Vintage Affair
Lone Star (in *Men Under the Mistletoe*)

Green Glass Beads (in *Irregulars*)
Blood Red Butterfly
Everything I Know
Baby, It's Cold (in *Comfort and Joy*)
A Case of Christmas

SHORT STORIES
A Limited Engagement
The French Have a Word for It
In Sunshine or In Shadow
Until We Meet Once More
Icecapade (in His for the Holidays)
Perfect Day
Heart Trouble
In Plain Sight
Wedding Favors
Wizard's Moon

PETIT MORTS
(SWEET SPOT COLLECTION)
Other People's Weddings
Slings and Arrows
Sort of Stranger Than Fiction
Critic's Choice
Just Desserts

HOLIDAY CODAS
Merry Christmas, Darling